"Writing that easily equals that of the Booker-winning Richard Flanagan . . . [and] as readable and gripping as any thriller. Only the thrills offered by this bright new star of literature are metaphysical and unexpected and will leave you thinking on a new level about the connections between men, women and places . . . A magnificently arresting, fresh prose style filled with brilliantly skewed impressions of nature and humanity . . . Effortlessly interweaving art, love, war, ageing and philosophy—the great themes of life—with equal respect and power given to element is a considerable achievement."

—*The Times* (UK)

"In this haunting debut, set in a starkly beautiful landscape, Hooper delineates the stories of Etta and the men she loved (Otto and Russell) as they intertwine through youth and wartime and into old age. It's a lovely book you'll want to linger over."

—Book of the Week, *People* magazine

"Quirky, offbeat . . . there's a fragmented, almost musical quality to [Hooper's] prose . . . There are few temporal or territorial signposts; instead, Hooper develops a complex patchwork of past, present and magical realist dream states . . . Those who love [director Wes Anderson's] stylized, whimsical film-making will probably love this book . . . [Hooper] offers a sweet, redemptive message here. Quests are generally reserved for heroic types: dashing knights, courageous hobbits. Now eighty-something Etta and her fictional counterparts are giving the myths a 21st-century twist. Modern life is full of people spouting rubbish about spurious emotional and spiritual 'journeys.' Etta's trek as she comes to the end of her life and reckons with the past has, in contrast, a real and worthwhile dignity to it."

—*Financial Times*

"Heartfelt . . . In simple, graceful prose, Hooper has woven a tale of deep longing, for reinvention and self-discovery, as well as for the past and for love and for the boundless unknown."

—*San Francisco Chronicle*

"Fictional journeys toward enlightenment and self-discovery fill miles of book shelves, but few are as freshly told as the road trip traced in *Etta and Otto and Russell and James* . . . Enchanting . . . The novel has a fairy-tale quality, one that lingers long after the story's dreamlike ending. It's filled with magical realism, whimsy and the idea that you're never too old to take risks."

—*Minneapolis Star-Tribune*

"[Hooper's] crisp, unadorned prose beautifully captures her characters' sentiments, and conveys with compassion but also a degree of distance their experiences of love and pain, longing and loss . . . Depictions of war, the way that trauma infiltrates even the most innocuous moments, are similarly brilliant and beautiful . . . Images like this evoke worlds of memory and feeling, and this novel pulsates with an energy that can best be described as raw but also highly restrained."

—*Chicago Tribune*

"Like a fairy tale, *Etta and Otto and Russell and James* is whimsical, even magical. A bit like the Canadian prairie, it is spare, yet beautiful . . . The texture that Hooper layers on—through almost remarkably small details, crafted in carefully chosen words—gives this novel a richness of character and an almost overwhelming sense of place . . . Hooper's writing is almost like poetry . . . The novel was a little like *The Unlikely Pilgrimage of Harold Fry* . . . it was also a little like *Life of Pi* . . . but mostly, I decided, it was about the Canadian prairie . . . and about even bigger things, like the lovely and terrible realities of being human."

—*Fort Worth Star-Telegram*

"To a Cormac McCarthy–like narrative—sans quotation marks, featuring crisp, concise conversations—Hooper adds magical realism . . . With beautifully crafted descriptions . . . Hooper immerses herself in characters . . . The book ends with sheer poetry, stunning and powerful, multiple short chapters where identities and dreams, longings and memories shift and cling to one character and then another within the 'long loop of existence.' A masterful near-homage to *Pilgrim's Progress*: souls redeemed through struggle."

—*Kirkus Reviews*, starred review

"Debut novelist Hooper's spare, evocative prose dips in and out of reality and travels between past and present, creating what Etta tells Otto is 'just a long loop.' This is a quietly powerful story whose dreamlike quality lingers long after the last page is turned."

—*Library Journal*, starred review

"Drawing on wisdom and whimsy of astonishing grace and maturity, Hooper has written an irresistibly enchanting debut novel that explores mysteries of love old and new, the loyalty of animals and dependency of humans, the horrors of war and perils of loneliness, and the tenacity of time and fragility of memory."

—*Booklist*, starred review

"Hooper's arresting debut novel, with its spare, evocative prose, seamlessly interweaves accounts of the present-day lives of its eponymous main characters with the stories of their pasts and how they first connected with each other . . . Hooper, with great insight, explores the interactions and connections between spouses and friends—the rivalries, the camaraderie, the joys and tragedies—and reveals the extraordinary lengths to which people will go in the name of love."

—*Publishers Weekly*, starred review

"Emma Hooper's assured first novel captures the stark beauty and unsettling openness of the western plains of Canada, where much of it is set. It gives its characters room to make their own paths through the world, and leaves gaps in their lives for the reader to fill in . . . A tender and poignant look at the way the end of life circles back to its earlier history."

—*The Columbus Dispatch*

"Hooper has conjured a character who is a gift . . . As the lines blur between Etta's and Otto's memories, and even between their physical bodies, readers emerge with a deeper appreciation for life and for its suffering against its backdrop of majesty. If you let it, the novel can encourage radical acceptance of the fact that everyone, and everything, is interconnected."

—*The Dallas Morning News*

"Lyrical . . . a touching reminder that age really is just a number."

—*Woman's Day* magazine

"You can see why publishers paid high sums for this first novel, whose shifting timelines, plots, and registers contrast starkly with its unchanging main setting, the featureless prairie of Saskatchewan . . . Hooper handles the tonal changes, narrative leaps, and gorgeous landscapes with an assurance beyond her years."

—Vulture.com

"The floodgates opened as I closed in on the last page of Emma Hooper's *Etta and Otto and Russell and James*. The ending she'd crafted was bittersweet, and desolated my heart in the loveliest fashion possible. However, it was knowing that this voice—this writer—was leaving me that stung the most . . . Hooper's story is a transparent glimpse into the roots and repercussions of a relationship with bittersweet, beautiful ends that are largely worth the separation-anxiety tears."

—Bustle.com

"*Etta and Otto and Russell and James* is incredibly moving, beautifully written and luminous with wisdom. It is a book that restores one's faith in life even as it deepens its mystery. Wonderful!"

—Chris Cleave, #1 *New York Times* bestselling author of *Little Bee*

ETTA AND OTTO AND
RUSSELL AND JAMES

EMMA HOOPER

Always and Always.
On and On.

SIMON & SCHUSTER PAPERBACKS

NEW YORK   LONDON   TORONTO   SYDNEY   NEW DELHI

Simon & Schuster Paperbacks
An Imprint of Simon & Schuster, Inc.
1230 Avenue of the Americas
New York, NY 10020

First Simon & Schuster trade paperback edition May 2015

SIMON & SCHUSTER PAPERBACKS and colophon are registered trademarks of Simon & Schuster, Inc.

For information about special discounts for bulk purchases, please contact Simon & Schuster Special Sales at 1-866-506-1949 or business@simonandschuster.com.

The Simon & Schuster Speakers Bureau can bring authors to your live event. For more information or to book an event, contact the Simon & Schuster Speakers Bureau at 1-866-248-3049 or visit our website at www.simonspeakers.com.

Interior design by Ruth Lee-Mui

Manufactured in the United States of America

1   3   5   7   9   10   8   6   4   2

The Library of Congress has cataloged the hardcover edition as follows:

Hooper, Emma.
Etta and Otto and Russell and James : a novel / Emma Hooper.
— First Simon & Schuster hardcover edition
pages cm
"Simon & Schuster Fiction Original Hardcover."
1. Older women—Fiction. 2. Memory—Fiction. 3. Friendship—Fiction. I. Title.
PR9199.4.H6495E88 2015
813'.6—dc23
2013045400

ISBN 978-1-4767-5567-0
ISBN 978-1-4767-5568-7 (pbk)
ISBN 978-1-4767-5570-0 (ebook)

For C & T
always and always
on and on

ETTA AND OTTO AND RUSSELL AND JAMES

1

Otto,

The letter began, in blue ink,

I've gone. I've never seen the water, so I've gone there. Don't worry,
I've left you the truck. I can walk. I will try to remember to come back.

Yours (always),
Etta.

Underneath the letter she had left a pile of recipe cards. All the things she had always made. Also in blue ink. So he would know what and how to eat while she was away. Otto sat down at the table and arranged them so no two were overlapping. Columns and rows. He thought about putting on his coat and shoes and going out to try and find her, maybe asking neighbors if they had seen which way she went, but he didn't. He just sat at the table with the letter and the cards. His hands trembled. He laid one on top of the other to calm them.

After a while Otto stood and went to get their globe. It had a light in the middle, on the inside, that shone through the latitude and longitude lines. He turned it on and turned off the regular kitchen lights. He put it on the far side of the table, away from the letter and cards, and traced a path with his finger. Halifax. If she went east, Etta would have three thousand, two hundred and thirty-two kilometers to cross. If west, to Vancouver, twelve hundred and one kilometers. But she would go east, Otto knew. He could feel the tightness in the skin across his chest pulling that way. He noticed his rifle was missing from the front closet. It would still be an hour or so until the sun rose.

Growing up, Otto had fourteen brothers and sisters. Fifteen altogether, including him. This was when the flu came and wouldn't go, and the soil was even dryer than usual, and the banks had all turned inside out, and all the farmers' wives were losing more children than they were keeping. So families were trying and trying, for every five pregnancies, three babies, and for every three babies, one child. Most of the farmers' wives were pregnant most of the time. The silhouette of a beautiful woman, then, was a silhouette rounded with potential. Otto's mother was no different. Beautiful. Always round.

Still, the other farmers and their wives were wary of her. She was cursed, or blessed; *supernatural,* they said to one another across postboxes. Because Otto's mother, Grace, lost none of her children. Not One. Every robust pregnancy running smoothly into a ruddy infant and every infant to a barrel-eared child, lined up between siblings in gray and off-gray nightclothes, some holding babies, some holding hands, leaning into the door to their parents' room, listening fixedly to the moaning from within.

Etta, on the other hand, had only one sister. Alma with the pitch-black hair. They lived in town.

Let's play nuns, said Etta, once, after school but before dinner.

Why nuns? said Alma. She was braiding Etta's hair. Etta's just-normal like a cowpat hair.

Etta thought about the nuns they saw, sometimes, on the edges of town, moving ghostly-holy between the shops and church. Sometimes by the hospital. Always clean in black and white. She looked down at her own red shoes. Blue buckles. Undone. Because they're beautiful, she said.

No, Etta, said Alma, nuns don't get to be beautiful. Or have adventures. Everybody forgets nuns.

I don't, said Etta.

Anyway, said Alma, I might get married. And you might too.

No, said Etta.

Maybe, said Alma. She leaned down and did up her sister's shoe. And, she said, what about adventures?

You have those before you become a nun.

And then you have to stop? asked Alma.

And then you get to stop.

2

The first field Etta walked across the morning she left was theirs.
Hers and Otto's. If there was ever dew here, there would still have
been dew on the wheat stalks. But only dust brushed off onto her
legs. Warm, dry, dust. It took no time at all to cross their fields, her
feet not even at home in the boots yet. Two kilometers down, already.
Russell Palmer's field was next.

Etta didn't want Otto to see her leaving, which is why she left
so early, so quietly. But she didn't mind about Russell. She knew he
couldn't keep up with her even if he wanted to.

His land was five hundred acres bigger than theirs, and his house
was taller, even though he lived alone, and even though he was almost
never in it. This morning he was standing halfway between his house
and the end of his land, in the middle of the early grain. Standing,
looking. It took fifteen minutes of walking before Etta reached him.

A good morning for looking, Russell?

Just normal. Nothing yet.

Nothing?

Nothing worth noting.

Russell was looking for deer. He was too old, now, to work his own land, the hired crew did that, so instead he looked for deer, from right before sunrise until an hour or so after and then again from an hour or so before sunset until right after. Sometimes he saw one. Mostly he didn't.

Well, nothing except you, I suppose. Maybe you scared them away.

Maybe. I'm sorry.

Russell had been looking all around while he spoke, at Etta, around her, above her, at her again. But now he stopped. He just looked at her.

Are you sorry?

About the deer, Russell, only about the deer.

You're sure?

I'm sure.

Oh, okay.

I'm going to walk on now, Russell, good luck with the deer.

Okay, have a good walk. Hello and love to Otto. And to any deer if you see them.

Of course, have a good day, Russell.

You too, Etta. He took her hand, veined, old, lifted it and kissed it. Holding it to his lips for one, two seconds. I'll be here if you need me, he said.

I know, said Etta.

Okay. Goodbye then.

He didn't ask, where are you going, or why are you going. He turned back around to face where the deer might be. She walked on, east. In her bag, pockets, and hands were:

Four pairs of underwear.

One warm sweater.

Some money.

Some paper, mostly blank, but one page with addresses on it and one page with names.

One pencil and one pen.

Four pairs of socks.

Stamps.

Cookies.

A small loaf of bread.

Six apples.

Ten carrots.

Some chocolate.

Some water.

A map, in a plastic bag.

Otto's rifle, with bullets.

One small fish skull.

Six-year-old Otto was checking the chicken wire for fox-sized holes. A fox could fit through anything bigger than his balled fist, even underground, even up quite high. He would find an opening and press his hand gently against it, pretending to be a fox. The chickens would run away. Unless Wiley, whose job it was to throw grain at the birds, was with him. But this time Wiley wasn't there, and, so, the chickens were afraid of Otto's fist. I am a fox. Otto wrapped his thumb around the front of his balled fingers and moved it like a mouth. I am a fox, let me in, pressing gently, but as hard as a fox, as a fox's mouth. I am hungry, I will eat you. Otto was hungry. He almost always was. Sometimes he ate little bits of the chicken grain. Good to chew on. If Wiley wasn't there.

He had checked three and a half sides of the wiring when three-and-a-half-year-old Winnie walked up in overalls with no shirt. Otto had put a shirt on her that morning, but it was hot, so she had taken it off. Dinner, she said. Close enough that he could hear, but not too close; chickens scared her. Otto, she said. Dinnertime. Then she left to find Gus and tell him the same. This was her job.

As well as a name, each child in Otto's family had a number, so they were easier to keep track of. Marie-1, Clara-2, Amos-3, Harriet-4, Walter-5, Wiley-6, Otto-7, and so on. Marie-1 was the eldest. The numeration was her idea.

1?

Yes.

2?

Yes.

3?

Hello.

4?

Yes, hello.

5?

Yes, yes, hello, hello.

6?

Present.

7?

Yes, please.

8?

Present.

9?

Hello!

Everyone was always present. Nobody ever missed dinner, or supper.

So, said Otto's mother, everyone is here. Everyone is clean?

Otto nodded vehemently. He was clean. He was starving. Everyone else nodded too. Winnie's hands were filthy and everyone knew it, but everyone nodded, including Winnie.

Okay then, said their mother, ladle propped against her round belly, soup!

Everyone rushed to the table, each to their own chair. Except today there was no chair for Otto. Or, rather, there was, but there was someone else in it. A boy. Not a brother. Otto looked at him, then reached across, in front, and took the spoon from him.

That's mine, he said.

Okay, said the boy.

Otto grabbed the knife. That's mine too, he said. And this, he said, grabbing the still-empty bowl.

Okay, said the boy.

The boy said nothing else and Otto didn't know what else to say, or do. He stood behind his chair, trying not to drop all his things, trying not to cry. He knew the rules. You didn't bother parents with child-problems unless there was blood or it involved an animal. Otto's mother was coming around, child by child, with the pot and ladle, so Otto, standing with his things, crying quietly, would have to wait for her to get to them. The other boy just looked straight ahead.

Otto's mother was spooning exactly one ladle of soup into each child's bowl. One for each, exactly, until, a pause, and,

I don't think you're Otto.

No, neither do I.

I'm Otto, right here.

Then who is this?

I don't know.

I'm from next door. I'm starving. I'm Russell.

But the Palmers don't have any children.

They have a nephew. One nephew. Me.

Otto's mother paused. Clara-2, she said, get another bowl from the cupboard, please.

Until recently, Russell's parents had lived in the city, in Saskatoon, and, until recently, Russell had lived there too, with them. But five weeks ago the banks announced that everything was absolutely broken, right there in the paper, for anyone who hadn't noticed yet for themselves, and three weeks ago, Russell's father, who owned a shop right in the middle of downtown, an everything shop with wrenches and lemon candy and bolts of printed cotton in rows, had turned a bit white, then a bit dizzy, then had to sit down, then had to lie down, and then, after sweating and sweating and Russell getting so much cold water from the kitchen, carried in the biggest bronze pitcher, hefting it up the stairs, hugging it to himself, so cold with the water inside, and bringing it to the bedroom where his father was lying, at first alone, and then, soon, with the doctor standing by, and then, not too long after, with the doctor and the priest standing by, while Russell's mother cooked for everyone and dealt with *all this goddamn paperwork* until, two weeks ago, while Russell was carrying a twelfth bronze pitcher from the kitchen, so cold against his stomach and chest, almost burning cold, Russell's father gave up and died. His mother sighed and put on her black dress, the one with the stiff lace collar, before closing up the shop for good, and going to work as a typist in Regina.

Russell rode part of the way with her on the train. He'd never been on a train before. The skinny-skinny cows zipped past so quickly. Russell wanted to lean out the window and open his eyes as wide as he could so that all the air hit them and dried them out, forever. But the windows didn't open. So, instead, Russell traced his finger up and down his mother's collar, following the twisting path of the lace, and let his eyes be wet. Almost exactly halfway between Saskatoon and Regina, the train stopped and Russell got off and his mother did not. You'll like the farm, she said. Farms are better.

Okay, said Russell.

They're better, she said.

Okay, said Russell.

And I'll see you soon, you know, she said.

Yes, said Russell. Okay.

Russell's aunt and uncle were waiting on the platform. They had made a small sign from the side of a milk crate. *WELLCOME HOME RUSSEL!* it said. Despite trying, they had had no children of their own.

That same year, the year Etta was six, it did not rain, not once. This was odd, this was bad, but what was worse was that it did not snow either. In January she could walk out of town through the tall grass and everything would look like summer, no frost, no powder, but, if you touched them, or a bird tried to land on them, the grass-stalks would crumble, frozen and brittle. Alma had taken Etta out for a walk, to where the creek was, when there was a creek. They were looking at fish skeletons, all of them strung out along the dry bed, the whitest things. If a beetle or worm had bored through any of the bones they would take them home and use them to make necklaces. The skulls, of course, already had holes in them, but Etta's sister didn't like to use these for jewelry.

They can come back alive when they touch your skin, she said. And start talking. Leave those.

Okay, said Etta. But when Alma wasn't looking she stuffed smaller skulls into her mittens, on the top sides of her hands so she could still bend her fingers.

Are your ears cold? said Alma.

A bit, said Etta. Even though they weren't cold at all. She was holding her mitten-hands to her ears to see if she could hear them, the fish skulls. To see if being against the skin of her fingers was enough to wake them up, to make them talk. The wind was loud that day, but if Etta pressed her skin against the bone against the wool hard enough, there was something. There were whispers.

What language do fish speak?

Alma was brushing dust from a beautiful rib, almost transparent; she did not look up. Probably French, she said. Like Grandma.

Etta pressed her mittens to her ears and whispered, Should I be a nun?

The wind blew and the insides of her mittens said, *Non, non, non.*

3

Etta sang as she walked. She never forgot the words.

We sit and gaze across the plains
and wonder why it never rains
and Gabriel blows his trumpet sound
he says, "The rain she's gone around."

She walked away from the roads, through the early fields. She knew the farmers wouldn't like it, but on the road every truck would want to stop and say hello and where are you off to and what are you up to, so she walked through the fields, trying not to crush any growth too badly. It was broad and mostly empty here, save occasional cattle, so she sang as loud as she liked.

She stopped for food in the rest-stop café in Holdfast. They had changed the tables and chairs since she was last there, with Alma.

Less color, cleaner. Nobody noticed her come into town, and nobody noticed her leave, except for the waitress and the boy at the till.

After eating three cabbage rolls, two pieces of white bread with butter, and one slice of rhubarb pie and paying for them, Etta left with ten sachets of ketchup and eight of green relish tucked into her coat pocket. Relish was vegetable and sugar and ketchup was fruit and sugar and either could see you through if you needed them to.

It was just starting to get dark when, little by little, the crops began to thin and the ground began to turn sandy and then to sand completely. And then, just as the sun sat down below the stretching orange of the horizon, Etta stopped walking; having made her way right up to a lake, right up to the water, just far enough away from the push of the waves to stay dry. She knew, of course, that she would encounter obstacles of smaller water before she was through to Halifax. She'd heard Ontario was full of them. But she didn't expect anything quite so soon. She sat down on the sand, a few meters from the wet edge. It felt good to sit. She wondered about swimming. How much energy it took; how far a person could go without needing to stop. She leaned back onto the beach and listened to the waves, a new kind of sound. Etta closed her eyes.

Oh my god I bet it's somebody dead.
　No!
　Maybe.
　Well, are you going to check?
　Come with me.
　Of course.
　I love you.
　I love you. And, look, not dead. Breathing.

I hear sometimes they do that, after death.

What, bodies? Breathe?

Yeah.

No.

Maybe.

No.

Etta woke at their footsteps, shuddering through the sand toward her, but she kept her eyes closed to listen as the couple approached. She breathed shallow. In sleep, her legs had burrowed down in the sand, and much of her torso too. The weight against her was comforting. She could feel it cracking and then coming back together as she breathed in and out. If I open my eyes they will ask me who I am, she thought. But if I don't open my eyes, they'll think I'm dead. Probably call the police. She pulled at her thoughts, tried to stretch open her mind, still with her eyes closed. Sand. The feeling of sand. Tiredness in her hips. Night. Voices. Light wind. A sister with black hair. A house in the city. Writing paper. Paper.

The couple were still talking, distracted. Keeping her eyes closed, Etta reached through to her coat pocket to get to the paper, fumbling through restaurant packets, triggering sand cascades. Not subtle, not unnoticeable. And there it was. Folded. She took it out. Unfolded it. They must have realized, now, that I'm not dead. They must be waiting. Or afraid. She opened her eyes. As it was dark, she had to hold the paper quite close to her face.

You:

it said.

Etta Gloria Kinnick of Deerdale farm. 83 years old in August.

Etta Gloria Kinnick, she whispered, to herself. Okay. Right, okay.

I'm not dead, she said, to the two young people standing beside her, staring. I'm Etta Gloria Kinnick. A person can't keep breathing after death.

Oh god! I mean, good! I mean hello, said the boy.

See? Told you, said the girl.

Are you okay? said the boy.

Yes, yes, I'm fine.

Oh, okay, good.

. . .

. . .

Do you need help getting home?

I'm not going home. So, no. No, thank you.

Are you homeless?

George!

Well, she just doesn't look homeless, is all.

I'm not homeless. I'm just not going home.

Where are you going?

East.

But that means across Last Mountain Lake.

Or around it.

But it's really long, right?

I don't know. Maybe.

It is. We have a map in our cabin. It is.

. . .

. . .

Hey, can we help you up?

Molly and George, the kids who found Etta, had come from a party; they had excused themselves quietly, separately, seven minutes apart, and then had met, a hundred meters further down the beach, behind the Lamberts' fishing shed. They were on their way back to the party, half an hour or so later, when they found Etta. And now that they had found her, and established she was not dead, and helped her to stand up and brush the sand off her legs and back, they were heading back there, to the party, both smelling of dry yellow perch nets, with indentations of gill lines across their backs and stomachs.

Hey, you know what? said Molly.

What? said George.

What? said Etta.

You should come with us. Back to the party. Come with us.

Yeah? said George.

Yeah? said Etta.

Yeah! said Molly, already taking Etta's hands, already moving forward down the beach toward the noise and the light.

Dear Otto,

I am on a boat. Just a small one, a cheap inflatable one, which is good, because I'm not sure how or if I'll be able to get it back to its owners, the younger twin sisters of a boy I met last night around a fire on the west beach of Last Mountain Lake. We were at a party. One girl said I was like her grandmother, now dead. I told her I'm nobody's grandmother and I'm not dead, and she said that made it perfect.

I am using a paddle we found on the beach. We don't know whose it is. I guess the twins never wanted to go far enough to need a paddle.

When I'm across I'll put the paddle in the dinghy and push them back onto the lake, with a note that says: Boat: property of the McFarlan twins. Paddle: owner unknown. I have already written it, on a napkin. I have other, real paper, (like this) but I don't want to use it up too fast.

As well as the boat and paddle, the kids also gave me two beers and half a forty of rye. Good in case I get cold, they said. They really were nice kids. Some of them were in love.

Remember to wear a hat and eat the spinach when it comes up.

Your,
Etta.

Otto got the letter five days after Etta had dated it. He was cleaning the oven, following handwritten instructions on a yellowed recipe card—

NEEDED:

Baking soda and water.

INSTRUCTIONS:

Apply, wait, remove.

—when the letter arrived with the morning mail. Etta had been gone for one week. The first day he had tried going out into his fields, as usual, but couldn't stop looking back, toward the house. Like Russell, with his deer.

The rest of the week Otto worked in the close garden plot or in the house. His stomach hurt whenever he got further away than that. He turned the garden soil and raked it out, then did the same the next day. Lining up the indents of the rake exactly, row to row. He would not plant anything, spinach or carrots or radishes, in the rows until Etta had reached Manitoba.

On his family farm, as a boy, Otto's before-dinner chore was check-ing the chicken wire. After dinner, he looked for rocks. Again he used his fist. If a rock was smaller than his fist, he left it. If it was bigger than his fist, he put it in a flour sack that he dragged behind him until it was almost but not quite too heavy to drag. Then he would take it to the edge of their land, to the ditch that separated it from the Palmers', and dump the rocks there. This was Rocksvalley, and on Sundays, when they didn't have to do chores, Otto and his brothers and sisters and, now, Russell, played Treacherous Journey there. If a rock was very big, too big for him to lift himself, he had to call out or run and get Harriet (4) and Walter (5), whose job was to drown the gophers who would otherwise dig and dig and dig their way through all the farm's soil. Harriet and Walter would also be working in the fields, and had stronger arms that could lift bigger rocks. Most of the time, though, Otto could lift what he found. Especially now that Russell came with him. He was only five months younger than Otto, so Otto's mother had taken to calling him Russell (7-and-a-half). She told him, you're welcome to eat here, Russell (7-and-a-half), I certainly don't mind; I bet it's lonely over there all alone; but, if you're here, you'll do your share of chores too. Right?

Okay, said Russell. He sounded afraid. This made Otto happy, even if it meant Russell tagged along with him now, getting in his way.

Don't your aunt and uncle have work for you on their farm? said Otto, his eyes scanning back and forth across the ground in front of him like a scythe, a system he had invented for finding all the rocks. Russell was walking a few steps behind, in case he missed any. This was Russell's sixth day of helping.

No. They don't believe in child-working, said Russell, someone could get hurt.

Hm. How're you going to learn to do the farm yourself then, later?

I don't know if I'm gonna. Besides, I go to school, said Russell. Because they were walking the way they were, one in front of the other, they had to say everything half-shouting. The wind blew crop dust up onto their tongues and the roofs of their mouths. Otto had taught Russell how to spit to clear it out, every ten minutes or so.

We go to school too, said Otto. Except in summer, like now, and harvest and Christmas and Easter. We can count up and down to ten. Even Winnie can. But that's not going to teach you how to keep away a fox from eating all your chickens so nobody gets eggs at breakfast or in cake.

Well, said Russell, we don't have cake much. He kicked a too-small rock. And I like school, he said.

Russell, in essence, became one of the Vogel children. He worked with them, ate with them, skipped school with them, and grew with them. Some of the younger children forgot or barely knew that he wasn't their brother, although he usually left at five o'clock in the evening to go home to his aunt and uncle's for dinner and prayers and bed. There was always a hot water bottle ready in his bed, even though water was scarce and his aunt had to rewarm it, out and then back into the bottle night after night. Apart from this, Russell was a Vogel. Which is why it was so shocking to the rest of them when they learned that he had never been on a tractor.

It's okay to not have driven one. We can't drive till we're ten for the girls, or twelve for the boys.

No, not just driving. He's never even *been on* one.

Never?

Never.

This was Otto and Walter. They were taking a break from their chores, going to get water from the house for themselves and for Russell and Harriet, whom they had left in the field looking for rocks and gopher holes, respectively. It was hot. Just past Dominion Day and dusty and dry and hot. Walter wore a hat too big for him. Otto always forgot his, so he wasn't wearing one. The sun was burning, again, the strip of skin where his hair parted. Later he would have to pick the peeling bits of it from his hair, and he'd hate it and go and find his hat and put it on the post of his bed to never forget again, but he would forget again. Much later this bit of skin would just stay red May through September, even when his hair was white and thin. Neighbors would use it as a sort of long-range calendar, planting spinach when it would first appear, covering up their tomatoes when it started to fade.

Poor Russell, said Walter.

I know, said Otto. Though, actually, he was glad.

Harriet!

What about her?

She's old enough! She's old enough to drive, right?

Yeah . . . but I don't suppose we should. There aren't any tractor chores right now. And you haven't found all the gophers.

We'll never find all the gophers. And you'll never find all the rocks.

We might. We're trying.

You won't. Let's get the water, take it to Harriet and Russell, then get Harriet to get the tractor, and then get Russell up on it. Let's do it! We can do it quick. Fifteen minutes, only, once along the side of the field, then back to rocks, and gophers. Yeah?

Maybe, said Otto.

Okay, said Harriet. Driving's easy. No problem.

Okay? said Otto. Are you sure?

Yeah, why not? It won't take fifteen minutes.

See? said Walter.

What do *you* think, said Otto, turning to Russell, who, thus far, had said nothing.

Okay, he said.

There was only room for two of them up on the tractor. Well, only room for one, really, just one molded metal seat, painted green, molded for legs much bigger than Harriet's, but there was a bit of space behind it where someone could stand and hold on to the driver's shoulders. If you were very small, you could also sit on the driver's lap, squeezed in before the steering wheel. Most of the Vogels had done it this way for their first time, on their mother's lap, or father's or Marie's, but Russell was too big and Harriet too small, so Russell would be standing. Walter and Otto would be watching, on the ground.

At first they cheered and shouted as Harriet steered away from them and down, along the side of the field. Then they stood and watched the back of the tractor for a minute or so. Then they could hardly see anything at all, so they turned back to gophers and rocks, walking slowly along the field in the sunken path of the tractor tracks.

Two large stones and one drowned gopher later, they thought they saw Amos—whose job it was, at this time of year, to pick wild Saskatoon berries into two big buckets, and whose fingers were always deep purple from it—running toward them, waving his berry-colored hands up over his head. They didn't realize it was Harriet until Otto saw the braids trailing out from under her hat. Her hands were more red than purple now, from up close. Her breath was like a machine's.

A coyote, she said. He was startled. It wasn't his fault, it wasn't mine. A coyote, she said.

She grabbed Otto's hand, and he grabbed Walter's. They ran together, back down the ridges made by the tractor tires.

Otto had seen plenty of dying things. Plenty. He had seen gophers, drowned, from when Harriet and Walter drowned them out, or shot, from when they didn't drown and instead ran up and away from the water, right to Harriet's gun. They were shot in the head, usually, and killed straightaway, except when they moved unpredictably and got shot in the side or leg, and would keep moving for a bit, keep trying at life, until Harriet could get in a good second shot to stop them hurting.

And he'd seen chickens, of course, half-left from foxes, and broken wild birds, from the windows or from cats.

And once, when he was younger, only four, Otto had found the very smallest kitten, a runt, brand new and abandoned in the tall grass behind the outhouse. It was gray and pink and very tiny. He kept it secret, because they weren't allowed to have pets just for themselves. He took the turkey roasting pan that his mother only ever used at Christmas, filled in with rags and pencil shavings to make a nice bed, and kept the kitten in it, tucked back in the high grass where he had found her. He kept the lid on when he wasn't around, to keep the kitten in and the foxes and dogs out. The kitten was so small that she hid easily under the rags and in the pencil shavings, and Otto would have to dig to find her each time he came with a small bit of milk or milk-soaked bread. He would hold her in one hand up to his face and tell her, You are small now, but you will be so big. You shouldn't be scared. You will be the queen of the cats. Don't be scared, don't be sad. You're gonna be great, great, great. He would stroke her with his little finger over her round wrinkled head and hope for her eyes to open. She would hold on to him with her claws that tickled more than hurt. He called her Cynthia.

But Cynthia's eyes didn't open. And she never ate the milk-bread and barely drank the milk. And she started moving less and sleeping more, only sleeping, and only barely holding on when Otto lifted her. He stroked her head and stroked her head and even tried, a little, to pull back the skin to open her eyes, but nothing worked. He would rock her, slowly, in his hand, and say, Cynthia, Cynthia, Cynthia, wake up, wake up, wake up, but she was sick, and he knew sick. Sick like a neighbor baby. So, one night, after using the outhouse, Otto lifted the roasting pan out of the grass, with sick Cynthia in it, and carried it carefully and quietly up to the bedroom. Amos, eight years old and wise, was awake when he came in.

Otto? he whispered. Others were sleeping all around.

Yeah?

Why do you have the turkey pan?

Don't tell?

I won't tell.

Come and see.

Amos got up, careful not to wake Walter, with whom he shared his bed, and they went into the hall. Otto put the roasting pan on the floor between them. It's my kitten, he said. Cynthia. She's sick. He lifted off the pan's lid. You hafta dig to find her, he said. She hides. He found her in the corner, in the shavings. He lifted her up in his right hand like he always did. She had shavings stuck to her back and head. She only sleeps, he said.

She's bald, said Amos.

Yeah, said Otto.

They both looked at her for a few seconds. From the room behind them they could hear everyone's sleep-breathing.

You know she's dead, said Amos.

Yeah, said Otto. His throat was dry. He was holding his hand so, so, carefully.

Okay, said Amos. He put his hand on Otto's shoulder and kept it there.

Okay, said Otto.

It was almost a year later, walking toward dinner after chores, when Amos said to Otto, You know Cynthia? She was a gopher, you know. Not a cat. She would have been killed anyway; she was a gopher.

Otto said nothing, just nodded.

And he had seen dead calves, the ones that came out wrong, some of them already dead, and some of them close enough that they soon died, with help or without, their eyes almost bigger than their heads, their legs spun around one another.

This was the thing Russell looked most like, on the ground, half under the tractor, legs spun around each other like licorice. Except his eyes were closed, like Cynthia's. Otto looked at him, and then turned around and threw up.

There was a coyote, said Harriet. She ran past us and Russell got scared and let go of me and I had to turn to not run over her and Russell slipped and it wasn't his fault and it wasn't mine and it wasn't his fault and it wasn't mine it wasn't mine, she said.

Everyone was wearing trousers except Otto, who had on a pair of Walter's old overalls, rolled up at the ankles. This was the biggest piece of clothing between them, so Otto took them off, and they lifted unconscious Russell up onto them, like a stretcher, still twisted, his eyes still closed, and carried him back toward the house, Harriet and Walter with one overall leg each, pulled taut, and Otto, in his shirt and underwear, in the back holding the straps and watching Russell's closed eyes.

Russell didn't die, but one of his legs did; his right leg forever twisted like a licorice lace, so that when you saw him walking across a field you always knew it was him, no matter if the sun was in your eyes. He folded down and in with every second step, the momentum following through in the direction of his bent right foot, taking all the strength of his other leg and back and stomach to pull himself true again, over and over. If you watched him walk across a big space it looked as if he was waltzing with himself.

Not too many years later, Etta and Alma drove all the way to Hold-fast in silence. Etta was fifteen. Alma at the wheel, in her beige shoes with heels. Her dancing shoes. Etta thought it must be difficult to drive in shoes like that, but she didn't say anything. The wind was louder, even, than the car. When they reached the rest-stop café, Alma directed them to a table against the wall. They ordered from a waitress they didn't know, and then,

I'm sick, Etta, said Alma. Her black hair was down; it was usually up. It changed her face shape like this, hid the stronger lines, hid her. The wind in the car had blown it messy.

You don't look sick, said Etta. She knew sick when people turned gray, or yellow, or coughed a lot or lost their voices or couldn't eat for one reason or another, but Alma was none of these things. Her voice was quieter, but it was there. Her face was hiding, but it was the right color. And she was eating. They'd ordered pie. Sour cream raisin for Alma, Saskatoon-berry for Etta. No one had had flu for a long time, years, not since they were very small. And that had been mostly the farm kids, not town kids like them with working lights and inside toilets. Still, Etta's heart beat harder. You look fine, Alma, she said.

Alma put her hands on the table, palms up. Etta had to stop herself from doing the same. Her first instinct was always to do like Alma. Instead she pressed her hands, palms up, against the bottom of the table. I don't have flu, said Alma.

Okay, said Etta.

I've ruined everything.

You have?

We have.

We have?

I'm not going to tell him though.

Who? What?

Jim.

Oh, said Etta. Her stomach dropped; her face went cold, felt green. She hoped Alma couldn't see it. Etta loved Jim. Jim took her out driving, along with Alma. Jim made her parents laugh. Oh, oh, oh.

The waitress came back with the pie. Thank you, they said.

Thank *you*, said the waitress, tilting her head while she said it, smiling. Then she turned around and headed back for the kitchen. Her shoes were like Alma's, only more worn, with scuffs on the heels and across the fronts. Etta looked at her sister. Not her face, but everywhere else. Her breasts, her arms, her shoulders. She couldn't see Alma's stomach, because of the table, but she imagined it, the white skin of it, pulling under the cotton of her blue dress.

I'm going to have to leave, said Alma. I've thought and thought and thought and, that's it. I'm going.

Going?

Yes.

Where?

To an aunt's.

But we don't have any aunts.

That's not what that means, Etta.

I don't, said Etta, then she stopped herself, looked down at the plate in front of her; a blue-flowered vine snaked around the edge. She wasn't sick, but Etta didn't want her pie anymore. Oh, she said. Will Jim go too?

I don't know. I doubt it. Why should he go?

But he—

That's not how it works, Etta.

Etta cut into the pastry with her fork. Purple-red. Can I come? she asked.

Etta, said Alma. No.

Alma ate some of her pie, sticky, dripping, so Etta ate some of hers. It was not as good as they could make themselves. We don't even go to church, said Etta.

They don't mind, said Alma.

We don't even really know how to pray.

I do. Now.

So, the baby will be a nun too. Etta pictured a tiny child wrapped up in a habit, surrounded by women with their hair covered. Everyone in black. It was almost beautiful. Everyone singing holy lullabies.

No, said Alma. They give it away.

They give it away?

Yes. And I pray.

Forever?

Forever. But you can visit. And not all the habits are black, there are some that are blue, light blue.

Etta closed her eyes. She could feel her heart beating in her eyelids. She tried to see past black to blue, light blue like the sky, like water.

Alma left less than a week later. So, you convinced her after all, Etta, said their father, walking back from the train station. Imagine, our Alma in a convent. Our Alma. Imagine. He was in front, then Etta, then her mother, strung out along the gravel path through brown grass, just close enough to hear one another.

I'm proud of her, said her father.

Yes, said Etta.

Yes, said her mother, from behind.

Etta did not know if they knew or if they didn't.

The convent was on Prince Edward Island. Such a long train journey away, and then a boat. The only boats Etta and Alma had known were ones made of paper that almost-floated in their mostly mud creek. That's miles, said Etta, on Alma's last night, across their dark bedroom to the place she knew Alma was, despite the blackness of night and drawn curtains. Why that one, so far away?

That's where the light blue habits are, said Alma.

4

Etta,

I am drawing a dotted line across our globe, starting from home, here, out along what I imagine is your path. I only put one or two dashes a day, small ones on our big globe, but it's nice to do, still, still, there is progress and I can watch it. Also, it can be like a Hansel und Gretel trail, leading you back here, should you forget the way. Even though I know you can't see it, or me, right now.

You must be in Manitoba by now.

I have planted the spring seeds. The spinach and carrots and radishes.

I am sending this to William, Harriet (4)'s son, who lives in Brandon. The accountant, you remember. In case you stop there, to sleep maybe, as you pass by, if you pass by, though I know you probably won't, and, probably, William will be confused by the name on the envelope, "Etta Vogel, c/o William Porter," and will post it back to me, but that's *okay. I'll give it to you when you get back; put it in a pile next to the pile I'm making of the letters you're sending here. They're on the kitchen table, because I hardly need all of it to eat at.*

I haven't been out to see Russell, in his field, since last week, when he suggested that maybe I shouldn't come back for a little while because I've got a cough, and it could scare away the deer. So I stay away. But sometimes he comes by after he's done looking, and we have coffee, or sometimes he leaves notes on our door as he passes by. He is well. I haven't told him where you've gone. I tell him you're out, that's all.

Here,
Otto.

P.S. I know you have gone to see the water, and you should see it, Etta, you should, but, in case there are other reasons you've left, in case there are things you have discovered or undiscovered that you didn't want to tell me in person, in that case, you can always tell me here. Tell me here and we can never mention it outside of paper and ink (or pencil).

Etta was in Manitoba. She could tell because the license plates had changed. She had been walking for fourteen days, so far. Washing her body and hair in rivers and streams when she could find them. If her clothes were dirty she would walk into the water with them on, not too far, just enough to let the current pull the dirt and sweat away, and then she would close her eyes and hold her breath and duck her head under, the feel of moving liquid through her thin white hair, against her scalp. At home she had kept it curled, to look like more than it was, but here it dried straight and fine and she tucked it behind her ears like a child. If her clothes weren't dirty, she would take them off and walk into the rivers naked. The cold hitting her in patches: knees, sex, belly button, breasts, mouth, hair. But there weren't always rivers and streams crossing her path; Etta would sometimes go for days dry.

Some months earlier, she had started getting pulled into Otto's dreams instead of her own at night. She would be pulled right in and would be there, in water, in trousers, standing on a gray beach with blood lapping up to her knees and men all around yelling and she would be there, sometimes with a spoon or a towel in her hand and sometimes with nothing. Night after night.

She tried to sleep without any part of her touching any part of him, so his memory couldn't find a contact point to slip into hers.

Because Russell waltzed instead of walked, maybe, or maybe because he usually slept back at his aunt and uncle's, so that he didn't hear and wake when the Vogel parents, late, late into the night, sat at the kitchen table with the radio or just with each other and talked about this thing rolling up and over countries, lots of them, rolling over people, homes, everything, sucking them up, young men especially, young men like them and like their brothers; because Russell didn't wake and put an ear to the rough floorboards, careful of splinters, to hear news from downstairs, or, maybe, because he waltzed instead of walked, Russell wasn't afraid like the rest of them the autumn he and Otto were sixteen, the autumn they had all finally begun going to school for real, really trying this time, now that there were fourteen other Vogels to share the at-home chores. Russell didn't seem to be afraid at all. He whistled when he waltzed to school, on the days that Otto didn't. They each went every second day, so long as their chores were done the day before. On even days Russell put drops into the cows' drippy eyes and lifted boulders of hay from here to there while Otto went to school, worrying, and Otto did the same on odd days while Russell went to school, whistling.

Otto shared his desk with a boy called Owen. He was only fourteen, but ahead of Otto in every subject. He had dark hair in tiny tight curls. He smelled like flower soap. He watched as Otto's hand shook, trying to keep up with the words Mr. Lancaster was writing on the blackboard. *HELLO. MY. NAME. IS. THANK. YOU. CAT. MOLE. FISH. SUN. RAIN. CLOUD.* Mr. Lancaster would say a word, loud and slow, then turn around and write it on the board, then turn back to them and say it again,

HELLO,

HELLO

HELLO.

Owen's assignment had been to write a two-hundred-word piece on a king or queen of his choice, but he had finished long ago. He had written about Boudica. Now he watched Otto's shaking hand. He watched Otto a lot.

Hey, he whispered. Look, there. He pointed to the space between where Otto had copied out *MY. NAME. IS.* and *THANK. YOU.* You've not done that right. You need to fill in that bit, put in your name, or it doesn't make sense. Here, he said, and drew a ^ in the place where he had been pointing. Write it up here, your name, just here. Quick though, before Mr. Lancaster comes to check your work.

They both looked up. Mr. Lancaster was still at the board, writing. Otto looked back down, at the ^. He was losing time, falling behind. At the board Mr. Lancaster had already written two new words: *SEE.* and *SMELL.* Owen was watching, waiting. My name, thought Otto. Mr. Lancaster had never written Otto's name on the board.

Okay, thanks, said Otto.

Owen smiled.

My name, my name, thought Otto. At the board, Mr. Lancaster was writing: *JUMP.* Otto had to write something. He wasn't stupid. He scanned the words he had written so far. *MOLE. THANK. RAIN.* They were all just made of letters. Everything was. But he had no idea which ones he needed. So Otto picked letters from the words he had. The *E* from *MOLE,* the *H* from *THANK,* the *Y* from *YOU,* and so on. Otto wrote, *MY. NAME. IS.* ^ *EHYFE. THANK. YOU.*

At the front of the class Mr. Lancaster wrote: *PINK.* PINK, he said.

Owen followed Otto out of the school at noon. Usually Otto and the other Vogels would walk home for dinner, where they'd tell their mother at least one thing they'd learned before she would give them soup or bread. But today Owen was following him, so Otto stopped.

I'm not stupid, said Otto. I can stop a crazy bull. I can change two diapers at once.

I never said you were, said Owen.

Okay.

Oma says Vogels are the smartest kids around.

Okay.

But, said Owen, but you should know how to write your name.

I wrote my name.

You didn't write your name. You didn't write anybody's name.

Otto kicked at the ground. The dust covered his boot, disappeared it for a half a second, then settled again.

Otto, I can show you. I won't tell anyone. Let me show you, okay?

Otto kicked with his other foot. Balance. He looked over to where Gus (8) was standing with all the other siblings, waiting for him, and waved them away, home. Fine, he said, and followed Owen to the dusty dry dirt patch behind the school.

It's great, said Owen, because your name starts with the same letter as mine. That's neat, hey? That's nice. He pulled up a mostly dried foxtail and used the pointed root end like a quill in the dirt. Look, he said, o. It's just a circle. It's easy. Your whole name is easy, in fact. It's just circles and signs-of-the-cross, like at your church. He traced three more letters in the dirt: *t t o*. He handed Otto the foxtail, and then put his own hand on top of Otto's and guided it. Circle, sign-of-the-cross, sign-of-the-cross, circle.

We don't go to church much, said Otto.

The next day was Russell's turn for school, Russell's turn to sit next to Owen. You're good at writing, said Owen.

Just normal, said Russell. But thanks.

The day after that, Owen showed Otto his surname. It's easy, see? Just an arrowhead, another circle, a fat man fishing, an apple with peel hanging off, and a line. *V o g e l.* See? Owen let Otto hold the foxtail by himself this time, putting his hand across his taller, older, pupil's shoulders instead.

On the days when Otto went to school, Russell would show up, between chores, at three-thirty in the afternoon to meet him and walk back to the farm with him. Sometimes Russell had a dog or younger sibling with him, but usually he came alone, so he and Otto could have some time to talk together, in peace. They walked slowly because of Russell's leg, but Otto didn't mind. Everything else at the farm moved so quickly. On the days when Russell went to school, Otto would meet him in the same way. Every school day, Owen would watch them walking away together, the trail of dust raised by their asymmetrical boot steps hot and dry.

Alma the now-nun wrote letters to her parents and to her sister, Etta, from across a slip of water and so much dusty land. Two a week at least. One to Mother and Father, in a regular, pale brown envelope, and one tucked inside that, in a smaller, but sealed, blue envelope, for Etta, only.

Dear Mother and Father,

Much love to you, Etta, the house. Things are well here, everyone is very kind, very quiet, though we do sing in the mornings. There is more than enough food, even if much of it is fish, which I am not yet used to eating. I have met a girl here called Patricia Market who has cousins in Bladworth; I told her you would surely know the family.

When we're not praying or singing or eating fish, we knit, mostly socks, for those that need them. Cold feet are a horrible thing, especially here, where it can be so wet. Big socks and small socks, but mostly big, for men, or boys who are nearly men. More and more are coming through, in their matching shirts, trousers, caps. But their socks don't match, as we knit with whatever wool we get on donation, sometimes orange sometimes green or red or white. So the boys only look the same until they take off their boots.

Although I know you don't mind one way or the other, I pray for you each day, between dinner and bed.

Your loving daughter,
Alma

And, inside, in the blue envelope,

> *Dear Etta,*
>
> *I'm not throwing up so much anymore. Food tastes so good now that I know I'll (usually) get to keep it. Etta, I love food. Even fish, now. You should try it sometime, if you can find any, out there. Don't let the eyes scare you.*
>
> > *Your Sister,*
> > *Alma*

After this, Etta went to her bureau and opened the drawer second from the top and lifted a small jar out from under two sweaters. She twisted off the lid and upended its contents, one fish skull, into her hand. She held it to her ear, very close. *Ne me mangez pas.*

Or,

> *Dear Mother and Dad,*
>
> *Did you know you can get a cramp just from knitting? A terrible cramp. And it won't be prayed away, even.*
> > *(Find, enclosed, socks. Three pairs.)*
>
> > *Your Daughter,*
> > *Alma*

And,

Dear Etta,

I am huge. I am so much bigger than I ever thought I could be. I never thought of myself as a big person, in any way. Not only my belly, but other things. My feet. My hair. My chest. It feels like my whole body is not mine right now.

The nuns are good at seeing none of it. They have trained for years, I suppose, at seeing nothing. I am training too.

But I still see some things. These boys who are passing through our tiny island by the hundreds now, weighing it down, taking our socks gratefully like they were from their own mothers, these boys all remind me of Jim. Of course they look nothing like him, but, still, I can't stop seeing him in them. We pray, heads down, at the window, from 2 p.m. to 3 p.m., and, while I keep my head down, my eyes stay up, watching them walk past, in twos, in threes. I don't know if I want to see him there for real, or not at all.

But I'm happy, I think. Or maybe not happy, I'm just here, and this is where I am. And that's Good. There is nowhere you can go on this island and not hear the rhythm of the water.

I miss you, of course. I know you are taking care of yourself and being smart and and being Good. Tell me about home, and you, when you get a moment.

Your Sister,
Alma

And,

Dear Mom, dear Dad,

I am thinking about coming home for a visit. We don't have much money, here, but what I do have, combined with the little you send me, should cover the return train and ferry fare. One month from the post date of this letter? Does that sound good to you? If you say yes, I will go and buy the tickets right away. I hope you will find me not too much changed, but holier, of course. And perhaps a little fatter, from all the fish. (And lobster. Lobster! Sometimes there is so much of it that we find them crawling up, out of the water, onto our dock or lawn. I would bring one back, for you to try, but I'm sure Etta would want to keep it as a pet and companion.)

Your Daughter, with love,
Alma

And,

Etta,

Very, very, very close now. In fact, we have passed over close, as I'm now one week and two days overdue. The nuns are keeping a quiet but close eye on me, all the time. They have assigned Sister Margaret Reynolds to sleep with me, in my room, beside my bed on a tiny, and one can only assume uncomfortable, mattress on the floor. I have offered to share my (also tiny, but, still) bed with her, but she has refused. Perhaps she thinks, with my current enormousness, she wouldn't fit. Or perhaps she thinks other things. She doesn't say much. Just waits silently until she thinks I'm asleep each night before sleeping herself. But I'm too huge and strange and hot to sleep now, so I lie there and pretend to sleep while she does the same. In the morning she is always first up, with her mattress folded and pushed under my bed, praying next to my sink.

I am so, very, completely ready for this to be done now. I have tried to think of it not as a child but as something that is happening to my body, just my body, not me, something that will be over soon, but the longer it draws out, the more I think about what it really is. I think of names, Etta, while I pretend to sleep, listening to Sister Margaret Reynolds' attentive, awake breathing. I have realized what a nice name Etta is. Or James.

There's a rock I found on the beach that's so ocean-smooth it's almost soft. I keep it under my quilt, usually, but, sometimes, if Sister Margaret is late or away in the bathroom, I'll lift its round coolness to my face or neck or chest. It's the size of, maybe, two fists together. It is so small but so heavy.

I hope to visit soon. Mother and Dad might have told you. In just over one month. Everything will be wonderfully normal then, and maybe, if we can find somewhere to do it, I will teach you to swim.

Love,
Alma

The next letter was from the same address as all of Alma's others, with the same type of stamp and postmark, even, but it wasn't from her. There was only one envelope this time. It was addressed, *To the Immediate Family of Sister Alma Kinnick.*

Toxemia. A word that starts so harsh and ends so gently. A word whispered from Etta's mother to her father before they had a chance to recognize all that they were learning. A word carried by Etta's father up the stairs, oh so carefully, like a baby bird, to Etta's room. He gave it to her more softly than she'd ever heard him speak. Etta took

it and held it in her ears at first, and then her head, and then, suddenly, and horribly, her heart. Her mother crept through the door and
they, all three, realized how little it meant to know things, to know
the truth of things, now.

It took them longer, a week or so, to notice the hole in their language that this new word had made. To grasp that there was no term
for a parent without a child, a sister without a sister.

Etta signed up at the teachers' college one month after this.

5

She had been in Manitoba for three days, three dry days, when Etta's boots started leaking. Not letting liquid in, but letting it out, leaving a rust-colored trail behind her. In the morning it was just a mist of fine dots, hardly distinguishable by sight, only slightly more noticeable by scent, for those that notice scent. But by noon the dots had become a constant, if thin, trickle: the trail of them conjoining into two fine lines, like spider silk pulling from Etta's feet. And by midafternoon the trail-lines had spread into tracks like a burgundy cross-country ski path. The scent, for those that live by scent, was overwhelming. At six o'clock in the evening, Etta noticed that her feet hurt. These are good boots, she whispered to nobody, to Manitoba, these are very good boots. But her feet hurt. And the boots were leaking, and she was starting to feel faint. Damn, she said. Etta didn't think there was any part of herself stronger than her boots. If her boots broke, anything could. She sat down, and untied her laces. The boots slid right off, wet. Her feet red with blood. Like Saint Francis, thought Etta, but she did not pray to him. She didn't pray to anyone. Instead she wrapped her feet in spare socks, wiped her hands off as best she could without water, and ate a bun; the top half with a sachet of relish and the bottom half with a packet of sugar. She imagined butter and cinnamon, the long, thick snake of cinnamon buns she made for Otto on Sundays.

Now that they were out of the boots, Etta's feet swelled up so they'd never go back in. And the boots were broken, now, in any case. Okay, thought Etta. Tomorrow I'll go to a town and get something new. Okay.

That night she slept in a mustard field and dreamt. She dreamt of water. And boats and boys and men and boys, breathing in the water, spitting out the water, and everything loud and so much color, but darkened and getting darker and this is no place for a woman you better get down get right down, down, deeper, deeper, deeper and the water lapped her feet and ankles, warmer than you'd expect, rhythmic, comforting. But I am not a woman, she reassured herself, but I am strong and surviving.

When Etta woke the next morning there was a coyote licking and licking and licking her feet. Her socks had fallen off and the bleeding had stopped. Hello, said Etta, not sitting up, not wanting to disturb things. Are you helping me or eating me? The coyote looked at her. Amber eyes. Dog's eyes. Well? said Etta. The coyote went back to licking. Thank you, said Etta. Either way.

The coyote stayed by her while she got up and peed and rinsed her mouth and her teeth, still her own teeth, every one, with water from a bottle and gathered up her things. It followed her as she started walking, carefully, slowly, in bare feet. It followed her, like this, for hours. It followed her to the outskirts of a town, and then into the town, along the sidewalk, moving carefully around broken glass and gum to the downtown, and into the sports shop.

No dogs in the shop, said the worker, standing beside racks and racks of white shoes.

It's not mine, said Etta.

But it came in with you.

I know. But it's not mine.

Well, said the worker.

Well, said Etta.

The worker moved toward the coyote. Go! Get! Get out!

The coyote stayed. It lifted its top lip, showed yellow-white teeth.

The worker stepped back. Madam, he said.

He's not mine, said Etta.

So the coyote stayed and watched while Etta looked at the rows and rows of sneakers, all of which were white, until she bought a pair. Stepping in them was like stepping on fresh moss. The coyote followed her out of the shop, along the sidewalk, through the outskirts and back into the fields. Well, said Etta, I don't know if you're wanting me as a pet or to eat me when I sleep, but as you're still here we might as well give you a name. The coyote stayed two steps behind her. She could hear it even when she couldn't see it. We'll call you James, she said. They both kept walking.

That night James did not eat Etta, just slept a little bit away from her feet. The next morning he ate a gopher while Etta ate mayonnaise on crackers. When they were both done, they starting walking again. East, always east. Come along, James, said Etta.

Yes, yes, coming, said James.

Will you be joining me for the entire journey, you think?

We'll see.

Otto went to bed that night without a proper meal. Just butter and sugar on bread. You wait and you work, he told himself while he undressed. His throat twitched, wanted to cough. Spinach grows up fast, and so do the weeds around it. You wait, and you work.

But the next morning, he did not go out and weed the spinach. The next morning, he got up after thick sleep, no dreams, and stood in front of the kitchen cupboard, unimpressed. Alphabet cereal. Corn cereal. Rice cereal. Nothing real left here, and nothing in the freezer anymore either. He was starving for real food. He had always been skinny; now he was becoming hollow. His skin getting thinner, more transparent. Etta's recipe cards were still where he had left them, arranged in perfect rows along the half of the kitchen table he didn't use. Beside the letters. They were faded; she hadn't needed them for decades, the balances of flour, butter, sugar, ingrained in her mind and hands. Otto picked a card out of the *breakfast/snacks* division:

CINNAMON BUNS.

(from Aunt Nondis)

NEEDED:

1 tbsp. yeast

1½ c. milk

¼ c. w. sugar

2 ~~tb~~ tsp. salt

½ c. shortening (butter is best)

1 egg, 5–5½ c. w. flour (all-p)

1½ c. b. sugar, 1½ tsp. cinnamon

INSTRUCTIONS:

Proof yeast. Scald milk and pour into a large bowl. Add sugar, salt, shortening. Stir until melted then cool to room t. Add proofed yeast, along with egg. Stir again, well. Beat in 3 c. flour, then remaining 2(½) c. until feels right. Turn onto floured board and knead into smooth ball. Rise. (Double) (PTA)

Punch down risen ball and divide into two equal, smooth balls. Rest (10 min). Roll each ball down into a rectangle and brush with melted butter (lots). Combine the b. sugar and cinnamon and sprinkle over the dough-rectangles. Roll and seal. Cut into 1-inch pieces and nestle close but not squished into baking dish or tray (tray messier). Brush tops with milk (and more butter/b. sugar, if for Otto). Rise. (Double) Bake at 375° for about 25 min.

In a drawer, beside the beige box where the recipes used to live, was an apron, folded. Otto took it out and let it drop out of its fold pattern. Etta's smell cast up, and then was gone. He put the top loop over his head and tied the center ties around his back, then picked the recipe card back up off the counter and squinted at it, moving it a little closer to his face in case some secret, clearer instructions might surface. Some smaller writing beneath the writing, maybe. But no. Just:

Proof yeast.

And the rest. Okay, thought Otto. We speak the same language, Etta and I; this should be legible, this should be easy. He put the card back down on the counter, opened a cupboard, found and pulled out the yeast. There it is, he whispered to himself, proved.

Otto's first batch came out extremely tough. Like jerky. The dough sitting dead in its bowl during each of the rise periods. Okay, said Otto, to himself, to the recipe card. More research required. Okay. He ate them with pouring cream and applesauce to soften them as much as possible.

Before his second try, a few days later, Otto looked over the grease-stained cards, organized alphabetically, he now realized, until he got to the second to last card,

YEAST, PROOFING

(For dry. To prove it's alive and get things moving.)

NEEDED:

dry yeast

warm water

w. sugar

INSTRUCTIONS:

Put yeast in a small glass of warm water. Add two/three pinches of sugar. Wait 5–10 min. Alive = bubbles and smells warm, dead = dead.

Otto got out the yeast and the sugar and heated some water. He combined them all and waited fifteen minutes. Nothing. He waited fifteen more, just to be sure. Nothing. And then five more. Still nothing. Okay, said Otto. Now we know. Dead = dead. Instead of baking that day he went to the Co-op and bought some new yeast, along with a bit of bread, cheese, and pickles for dinner.

Batch two-point-five was better, the yeast proofed and smelled wonderful and the dough rose in the bowl for him to punch back down. Kneading, Otto thought as he moved his hands up and down in the dough, was the best part. It was the connection point, between you and the food. It was gentle and brutal at once, punching, but gently, carefully. Rhythmic, like marching. Once you got started, it was automatic and comforting. On, and on.

This batch was better, but still too tough, like the buns were three days old, even when they were still oven-hot. These went to the birds.

How long you knead 'em for? asked Sheryl. She was checking the expiry dates on cigarettes. She had them all out on the Co-op counter, sorted according to brand, so that the colored packets made layered stripes in front of her like a rainbow.

I'm not sure, said Otto. Maybe fifteen minutes? Maybe twenty?

Twenty! cried Wesley. He was in the back by the baked goods, sweeping crumbs.

That'll be your problem there, said Sheryl. No question. She held up one hand, five fingers. Five minutes, tops, she said.

Yeah? said Otto.

Tops! called Wesley.

Otto's third batch was soft and risen and sweet. He watched the orange-hot window of the oven like a film. Once they were cooled, he walked across the field and knocked on Russell's door. Some time, some noise, and then Russell answered,

Oh, hello, Otto. His body blocked the doorway so Otto couldn't see inside.

Hello, Russell, hot out there today?

Awfully.

Any deer?

Not today.

Maybe tomorrow.

Yep. That's what I say.

Well . . . I baked.

Russell didn't respond, took a moment, so Otto continued,

I baked. I brought you some cinnamon buns. They're fresh.

Russell eyed the bundle under Otto's arm, wrapped in a blue and white cotton towel. He shuffled back a bit. Well, he said, you'd better come in then. He moved aside just enough for Otto to pass.

Russell's kitchen was tiny, with boxes of things everywhere. Boxes of car and truck and tractor parts, boxes of books on animals, boxes of screws and nails and tacks. Russell moved a box of cleaned-out jars to get to the oven so they could warm up the buns. They ate them plain, without butter.

They're good, said Russell. Thanks for bringing them.

Well, Etta brings you these things, sometimes, I know. So.

They're almost as good as hers.

They ate in silence, both watching the window; the sun was going down in orange and red. They finished eating and Russell got up to turn on the overhead kitchen light.

Otto, he said, I know. I know Etta's gone away.

Otto turned from the window. You do?

She wrote me a letter, weeks ago. Russell pointed over Otto's shoulder to a bulletin board. The letter was tacked there, faded a little.

My dear Russell

it said,

I have to be away for a while. Please watch over Otto. I know that's something you know how to do.

Your
(friend)
Etta

Just like that. Beside the letter, also pinned to the board, was the envelope it had come in, with Russell's name and address written in Etta's hand, postmarked Strasbourg, twenty-two days ago.

But. But, you didn't say anything, Russell. You let me lie about it.

I didn't want you to feel awkward. And, I was angry.

That I didn't tell you?

That you let her go.

Are you still angry?

Russell thought. Yes, he said. But less so. You're thin, Otto. He hesitated for a beat, and then, Will you tell me where she is?

Otto couldn't. He didn't know. And he didn't want to know and he didn't want Russell to know either. So, instead, he told him about the first letter, about Etta's walking, about the water.

And if she forgets? asked Russell. Her name, her home, her husband? To eat or drink or where she's going?

People don't forget to eat or drink, said Otto.

It's like before, said Russell. It's like before but swapped. You and her, swapped. And me, I'm always just here.

More than seventy years earlier, a few months before the banks had died and taken Russell's father with them, it had been Russell's sixth birthday. To celebrate, his father had taken him downtown to the family store, to pick out one thing, anything at all, to have and keep, as he had every year since the boy turned two. On his second birthday Russell had chosen a lemon candy. On his third, a beautifully shiny roll of aluminum foil. On his fourth, a shovel that was too big for him but that his mother promised he could use when he was eight. On his fifth, he chose another lemon candy. This time, on his sixth birthday, Russell found a book tucked in between the recipes and the newspapers. It was hard-backed and heavy, with a group of animals, a wolf and a bird and a deer and a snake on the cover, all together, like friends. The cover was cloth; Russell ran his fingers up and down, against the grain and with it. This, he said.

Tracking and Hunting the Animals of Western Canada? said his father. You're sure?

Russell ran his fingers over the wolf, bird, deer, and snake. Yes, he said. I'm sure.

That evening he sat on his father's lap as they looked through the book together. It was mostly words, but in the middle there was a section of black-and-white drawings depicting the various types of animal tracks in alphabetical order by species. I like those ones, said Russell, pointing. They're like faces of rabbits. But without mouths.

Deer tracks, said his father. The whole deer family has similar tracks, all rabbit faces. See? He pointed down the list: Caribou, Elk, Moose, Roe, White-tail . . .

And if you find those and follow those you find a deer? asked Russell.

If you're very quiet and gentle and patient, then you just might.

Wow, said Russell.

Though there aren't many in town, I shouldn't think, said his father.

But maybe one or two?

Maybe one or two.

Wow, said Russell. Wow wow wow.

Otto walked home carefully and slowly across the dark field that night. Too dark to see the best path through the grain. It reminded him of walking home drunk, either through the Vogel field with Russell, or else through troublingly quiet French villages with near strangers, or, just the once, with Owen. He didn't drink much after, with Etta.

Otto went straight to bed; it was later than usual. He slept for three hours and then

Otto!

Banging wood. Kicked wood. And yelling.

Otto!

He sat up. Established where he was, what time it was. In bed, just after three a.m.

Otto!

It was Russell. Russell's voice yelling, Russell's boots kicking the door. Russell drunk? Maybe. Because of his bad leg he had to lean into the frame before each kick. Otto could hear the soft creak of his lean. Creak and bang. Otto! Creak and bang. Otto drew the curtains and opened the window by the bed. It faced out, in the same direction as the door. He leaned through it.

Russell. My God. Three in the morning.

We need to go! said Russell. I'm not drunk. Don't think that I'm drunk, Otto. I'm here and we need to go! Now! We need to go find her. Otto. Otto! She could die out there! She could be dead already! Put your boots on. I've brought the truck around. We can make the Manitoba border by morning.

Otto leaned his torso across the wooden window frame. White paint flaked onto his stomach. He wasn't wearing a shirt. It's a huge country, Russell, he said.

I know, I know, that's why, Otto. That's why!

No, said Otto.

Otto! said Russell.

No, said Otto.

But, goddamn, Otto!

No, said Otto. No, Russell, I'm not going.

Some husband, said Russell. Some fucking husband. He kicked the door again, harder. The force of it knocked him off balance and he stumbled back, toward his truck. I'll go alone then. Right now, alone. Some fucking husband. He turned around, away from Otto.

It's not what she wants, Russell, said Otto, but quietly. Too quietly for Russell, who had already waltzed himself back to his truck, turning the lights on so they lit up the porch like morning, to hear.

One late night, with ears squished to sock-worn floorboards, the Vogels listened to their parents, directly below, in the kitchen. They heard:

. . . you can't throw away the radio! It was expensive.

It wasn't, you made it from scrap, mostly.

Yes, but, radios are expensive in general, most of the time. . . . You know it can't stop anything, throwing it away, not really.

The boys will hear and then—

The boys will hear regardless.

Maybe not.

They will.

Maybe not so soon.

They're hardly boys now, some of them. Amos, Walter, Otto. . . . You can't stop them growing.

But I can stop them going.

Maybe.

The Schiffs in Kenaston only have one. Just skinny Benedict. Sixteen. And he's gone.

Well, we've certainly got more than one . . .

. . .

It was a joke.

I know.

You know I don't want them to go either.

Yes, I know.

The sound of a cup stacked on another cup.

Let's see if we can find some music . . .

There's no music, only news.

Let's try.

The fuzz and stutter of channels, until, finally, fading in from static, the slow-motion swing of clarinets, muted horns, piano. This, under the sound of carefully stepping feet, in time, together.

As his brothers and sisters dispersed to their beds, one side of their faces red with the grain of the floorboards, Otto, coldly and suddenly, realized it was him. The thing his mother was so afraid of was him, or undeniably within him. Was why he'd been so afraid himself. Otto realized that, sometime not too far from now, he would go. And, although he didn't tell anyone, not even Russell, it made him terribly sad and terribly excited.

The next day was Otto's turn to go to school, walking in a shuffling, sleepy gang with the others who were off chores that day. When they arrived, however, the school's front door was closed, and all the other students were standing about outside in the dusty yard. The door's locked, said a thin girl with dull yellow braids. We all tried, but nobody can get in.

Where's Mister Lancaster? asked Walter. He was the oldest, the biggest, by years, by a head. The girl closed her mouth tight, shrugged, and ran back to her friends.

Another girl, from a bigger, older group, one that spent a fair amount of time talking about and looking at Walter, shouted across the yard, The dust. It's gotta be the dust, Walter. Then she spit.

Nobody was very surprised that Mr. Lancaster had gone. He had been teaching in silence for the past three weeks. He had taught, always, with the door to the schoolroom open, for air and for light, and had done so for his entire career at Gopherlands school. This meant that, every day, all day, the prevailing northwest wind would blow dust up off the fields for miles and miles, straight into the teacher's mouth, which was most often open with teaching. Mr. Lancaster had come from a city; he didn't know about spitting. He would sleep, at night, curled against his wife's back, breathing dust like a dragon, so she would have to bang out her hair like a chalkboard eraser each morning. Over the ten years he taught at Gopherlands, Mr. Lancaster's voice got quieter and quieter until one day it was just gone. He taught with gestures and chalk drawings as long as he could until the school board found out.

So the students sat teacherless in little clubs and clusters on the dry grass, backs of necks burning in the sun, keeping themselves entertained with chats and games and naps for the hour or so until a sweating man in a full navy blue suit trod heavily toward them from the same direction as the sun. Yes, hello, sorry, sorry, he said. He let them into the school with a key on a ring with dozens of keys. It made a lot of noise. Please sit down, please don't fuss, he said. He wrote five number problems on the board. There, he said. I will explain everything in a moment. But first, please, numbers! Numbers. He had the students work on the problems with their heads down in silence while he frantically pulled and pillaged through the drawers and papers of Mr. Lancaster's desk, still sweating.

Otto found numbers quite easy. He had been counting siblings all his life, dividing chores, multiplying portions. He was finished, with nothing to do, when Owen passed him a folded piece of paper. Otto unfolded it.

What is your name?

Owen had written this at the top of the paper, leaving lots of space underneath. Otto wrote his full name and folded and passed the paper back to Owen. Owen unfolded it, wrote something new, and passed it back. And so on:

What is your name?

OTTO VOGEL

Are you well?

I AM ~~BOARED~~ (bored)

Me too. This man is disgusting. Like an animal.

~~MAY-BE~~ A DOG OR A HORSE. (maybe)

I am afraid of horses.

I KNOW.

Can I walk home with you today after school?

YOU LIVE WEST(erly), WE LIVE EAST(erly), SO IT
   ~~DOE'SNT~~ MAKE SENSE. (Doesn't)

I like walking.

WE WALK VERY SLOW ME AND RUSSELL. YOU WILL
   BE COME ~~FUR FRESTE FURESTR~~

Owen took the pen from Otto's hand. *FRUSTERATED*, he wrote.

At the front of the class, the man in the suit had found what he was looking for and was now hastily scribbling something on the back of an assignment a student had handed in about what-is-the-true-meaning-of-God-Save-the-King? When he finished, he stood up. Students! he said. I hope you have finished your sums. I have sad news. You may have noticed that Mr. Lancaster is not here. Mr. Lancaster will not be here anymore, ever. As you may have suspected was the case, his voice has turned to dust, and he is now unfit to teach and has gone to fight the war instead. I'm sure this is troubling for you and I am sorry for that. Now, can I please have a strong-legged volunteer?

Winnie, whose legs were cramped under her desk and whose stomach always got squirrels and butterflies in it when she sat in one place for more than ten minutes, shot her hand up into the air. She was the only one. So, the sweating man from the school board sent her to run the eight kilometers into town with a notice to deliver to the college there. Winnie was out the door before he even finished the directions. There was only one road, anyway.

Halfway, after about thirty minutes, Winnie stopped for a break and to eat the apple that was giving her left hand a cramp. The notice was in her right hand. While she ate, she opened the not-terribly-well-sealed envelope to read what she was delivering. Mr. Lancaster had told them the story of Hamlet; she thought she'd better find out what the notice said, just to be sure. It was in dark thick ink, written hastily,

IMPORTANT/URGENT:

it said,

Gopherlands General School Immediately Requires:

   One Teacher. (For all levels.)

Must:

   • *Have appropriate training.*
   • *Be willing to live on-site.*
   • *Teach with the door closed. (Certain south- or east-facing windows optional)*

Applicants please contact WILLARD GODFREE,* Larger Area Super-Intendent, ASAP.

*To be contacted either by telegram, written letter, or else in-person at either the Civic and Meta-Civic Bureau Office (143, Main) or else at the third house on the left-hand side as you come into town (yellow door). Please do not call after 9 p.m.

Winnie, assured of her safety, refolded the notice and resealed the envelope using the stickiness left on her fingers from her apple. She kicked a hole in the earth to drop the core into, kicked soil back over it, and ran the remaining four kilometers down the road.

The girl who answered the door at the college looked about the same age as Winnie, but cleaner, and with braided hair. Yes? she said.

A notice, said Winnie. She handed the notice to her with her right, less sticky, hand.

Thank you, said the girl. A young woman, really. Some others, all dressed the same as the girl at the door, walked by, trying to look like they weren't looking.

Would you like—started the girl. But Winnie made like she didn't hear and started back, running down the road out of town, toward the school. She didn't know whether she would like or not.

The next day, Russell's turn for school, classes were canceled. A notice on the door.

Sorry—

Classes canceled today. Please call tomorrow.
Thank you. Sorry.

The day after that, Otto's turn, the school was open again. There was a woman no one had ever seen before standing at the front of the class. Once all the too-tiny desks were full with too-big legs, she walked to the back of the class and firmly shut the door. As she marched back up to the front, Otto watched her calf muscles. Great calf muscles. She couldn't be much older than him. Younger than Amos or Marie for sure. Back at the front she clapped her hands together, once, twice, and cleared her throat. Well, she said, hello, everyone. I trust you're well and ready to learn. I'm going to help you with that. I am Miss Kinnick, Miss Etta Kinnick. And I am your new teacher. Then she smiled.

There were fifteen girls in Etta's class at the teachers' college. They all wore the same burnt orange skirts, pleated like a Scotsman's kilt. They could choose their own blouses, so long as they were white, and ironed. Some of the girls lived there, in dormitory rooms set above the lecture halls. When they were late, in the mornings, Etta could hear their hurried feet above her head, crescendoing down the stairs. Etta, though, continued to live at home with her parents. It was only a twenty-minute tram ride or a forty-five-minute walk in the mornings and evenings. It was cheaper, living at home, but that's not why she did it. Etta knew her parents' house would be too quiet, too still, with both daughters gone.

She was in her second year, of two years, when a junior called Caroline answered the door to a dusty, panting girl from one of the farms. Etta saw her while walking between classes; she looked terrified.

That afternoon, in Elements of Discipline, their lecturer read a notice from Gopherlands school aloud to all fifteen second-years. The sharp white noise of pencils taking down the details and of shortened breath around her prickled Etta's ears like an itch. A job hadn't opened up in the area for years. The vast majority of the college's students graduated, got married, had a child or three, and stayed home kneading bread and singing lullabies for the rest of their lives. After reading the notice, the lecturer placed it on the front corner of his desk for students to examine, if they wished, after class, and continued with his lesson on Sticks and Stones. In her head, Etta counted up to one hundred, then back down again. When she got to zero she raised her hand, even though no question had been asked. The lecturer noticed her at the end of his phrase, when he looked up from his notes. Yes, Miss Kinnick? he said. The class turned from various directions to look at her.

May I please be excused to go to the bathroom? asked Etta. Her voice was tight with anticipation.

Yes, yes, of course.

The other students, now uninterested, turned back to the front of the class, their books, their own thoughts.

Once the door to the classroom was closed behind her, Etta broke into a run; out of the college, down Creek Lane to Victoria, down Victoria to Main, and then along Main, counting up the numbers: 121, 123, 125, 127, 127A, 129, 131, 133, 135, 137, 139, 141, and, finally, 143. She caught her breath. She repinned her hair. She wished she had thought to bring a hat. She counted to three and walked into the Civic And Meta-Civic Bureau Office.

I'm here about the position at Gopherlands. Her hands, held together behind her back, shaking. Her face composed, almost stern. Grown-up.

Oh, oh, yes, excellent. You're from the college?

Yes.

You're old enough?

Yes. Although Etta didn't know how old was old enough. She felt old enough.

You can teach with the door closed?

Yes.

Okay, that's fine then. Good. You'll have to sign these papers. You'll have a day to collect your things and move to the tutor house. You'll start day after tomorrow.

Just like that. Etta signed the papers, shook Willard Godfree's hand, and walked out of the office, back onto Main Street. Then she blinked once, twice, and broke into a run back to the college.

After the day's classes, each of the other fourteen girls went to 143 Main, and each found the same—

Thank you, Teachers, but:

The position has been filled.

> *Sorry.*
> *W.G.*

—note on the door. Some of the most eager also visited the third house on the left on the road into town, but there, on the yellow door, was another copy of the same,

Thank you, Teachers, but:

The position has been filled.

> *Sorry.*
> *W.G.*

6

James liked singing; he was always singing. Coyotes have voices a bit like oboes; they are not unpleasant. Etta would sing along with him sometimes, and sometimes she would just listen. Mostly he sang cowboy songs. Sometimes he also sang hymns or radio songs that he'd learned from dogs, but mostly not, mostly it was cowboy songs:

> *O bury me not on the lone prairie*
> *Where coyotes howl and the wind blows free*
> *In a narrow grave just six by three—*
> *O bury me not on the lone prairie*

Etta was humming along, they were taking small steps, the kind of steps they took in the late afternoon, tired, but directed. The days were getting longer and hotter, the sun now up before five-thirty in the morning and out long past nine at night. Etta kicked a rock. There were more rocks now. They were pulling toward Ontario; James recognized the smells each time he stopped singing momentarily for a breath. The next time he did, after *O!*, Etta interrupted his song,

Do you think Amos will mind if we don't show up until morning? she said, stopping suddenly, I'm really tired.

James, who was trotting ahead of Etta, slowed so he was at her side. *I'm sure he won't mind,* he said. *Let's stop now, continue in the morning.*

After Etta had fallen asleep but before he curled into a tight ball himself, James dug into her bag and pulled out a piece of paper, careful not to leave deep teeth marks.

You:

it said.

You:

Etta Gloria Kinnick of Deerdale farm. 83 years old in August.

Family:
Marta Gloria Kinnick. Mother. Housewife. (Deceased)
Raymond Peter Kinnick. Father. Editor. (Deceased)
Alma Gabrielle Kinnick. Sister. Nun. (Deceased)
James Peter Kinnick. Nephew. Child. (Never lived)
Otto Vogel. Husband. Soldier/Farmer. (Living)

James tucked the paper, as best he could, under Etta's arm, for her to find when they woke up again, around five-thirty the next morning.

Four months earlier, Otto woke up because he ran out of air. Dreaming of water. He sat up and pushed the blankets away like the tide, kicked his feet out. It was still dark, and cold. He felt his way to his robe—warm around him, it hung too long off his arms, too long over his feet, like a bridal gown—and slipped out to the kitchen. He took ginger cookies from a jar in the freezer and sat at the red and starry table pulling himself out of the drowning of his sleep. The huge water and moving sky.

Otto woke when Etta left the bed. Without her the cold got in, almost immediately, as soon as he inhaled. He listened with eyes closed as she struggled with the fabric of his robe and opened and closed the door. He waited for the sound of water from the bathroom, for her return. He counted to two hundred and fifty, listened, and did it again. Then he got up too.

Etta was at the kitchen table, in his robe. Etta, said Otto, Etta.

Etta? said Etta. She put down the cookie she had been lifting toward her mouth. She looked at her husband like a ghost, like a mirror.

So what shall we do? Otto said the next morning at breakfast, cinnamon buns, oranges.

Maybe I should go away, said Etta. A place for people who forget themselves.

But I remember, said Otto. If I remember and you forget, we can balance, surely.

Maybe I should go away, said Etta, again. Her hair was white and undone. The piece of it that fell toward her mouth reminded Otto of baby geese. A return to down.

I could hurt someone, she said. The cinnamon bun on her plate a perfect spiral, tucking into itself, away and down. Perfect.

You won't.

You know I won't?

I know you won't.

They ate, for a while, and then Etta said, What will you do today?

Go to Palmer's, I think. Help out there a bit.

Wear a hat. The sun.

Of course. And you?

Etta had one hand on the table, her left, she spread the fingers flat. Pickles, she said, carrots and garlic and cucumber.

It's a long time till winter.

But it never really is.

No, I guess it never really is.

Russell drove and drove. The dark roads were very quiet. He only saw three other vehicles before Last Mountain Lake, and he didn't recognize any of them. The windows to his truck were rolled down and the wind made him feel awake and alive. He couldn't stop smiling. He drove over the Manitoba border just after sunrise, the furthest east he had ever been.

While Russell drove, Otto tried to go back to sleep, but couldn't. So he went to the kitchen and closed his eyes and let his finger fall at random onto one of the recipe cards.

DATE SQUARES
(a.k.a. Matrimonial Cake)

He got out the flour, the sugar, the butter.

The day after Etta Kinnick's appearance at Gopherlands, Otto went to meet Russell after school. He had finished giving the cows their drops. Without them their eyes got so dry with dust that the lids stuck together, shut, blinding them. When he put the drops in they cried brown, appreciative tears. They cried and cried, sometimes for hours. It was some time yet until Otto had to supervise dinner's peeling and chopping, so he had time to walk with Russell. He waited, leaning against the overlapping wood of the school's siding, along with all the dogs from the various farms that came to meet their masters. He stroked the head of an especially tall golden mixed breed. It was hot, and all the dogs' tongues hung low and loose out of their dry mouths. Together they all listened to the scraping and gathering of students at the end of their day.

The first one out of the school was Owen. He navigated through the dogs to Otto. Hello, Otto, he said. Missed you today.

Russell was right behind. Otto! he said. This new teacher! This new teacher. . . . Come on, let's head home now. I want to talk to you, now, away from here a bit. He put a hand on Otto's shoulder, steered him away.

Okay, okay, said Otto. Let's go. And then, three steps later, twisting his neck back toward the school, Bye, Owen. See you tomorrow.

Otto, she's wonderful, said Russell. They were far enough away from the school now, a good hundred meters away. Why didn't you tell me she was wonderful?

I told you we had a new teacher. I told you she was nice.

Nice isn't the same as wonderful.

No, I guess not.

I asked so many questions. I'm going to be noticed, Otto. I'm going to read all of the books I can find. I'm going to be the best student she's had. . . . Otto, don't you think she's wonderful?

Otto shrugged. He wasn't sure, really. Miss Kinnick seemed to be a good teacher. And she had nice calves. But she was a teacher. Their teacher.

I think she's wonderful, Otto, said Russell. Just that, wonderful.

Shut up, Russell, said Otto. But he was happy. Russell didn't get excited very often. It was nice to see.

It wasn't that Otto didn't know about women, or didn't like them. He did and he did, he definitely did. At night, trying to fall asleep, his body and mind pulled him between images he'd seen on grainy postcards, and the neighbor when she rode with no saddle, and sweat through printed cotton on women in town on the hottest days, between all that, and the sirens, stomping and shouting on the radio, at night, when his parents didn't know they all were still awake, still listening. What the noise on the radio meant and where it could lead him, if he let it. Between these two things, he knew that he wanted things quite badly, but still wasn't exactly sure what.

But, Otto, did you see how she—

Russell, said Otto, interrupting, Miss Kinnick is wonderful, it's true, yes, and will continue to be, and we can talk about that lots and soon, but, right now, I need your help. I need to steal the radio.

Russell stopped, looked up.

Not for good, just for half an hour or so. I need you to distract Mother so she takes her eyes off of it for just long enough. Just long enough for me to take it and listen properly. Not midnight through floorboards. Really listen. Half an hour. Then I'll put it right back.

It's because you want to know about this thing.

Yes.

This thing she doesn't want us to know.

Yes. But, don't you? Want to know?

No. Maybe. No, probably not. I trust your mother, Otto.

. . . But, you'll help me? Still?

Yes, yes of course.

Otto's mother loved all her children ferociously, and Russell like one of her own, except that she loved Russell just a bit more softly. She knew what her children were made of, she knew they could be handled roughly and would live and learn through it, but Russell was made of something unknown; he could break, or, perhaps, was already a little bit broken. This was why Otto needed his help, specifically. His mother, if she was going to bend at all, would never do it for him, but she might do it for Russell.

The thing was, the radio, made as it was from scrap parts and just the little bits of time Otto's father could fit between the duties of farm, father, husband, was impressively functional, but lacked certain refinements, such as volume control. If someone in the house was listening, the whole house was listening. It was quieter upstairs, but, still, it slid up through the ceiling, the floorboards, it could be heard. Especially by Otto's mother, it could be heard. So, what Otto needed was to get his mother out of the house altogether, and, preferably, out of the yard too, for long enough that he could find and hear from the radio whatever it was he was trying to find and hear.

So, how do I do that? said Russell. They were almost home now; the other Vogel students, whom they'd let pass them, were already walking up the drive.

The chickens, said Otto.

The chickens?

Yes. I've got a plan.

They were going to put a chicken in a tree. One of the wind-break trees, one near the end of the row, away from the house. Pretend it escaped, flew up there, terrified, and could not get down.

Mother has a way with the chickens. She's the only one. She'll understand, she'll come and help, if you ask her.

So you're asking me to ask her?

Yes. Please.

Okay. Okay, Otto.

Thank you. But, first, now, we have to get the chicken up the tree.

Because of Russell's leg, Otto did the climbing. Russell carried the chicken under his coat as nonchalantly as he could from its yard, past the house, down the line of wind-haggard trees to the second-last one, his arms clutching in such a way as to try to minimize, as much as possible, the scratching and pecking damage to his chest and stomach. Otto was already up in the tree.

This animal is not happy, Russell called out and up as he approached. This animal wants to kill me.

It won't. Just don't kill it. Don't squeeze too hard. Don't suffocate.

I'm not.

Okay.

By this point Russell was standing under the tree, under Otto, whose legs dangled down just above his head.

Okay, said Otto. Pop her out and pass her here.

It wasn't difficult at all for Russell to convince Otto's mother to leave the house, to come and help the stranded chicken in the tree.

I call it, ma'am, he said, and it just hops up, to a higher branch. But I reckon you could call it down. I reckon it would listen to you.

Of course, Russell, it will. Chickens, children, they're all the same. Give me one minute and I'll be out with you.

Russell waited just outside the front door. One minute later, Otto's mother appeared. She was carrying two bundled blankets. In case we need to catch it, or wrap it up for stress, she said, and strode past him, toward the trees. Once they were ten steps away, Otto, quiet as a fox, slipped into the house and closed the front door behind him.

The radio was a beautiful thing. It was hodgepodge and patched up on the outside, but on the inside it was filled with voices, filled with people and music and ideas from away, from far away. Otto took a breath and turned it on.

And it did nothing.

Otto twisted the dial-in knob all the way around and back again. He turned the whole thing off and back on again.

And it did nothing. Otto looked at the radio and it looked back at him, silent, stony. He didn't have much time to begin with, and now he had less. He ran his hands over the sides of the radio, but there were no new or unexpected knobs or switches or panels. He carefully pushed his body weight into it, pivoting the machine around, to expose its back. There, on the back, was the compartment his father had fashioned to fit the True-Tone battery. And there, in the compartment, was nothing.

Over by the wind-break trees, Otto's mother and Russell wrapped an irritated and exhausted chicken in one blanket. In the other, still bundled and held firmly under Otto's mother's arm, against her side, was the battery.

Dammit, said Otto. Dammit dammit dammit.

She's smart, your mother, said Russell. I told you, she's smart.

I know she's smart. Dammit.

You're lucky the chicken didn't jump down and kill itself.

Chickens aren't stupid either, Russell.

They can be.

Not like that. Dammit. Damn! Now what? Nobody else round here has a radio. Only in town. And they lock their doors in town.

Well, said Russell. Some people do.

Lock their doors?

No, have radios.

Which people?

Some people. My aunt and uncle. They have a radio. We have a radio.

Otto stopped walking. They weren't walking anywhere, just walking. What? he said. *What?* His face got hot, like it had been in the sun too long. Russell! he said. Goddammit. Why didn't you say?

I trust your mother. She knows how to keep things, kids, alive.

Goddammit, Russell. No one's gonna die from radio-listening. We're going to your aunt and uncle's. Right now.

Russell's aunt and uncle's place was very different from the Vogels'. Everything was very quiet and breakable, decorated in blue and white. Otto had only been inside once before, when Russell was recovering. It felt then as it did now, like a hospital. Or, the way Otto imagined a hospital would feel, at least. They sat on the floor, in the middle of the living room, and listened to the low, steady voice of the CBC overseas report, looking straight ahead, not at each other, Russell growing colder and colder with each image the radio voice threw out at them, Otto growing hotter and hotter, while Russell's uncle made them coffee in the next room.

You're not old enough. They were hurrying back across the field. They were late for dinner help, the sun was setting.

We almost are. We soon will be.

No point thinking about it until then, though.

Planning, Russell, we'll need to plan. How to tell the family, your aunt and uncle, what we'll pack.

What you'll pack.

What we'll pack. Russell, I'm seventeen in two months, then five more and you are too. I can wait the five months.

You can wait forever, they won't take me.

Of course they will, Russell, you're smart. You're smarter than me.

They won't. It's not about smart. You know they won't.

Otto stopped because Russell had stopped, and was now three steps behind him. But, Russell, he said, if they don't take you, what will you do?

I'll stay here, I'll wait. I'll go to school. I wouldn't be worried about me.

Russell, I'd go crazy, staying here.

But I won't.

Well, we'll see. What they say.

They'll say no.

We'll see. In seven months we'll see.

After the students left on her first day of teaching, Etta stayed at the front of the class, facing the emptied desks, remembering, matching names to places. She went round three times, then wiped the chalk from her hands onto her skirt, picked up her things, and left the school, walking the fifty meters to the teacher's cottage. To her cottage.

When she'd arrived the day before, she'd found neat piles of things laid out for her. A folded towel, kitchen linen, bedsheets. A teapot, a teacup, a teaspoon. Like an archaeologist's carefully sorted evidence of civilization, of habitation, but whomever had laid it all out was gone. There was no one but Etta, the towels, the spoons. She considered leaving the door open so the wind could pass through, keeping her company with its humming and shuddering, but recalled the previous tenant and did not.

Now, after her first day's work, everything was just as it had been. Careful piles, undisturbed. She took off her boots, sat at the table, and, in the dust that had gathered there—that gathered each time she went out, or came in—she drew a chart:

MONA–STUART	JOSIE–RICHARD	EMMETT–STEVEN
LUCY–ELLIE	GLEN–ELLA	JOSEPH–BETH L.
WINNIE–BERNICE	CELIA–BETH M.	OWEN–OTTO
WALTER–SUE	SARAH–AMOS	

She ran her finger under each name, a thick smudge, and remembered: Mona: blond braids, can't add yet. Stuart: missing teeth, very silent. Josie: wonderful laugh, starting to count. And so on. Owen: curly hair, tries very hard. Otto: happy, sunburnt.

That night she lay in bed, not sleeping, listening to the gaps in the sound around her where she was used to footsteps, hushed voices, breath. The fullness of the silence here was heavy. The only sounds were her own. She listened to three thousand, one hundred and twenty of her own heartbeats before falling asleep.

She slept late. She had forgotten to open the bedroom curtains for the morning sun. Most of the students were already milling around outside the school when she got there. In her rush, she hadn't had time to unpack her chest to find clean stockings, so her bare feet stuck at the leather of her boots as she walked through the students to unlock the school's front door. She stood to the side and let the students pass her, filing in to their desks. Her students. Except, they weren't. Or many of them weren't; almost half of them were new, unknown, and almost half of the students from yesterday were gone. One of the new students, in the back, already had his hand up, before she'd even reached the front of the classroom.

Yes?

Hello, Miss. I'm Russell. New from yesterday. I just thought I should introduce myself.

After that six more hands went up, and Etta learned the names of six more new students. In her head she smudged out the old dust chart, and started a new one. Charts and lists. She was fine so long as she could make a chart or a list. Names, places, faces.

Okay then, she said, welcome to some of you and welcome back to the rest. Sarah, if you wouldn't mind closing the door? Everybody else up too. It's good to start the day singing, I think. We'll start today with "The Maple Leaf Forever."

All the students stood up, but Russell, despite his leg, stood up the fastest and straightest of them all.

7

Russell drove and drove until his eyes wouldn't let him anymore and he had to pull over and sleep. When he woke up, he assessed the situation. He was a fair ways across Manitoba. He would need to get gas again soon, and food for himself too. And, most important, he was going to have to refine his plan. Find a way to find Etta now that they were, hopefully, in the same region. A plan. Russell wasn't so good with plans. Usually other people had them and he just rode along. He opened the glove box, just to check, but there were no maps. Of course not. He'd never had maps, never needed maps to know the way from his farm to Otto's or to town. Well, east then, he figured. Until the next Shell station.

Half an hour later, starting into the outskirts of somewhere, there was a gas station with a diner. Russell pulled in.

The waitress was tiny. Ten years old, eleven, maybe. She held his plate of eggs and toast straight out in front of her as she walked it to him. No tomatoes today, she said. This normally comes with cooked tomato but none today. Sorry.

Oh, said Russell, that's okay. There were no other customers in the diner yet; it was still very early. Thank you.

No problem, said the girl. You want something instead? Instead of the tomato? I think we have bananas in the kitchen, and carrots and cookies . . .

Um, a carrot? said Russell.

For breakfast? said the girl.

Yes . . . well, with eggs and toast? No? Should I have the banana instead?

I'd have the cookie, myself.

So Russell had the cookie. The child went into the kitchen and brought it to him, arms straight out. It was oatmeal-raisin.

Thank you, said Russell.

Oh, no problem, said the girl. She rested one hand on the table, made no move to leave. Russell cut a bit of egg, put it on a bit of toast, and lifted it to his mouth. The girl watched him, a little bored.

Good? she said.

Yes . . . thanks, said Russell. Thank you.

It's not hard, she said, to cook an egg. I've been doing it forever.

Oh, yes, said Russell. But still. He cut another piece of egg, accidentally piercing the yolk. It spread across his plate. Say, he said, shouldn't you be in school today?

Nah, said the girl. I don't go to school. Home-learning. Teach myself. Post it in. You know? So I have time to run this place. It's important, though, I know, learning, especially math, for adding the price of eggs and the price of toast and the price of a hermit cookie, right? Then for figuring the amount you give me minus that amount for change. Then to figure out if you left a good tip or not. It's important, I know, just not to be there. I can be around kids whenever

I want. Wednesday's kids-eat-free-with-paying-parents, for example. Lots of kids around then.

And your parents?

In Toronto. We've been running this place on our own for four years now. Speaking of which, I guess I'll go check on the pies. You won't be lonely?

Oh, no, I'll be fine. But, can I ask one more thing?

Yeah, course.

Have you seen an older woman, on her own, dusty, probably, walking through here or past here? . . . Wait, I've got a photo. Russell took his wallet from his back pocket and pulled a haggard black-and-white picture from between two five-dollar bills. That's her, he said. A little while ago though. Just the lady, not the man.

In the photo, Etta was wearing a sort of ivory dress suit. Narrow skirt, blouse, tapered jacket. She was smiling. It was her wedding photo. Russell had taken the photo himself.

So, about sixty years older than this. But still, her, said Russell.

That's not you, said the girl, pointing at the man in the photo, at Otto.

No, said Russell, that's Otto.

How strange . . . said the girl. No, I haven't seen her. But I don't get out of here much. Hold on, I'll get the dish boy and ask him.

Russell ate as much of his eggs and toast as he could while the waitress went back into the kitchen. When she appeared again, she had a little boy with glasses and freckles with her. His glasses were all fogged over. My brother, she said, he does the dishes. She turned to the boy. Tell him what you told me, she said.

My window, said the boy, by the sink, it looks over the road and the fields behind it. I see loads of trucks and tractors and combines and stuff. And animals sometimes too, sometimes deer—

Deer? said Russell.

Yes, yes, said the boy, mostly girl ones but sometimes also big ones with antlers and sometimes baby ones too, I know they're babies and not just small because—

Monty! said the girl, punching him in the arm. Stop rambling! Tell him what you told me.

Oh, no, said Russell, it's not—

—and, said the boy, and, and also I saw a lady, I think, yesterday morning. I thought she was maybe a witch or maybe a lady-Santa-Claus.

Russell's chest clenched. A lady? An older lady? Did she look okay? Was she hurt or anything?

She was singing, I think. She was fine. She was magical.

Andwherewasshe? Russell's words were racing his heart. He stopped, tried again, And, (breath) where was she going? (Breath.) Which direction? (Breath.) Could you tell?

East. Toward the sunrise.

That's good, that's very good. That's great. Thank you. Thank you very very much, Monty. And you too . . .

Cordelia.

Cordelia.

The girl ushered her brother back toward the kitchen, but he stopped halfway. Um . . . he said.

Yes? said Russell.

Um, well, if you find her, when you find her, can you tell her I've been good?

Yes, Monty, yes, of course.

Back in his truck, Russell opened the map he'd bought in the gas station shop. MANITOBA AND WESTERN ONTARIO (to scale)—(Including

Bike Routes and National Parks). What a lot of lakes Manitoba had. And Ontario even more. This country got bluer, wetter, the further east you went. Assuming Etta knew this, or had a map, she would stay south, below most of the water. How far could she have walked in a day? Twenty kilometers? The days were pretty long now. Russell stared at the map a little bit more, calculating, then placed it on the passenger's seat, still unfolded. He went back into the shop and bought an OK MANITOBA! backpack, five packets of salted peanuts, six bottles of juice, a family pack of crackers, two large chocolate bars, and a flashlight. He had a plan. He'd drive twenty more kilometers east along the fields adjacent the diner, and then he'd get out and walk. He'd tracked deer before. He knew how to find footsteps, how to follow.

From the window of the diner's kitchen, Monty and Cordelia watched him drive away. Monty waved with a soapy hand.

Etta and James had just finished eating lunch. Hot dog buns with peanut butter and wild berries for Etta, a caught mouse and a sleeping moth for James. They were resting in the shade until the sun calmed down a bit. Etta had out her papers, her pen.

What are you doing? said James.

I'm writing a letter.

To who?

To Otto. But you don't know him.

I might.

He lives far from here. A long, long way, even for a coyote.

But not for you?

A long way for me too.

Where?

Back in Saskatchewan. On the other side of the long lake. And then some.

But, said James, *then you're going the wrong way. We're going the wrong way.*

Etta thought about this for a moment. And then, It's a loop, James, I'm going out this way, then coming back that way.

I see, said James. *A long loop.*

Have you seen the ocean, James?

No.

Me neither.

But we will.

Yes, we will.

Etta put away her papers and pen, brushed the hot dog bun crumbs off her lap for the birds, and they started walking again, away from the sun. They sang "Johnny Appleseed" and "A Fair Lady of the Plains" as they went. Sometimes Etta did harmony.

After a few hours, a forested lake began to come into view in front of them, to the north.

We'll have to stay south, said Etta.

Yeah, said James. *I'll bet we'll be coming into Ontario soon. Another day or so, I bet.*

That's good, said Etta, that's very good. Her feet weren't even hurting today.

Yeah, it is, but, Etta, said James, *Ontario is not like the prairies. Things are bigger there.*

I'm used to big things, our big sky, big fields.

Other big things, though. Rocks, bigger rocks. And lakes and trees.

How do you know all this?

The skunks. They move around a lot. They tell stories.

It will be fine, said Etta. Rocks are negotiable, and trees are friendly, and lakes, well, perhaps we'll get a boat. One of the little inflatable ones, easy to carry. Can you go in boats?

I don't know. I've never tried.

Well. We'll see. I hope so. We'll just have to be careful of your claws. It will be fine. Ontario will be fine.

Okay. It will. But, also, Etta, there is rain, there, more rain. Even in springtime and summer. You have to think about sleeping in rain.

But you said the skunks said there were big rocks and trees?

Yes.

Well that's shelter for night. And maybe we'll get to cool down somewhat in the day. Rain is good, James, when we open our mouths to sing it will be like drinking.

Dear Etta,

I guess it's worse to keep a secret from you than to spread a secret you've given me. What do you think? In any case, I've already done the latter, so I'm not going to do the former. I told Russell, Etta. I told him about what you're doing and, as rough as I know, where you are. I'm sorry. It's hard to keep closed-up to Russell. You know this. Now he's upset, a bit, with me, and has left, gone east, to try and find you. He's in his truck, the silver-gray; you know it. Look out for it. He wants to help you, he's worried about you. I told him I'm not worried, not like that, and that if I'm not then he shouldn't be, but still, he was. He got excited. More than I've seen him be in years. So, he's out there, now, east, looking for you. I don't know what you'll make of that, but I thought you should know. I know he won't stop you if you don't want him to.

I am fine. Still here. I made the most beautiful Saskatoon-berry pie the other day. Sugar-glazed the pastry, flour-thickened the filling, everything. Will have to go to town tomorrow as we're out of flour and butter.

I am waking up earlier and earlier. The sun comes up at five and I'm up to greet it. I sit in our kitchen with a decaf and wait for it to come up. And going to bed later and later. My eyes don't like being closed when it's dark out, I guess. My body aches with tiredness through the day, so I nap, sometimes, when things are in the oven. Sometimes even in the kitchen, with my head on the table where the sunlight hits. I know it's not hygienic, but I always wipe it down before eating off that spot.

Okay. I'm going to check on the weeds. We've got thistles this year that pop up to your knees whenever you're not looking.

I hope you're well. Keep to the shade. Write when you have time. I read your letters out loud so there's a voice in the house.

Yours, remember,
Otto.

Otto folded the letter into thirds and put it into an envelope, even though he had no address to send it to. He wrote his wife's name on the front and put it with the others, in a neat stack on the corner of the table, beside the letters that came in from her.

They started spending a lot of time at Russell's aunt and uncle's, on the floor, in the middle of the blue and white living room, whenever they had breaks between school, chores, sleep. They would both sit facing the same direction, toward the radio, as if it were a person. After half an hour or so, Russell's uncle or aunt, or sometimes both, together, would knock gently on the door and slip in with a tray of coffee and buttered brown bread. Then they would all sit listening. One by one they drew in and soaked up the reports, the predictions, the analyses, the lists and lists and lists of sometimes-foreign and-sometimes-familiar-names, and the interviews. All of these in the steady, reassuring voice of the radio announcer, the vowels long and consonants precise, the strong, solid inflection leaning more toward England than home, all of these except the interviews, where, suddenly, starkly, they heard voices like their own. Sometimes the interviewer, calm, measured, would interject with questions or little comments, like breaths, between phrases: No? Yes, I see, Ah, Oh, oh, oh, but usually, mostly, they receded and let the interviewees tell their first- or second- or thirdhand stories in voices that could have been their cousins', their neighbors', their own.

They heard one story about prisoners who had been taken from their homes and jobs, pulled away from cash registers, books, stoves, cats, bosses, friends, and put all together in a very small room with no windows except one, extremely tiny and high up, higher than anyone could jump or anyone could reach even when three went on each other's shoulders like a totem pole, teetering, with a crowd of hands reaching, waiting for the top to fall. There was no food and no toilet and everyone was so close to everyone else that they'd sleep standing up, supported by bodies on every side, with blankets of their neighbors' clothes and hair and breath. They were like this for three days, taking turns standing in the corner that they'd designated for their waste, the smell of it choking and repulsive at first, but hardly noticeable by the end of your three-hour turn, counted out loud in seconds, as everyone had their watches taken off them, craning their necks higher and higher, toward the air and light of that one window, stomachs louder and louder, competing against the counting. It had been three days, three days like any, like many, others in very similar rooms with similar prisoners all over the region, all over the past few years, when, all at once, at what they figured was close to noon based on the light from the window, all the children and all the babies started to rise, so hungry and so light that they floated. And once they started floating and realized what they were doing, what they could do, they waved their arms to steer, and directed themselves up and straight to that one window. One of the children, the seven-year-old daughter of Aaron and Thilde Bloomberg, locksmiths, slipped her narrow hand and wrist through the grate to release the latch holding the pane in place, and pulled it away. The children passed the square of glass, roughly two square feet, down between them, back to the adults below, so it wouldn't fall on anyone's head. Then they floated back up and took turns gliding out of the hole where the window had been, the older ones holding the hands of the infants. No one knew, said the radio, where they'd gone, or where or if they'd landed, though it was speculated to perhaps be Switzerland or perhaps Central Africa.

They heard another story about a field that had once been yellow with grain that had turned completely red. Painters and scientists were sent in to examine it, but they always came back completely red themselves, head to toe, skin and clothes, if they came back at all. Due to the fate of the painters and scientists, no one was willing to eat or buy the red grain, and the field was deemed unusable and irreparable.

Every day there were new interviews, new stories, every day more.

Soon enough it was Otto's birthday. A Saturday. Winnie made an apple cake for dinner. Everyone sang a song about birthdays that they'd learned in school, from Miss Kinnick. After dinner Otto's mother gave him the rest of the day off chores, the traditional luxury reserved for birthdays. Otto lay in a soft bit of wild grass, in the shade of one of the wind-break trees. Russell, after dishes, found him there. Otto, he said, you should go.

No, said Otto.

Go, said Russell.

No, said Otto. Nope. I'm waiting for you, Russell. And that's that. He crossed his legs and closed his eyes. Five months, he said. Just five.

Otto went to school and did farmwork, learned more and more shaky letters and words, songs and numbers, forced ticks off horses and weeded row after row after row of sandy earth while the knotted ball of anticipation in his stomach shuddered and stretched and kept him awake long into the night, until, soon enough, it was five months later, Russell's birthday, and he and Russell were in town, in the doorway of what was a dance school Monday, Wednesday, and Saturday afternoons and, now, was the nearest recruiting office. It was a large gymnasium, with a man at a desk in the middle. Other than him, Otto and Russell were the only ones there. The man at the desk was in uniform. Dark green with a triangular hat like the boats they used to make of paper. He stood when they entered. He did not speak. He picked up two papers from his desk and held them out mechanically at Otto and Russell, looking over their heads.

There wasn't space on the desk, so Otto and Russell spread their forms on the floor. Otto looked over the pages, carefully sounding out the questions in his head.

FAMILY NAME?

CHRISTIAN/GIVEN NAME?

BIRTH DATE?

POSTING ADDRESS?

REASON FOR JOINING UP?

REASON(S) FOR NOT JOINING UP (IF ANY)?

He slowly rounded out letters into the first and second spaces. V-O-G-E-L. O-T-T-O. Wobbly. Childish. He looked over to Russell, who was tapping his pencil on the floor, already finished. Russell, he whispered, head down low toward his papers so the officer couldn't hear. Seeing as you're finished, could you, maybe, help me?

Russell took Otto's forms and filled them in with decided, quick strokes. What should I put for this? he asked, pointing with the pencil end to the last two questions.

Put "Because otherwise I will explode," said Otto.

I don't think I can put that, said Russell.

I know, I know. Okay, put "To see beyond this place."

Russell wrote it in. And for the next one?

Write "None," said Otto.

While Russell was writing, Otto saw that on his own form he had put, for the last question:

Dead leg. (2) Do not want to.

He hadn't written anything at all for the second-to-last question.

While they wrote, the officer sat and pushed the papers on his desk to align exactly with its sides. He kept his head down while they placed their completed forms in the pile on his left, but lifted his eyes, just a little, just a tiny bit, up toward them. I know you're worried, he whispered, but don't be, don't be. It will all be okay, I promise. It will be fine.

Three weeks later they got their letters in the post, in envelopes dyed a muted uniform green. Otto was to report to the Regina office for dispatch in four days; Russell would not be needed.

Etta, in the new openness that surrounded the schoolhouse and teacher's cottage, learned to listen differently. As the months passed, her ears learned to distinguish shapes, patterns, life, in the big silence of this place. Smaller sounds, broader sounds. Insects calling against or with the wind, the conversation the wooden walls of her room had with the sun, the tread of boots on gravel miles away. And, of course, the calls of children and their dogs across the fields as they made their way toward her, toward the school. The brushing of the grain away from their bodies as they passed through.

And she'd figured out the scheduling of the switching students. The Vogels and Russell, who took turns, each day, back and forth. She asked Russell, one morning, as everyone was settling in, finding their seats, Why you too, Russell? You're not a Vogel. Before he could answer, Addie interrupted, from a front desk,

Oh, he is one of us, just with a different name. Mom calls him Otto's twin.

Russell smiled and flushed. Owen, his desk-mate, grimaced and mumbled something. The students in the desk in front of them giggled. Bolstered, Owen whispered something more, a little louder this time. More sniggering. The girls on their left looked over, downward, toward the boys' legs. Russell straightened up, looked directly ahead.

Right, said Etta. Okay. That's enough of that. Everyone up, today we're starting with "Johnny Appleseed." Russell you can be on clapping, Gus and Beatrice, you do the stomps. Nice and loud, get the dogs howling. Ready?

In the months since coming to Gopherlands school, Etta had

started to hear new things, and so did all the neighboring farms. First thing in the morning the wind would carry the belted song of twenty-two children out across the land, through the cracks in the barn where Mabel McGuire was milking, over the hum of the tractor Liam Rogers was driving in no fixed pattern, under the warped door of the farmhouse where Sandy Goldstein was still working her ancient body slowly, carefully, out of bed. If the song was one they knew, they'd sing along, passing it further and further.

The next day, before class, Etta was in the yard being introduced to Lucy and Glen's new skinny gray dog when Otto and the other Vogels marched up the road to the school. Owen broke out of the circle of children around the dog and hurried up to Otto. Hey, Otto! he said. Good morning! Want me to fill you in on yesterday's lessons?

Otto hesitated, opened his mouth like he might say something, then, instead, swung his arm around, a closed fist. Owen flinched left, clipped in the shoulder. The others turned away from the dog, began to yell out. Otto lunged again, this time at Owen's chest. Don't you, he said. Don't you ever, ever— The smaller boy stumbled back, lost his footing, fell down, head cracking the gravel. Otto fell on top of him. A blur of dust rose around them.

Etta saw all this over the head of the dog and the heads of the students, played out before she even realized what was happening, before Owen did either.

Jesus Christ! she yelled. The students whipped their heads back to look at her; a blaspheming teacher was as exciting as a fight. She broke through them to where Owen was, on the ground. Knelt down beside him. Breathing shallow, eyes open, stunned, a bit of blood here from his nose, there from the back of his head. Otto stood and stepped back, arms fallen to his sides. You, said Etta. You will not come to classes today, Otto Vogel. Go home, just you, by yourself, and come back to speak with me at the end of the day.

Otto said nothing, just turned and walked back toward the farm. His brothers and sisters watched him. Winnie took a step, like to go with him, but Walter put an arm out to stop her.

Etta did her best to lift Owen back to his feet. He was surprisingly light; she could feel his shoulder blades through his shirt. Thank you, he said, but I'll be fine. He wiped at the blood under his nose with his shirtsleeve, staining it dark.

I would like to make it clear, said Otto, in the doorway to the classroom after all the students had gone, that I am here with an explanation, not an apology. He crossed to where Etta was waiting, at her desk. He was taller, older close-up. Etta could feel the heat off him, angry.

You should sit down, she said. Sit and explain.

Russell, said Otto, is the smartest one here. Smart and kind to everyone and thoroughly capable—he was still standing, like he was giving a class presentation—of everything. Everything except standing up for himself. So I did that for him. So we do that for him. Prepared speech finished, Otto relaxed a little, leaned a bit on the heavy wood teacher's desk between them.

What did Owen say about him?

Does it matter?

Maybe.

People could say things about Owen. They could. But they don't. We don't. Words are strong. The strongest. Worse than bruises on gravel.

Etta considered this. Things people had said, whispered, when Alma left. The deep and unexpected urge toward violence she'd felt. To throw her body in the way of the words. Not something covered in teachers' college. You can't hit people, she said, finally. Though she wasn't sure. Her fist into the soft, stupid mouths of former friends, bursting, realizing, something. You can't do it here, anyway, she said. You, you should have told me. I could have spoken with Owen.

It's not your responsibility.

Surely it is. As much as yours.

It's not.

. . .

. . .

Well, what will Russell do, if you're not there? When you're not there?

I will find a way, said Otto.

Etta rearranged the seating so that Otto and Russell no longer sat with Owen but on the opposite side of the room, at the back. Owen, a dark smear swollen from one side of his nose to just under his eye, kept his head fixed forward through the lessons and went home, by himself, for dinner. His new desk-mate, Sue, whispered soft words of consolation at him, lightly touching the place where his hair had had to be shaved away, but Owen ignored her, steadily working through his lessons on his own.

A week later, after class, when the students and dogs had dissipated, away, back toward various homes, and Etta had finished bundling up the second- and third-year assignments on Why I Would Like To Be Queen Or King and Why I Would Not Like To Be Queen Or King, respectively, she noticed that Otto was still there. In his new desk at the back of the room. Sitting, this time.

I thought I should apologize, he said. Not for what happened with Owen, but for how I spoke to you the other day. I thought I had better say sorry. I wouldn't talk that way to my father or mother, and so I shouldn't to you either.

Thank you, Otto. That's good of you to do. I was just planning to fail all of your assignments for three weeks.

The room fell silent.

Oh, Otto said. Well, yes, yes, I am sorry.

Etta smiled. Apology accepted. You can go home now.

But Otto didn't go anywhere, he didn't move.

Otto? I need to lock the school.

Yes, sorry. Of course. It's just that, I was wondering, I have a favor to ask.

Etta put the assignments back down on her desk.

You've noticed, I'm sure, said Otto, that I am not the best at words. At reading and, even more, at writing. I mean, I could be, I will be, but it's still quite new, and it's harder, starting late. The younger kids can get it right away, their brains still have space. But mine's already part-full. So,

And then Otto told her about Owen, about the lessons Owen used to give him. First in the dirt with sticks, then at dinner with paper, pencils. And, said Otto, he was going to write me letters. I'm, I'm going away . . . to fight, and he was going to write to me, so I could write him back. So I could keep up practice, over there . . . He stopped. Didn't go so far as to ask Etta anything outright.

Under the desk, Etta's right hand clenched. It was just as Alma had described. Little by little, all the young men from all over the country heading east, marching past Alma's convent in mismatched socks, draining out like a hot summer's stream. Etta looked at her student, his hands folded into each other, calm, still at his desk. Just like that, she thought; it's that easy, they go just like that. She felt very heavy. When are you going? she said.

Saturday.

In two days.

Yes.

So this was your last day of school.

Yes.

An apology, a request, and a goodbye, thought Etta. All in one. Okay, she said. I can write to you, and you can write back. My mailing address is easy, it's here. She went to the blackboard, picked up a nub of chalk:

The Teacher's Cottage
Gopherlands School
Gopherlands, Sask
Canada

Oh, and, she lifted her arm back up to the top of what she'd written, squeezing the letters in:

Etta Gloria Kinnick

That's me.

Etta, said Otto. That's easy to spell. Good. He wrote the address out carefully in his book. On the inside back cover. I don't know mine yet, he said. But I will send it to you.

They said goodbye, polite, formal, a handshake, and Otto walked to the door.

Oh, and, Miss Kinnick . . . Etta? His body was blocking the late-afternoon sun, a cut-out of light around him.

Yes?

Keep an eye out for Russell, okay?

Yes, Otto, of course.

8

A photographer from Kenora, who worked taking photos for a local but not unremarkable newspaper, was taking his daughter, his only child, for a light-aircraft flying lesson in the flattest, longest place he knew, when, a hundred or so meters away, he saw Etta, all dust and sun, all eighty-three years old, hair winding out behind her, with a coyote trotting at her side, its head only just above the grass-line. Well, he said, look at that. And, because he was always ready for something like this, he pulled his camera up from where it hung, almost always, around his neck, and took a picture.

When the photographer, whose daughter was proving to be a better pilot than any other her age, perhaps than any other ever, gave the photo of Etta to his editor, the editor said, What's the story?

And, although the photographer said he didn't know the story, the editor still liked the picture and agreed to publish it in the weekend paper's Out & About section and gave the photographer fifty dollars, which the photographer spent almost immediately on a small but good-quality camera for his daughter to use in the air, while fly-ing. Which is why, two days later, she came home from her lessons, still in her helmet, and said,

I took some pictures. Mostly of the coyote-woman. She's still out there, still walking east. I don't think she's even stopped. I don't think she's going to stop.

Which is how the photographer got the story. And, soon enough, how everybody got it.

And so, one day, not too long into the rocks and trees of Ontario, a man and a woman, both in office-type suits, one burgundy and one navy, stepped out from behind a tree Etta was approaching. Pardon us, Miss, said the man. Have you got a couple minutes to spare? We would love to talk to you. The woman nodded and smiled and held a microphone out in front of her casually, like a cup of tea.

I don't really have very many minutes, said Etta. I am eighty-three years old.

The man took a pen from one pocket and a notepad from an-other and began scribbling.

But, continued Etta, I suppose you could walk with us for a bit, if you can keep up.

James said nothing.

And you've been walking for how long? said the woman. They were scrambling over some low rocks; she had rolled the bottoms of her burgundy suit pants up so as not to get caught and was now manag-ing to keep her balance by holding one arm out to her side, to coun-terbalance the other, out toward Etta with the microphone.

Since before the spinach, said Etta.

The man was a little ways behind them, as he kept having to stop to scribble. But, Etta, he called up to them, why? And then louder, in case she hadn't heard, *Why?*

Etta thought, stepped around a root, turned, and said over her shoulder, I don't remember.

You don't remember? said the woman, low, too low for the man to hear.

Sometimes I remember, sometimes I don't. It's nothing personal. Right now I just don't.

Can we stay with you until you do?

They made camp between some birch trees. The man couldn't decide whether to have his suit jacket under him, as a bed, or over him, as a cover.

There are flies, said Etta. I'd go with over. There was a lake nearby, as there almost always was these days. They could hear its twilight birds.

Etta, what *do* you remember? asked the woman. They were laid down now, looking up through the branches.

I have a sister, said Etta. Alma.

Back from catching, killing, and eating a small brown mouse, James curled up into the soft indent of Etta's waist on the far side from the reporters. Still silent.

That night Etta dreamt of water. And boats and boys and men and boys, breathing in the water, spitting out the water, and everything loud and so much color, but darkened and getting darker and this is no place for a woman you better get down get right down, down, deeper, deeper, deeper.

*   *   *

In the morning, over a berry breakfast, Etta said, Water. That's why. I'm trying to get to the water.

Before they left, the woman whispered to Etta, while the man was looking away, scribbling, I wish I could come with you.

You can, said Etta.

I can't, said the woman.

They were picked up by a half-car-half-truck with giant wheels that pulled up through the trees. You can, said Etta.

Maybe, said the woman, across the rolled-down window of the passenger seat.

Russell was looking for Etta's boots. For the treads, in the dirt. It hadn't rained since he'd started, so the tracks should have been there, somewhere. He looked for a folded-down parting in the foliage, and for the treads. He knew them, he'd seen them hundreds of times, thousands of times. And he'd followed them before too. Twice.

Once was fifty-five years ago, almost. That year of mud, maybe the last, maybe the only. It wasn't raining, but it had felt like it might. That was rare enough. He had followed them across his flax to the yard behind his Quonset, where he kept his collection of big metal. Mostly broke-down things, though some of them would still go, if he was patient enough. At first he thought she was an animal. A dog or coyote, the way she was bent down, low, crouched. Her arms were around her stomach, clenched. She was rocking, slowly, subtly, back and forth. Her head was pointing down, at the mud; she didn't see Russell.

He took a step back, behind the cover of a rusted thresher's cylinder. If she was here, he reasoned, it was because she didn't want to be seen. This place, in the shadows of gently stagnant machines, was where the foxes came to give birth, where the cats came to die. Sheltered. Private. But Etta didn't look right. Not normal, not okay. She might need him. He deliberated. Then, without moving, without deciding, he said, Etta, I am here, behind the thresher. I can come around to you, or go back home, or just stay here, just here. Whatever you want.

There was a long silence, and then, without looking up, Etta reached one hand out toward him. Open. He walked over, knelt down in the mud, and took it. She said nothing and he said nothing, just let his hand be pulled away from him and back and away and back as Etta rocked. Her eyes were squeezed shut. After a minute, barely a minute, she let go and said, Okay. I think I'll be okay now, Russell. You should go home.

Her voice had too much air and not enough sound.

You're sure?

I'm sure.

Okay, said Russell. He stood up. The knees of his jeans were wet and heavy with mud. He turned around, away from her.

And, Russell, she said, thank you. For now and for then and for always. You're so quiet, so gentle, so patient. So, so, so. The sibilance of her words barely there, o, o, o.

Russell followed the treads back to where they'd passed his front door. Otto had been home for a few years now, he reminded himself. He didn't need to worry about Etta so much, now. Still, a few hours later he went back to the place behind the Quonset just to be sure she wasn't still there, and to see if, maybe, she'd left anything behind. The grass was wetly matted down where she'd been, and the mud kicked around a bit, but that was all.

That night, after sunset but before bed, Russell went for a walk. He knew the route by heart and by feet and could look up at the star-full sky more than down at where he was going. He walked until he got to Otto's truck, parked up along the southeast corner of Otto and Etta's house. The truck was unlocked. It was always unlocked. Russell opened the door furthest from the house and slipped in and across to the driver's seat. The truck's interior was still and hot and smelled of the rough white soap that Otto and Russell had both used since they were kids on the Vogel farm, scrubbing up hands and fingernails be-fore lunch. Warm-yellow light from a kitchen window shone through and bounced back off the truck's side, making Russell invisible and illuminating the inside of the house like a silent movie. He made up his own soundtrack, imagined the sounds, silence, words:

Otto is sitting at the table, reading a newspaper. Quiet. Then he gets up, his chair scraping across the floor a little as he does, opens a drawer, gets a pencil, and sits back down. He continues reading, every now and then drawing slow, careful circles around words. The pencil scratching lightly. After twenty-seven minutes, Etta comes in, walking with her body held, careful, like a heavily pregnant woman, except thin, empty. Does Otto notice this? She puts the kettle on, leans against the counter. Otto turns so his good ear faces her. Does Etta notice this?

I'm sorry, says Otto.

Etta looks up, away from the kettle. Otto taps his finger against the newspaper.

I'm sorry, I'm so sorry, he says. *You should have stayed with Russell. This would not have happened with Russell.*

Etta walks across to him, looks over his shoulder at his hand on the paper.

Maybe, she says. She sits in the chair next to him, next to the good ear. *But it's too late now, isn't it.*

They sit in silence, both looking down, at the table, the paper, for four minutes. Then Otto picks up his pencil again and draws a circle.

Etta, he says. *Do you think this happened because you still love him?*

Maybe, says Etta. She points at the circle. *Maybe*.

The kettle lets out a short, small whistle. Etta looks around to it and Otto follows her gaze. Then it's silent again and they both look back down at their hands, the paper.

That was a long time ago. But Etta always bought the same boots.

Now, however, Russell couldn't find their tracks. He crossed all the way up across the swatch of land that she'd almost certainly have to have crossed, between two lakes, along the same corridor as Cordelia and Monty's café, eyes to the ground, checking carefully, and then back again. There were many other tracks, some human, farmers or hikers probably, and some animal, mice, deer, dogs, coyotes, but no Etta. No Etta as he knew her, at least. It had taken him two days. He'd eaten most of his peanuts. He walked back to his truck. He could track and trace, yes, but Russell knew that he couldn't keep up with Etta walking. He couldn't keep up with anyone. He swung his legs into the cab, bad then good, and set off east again, on small and smaller roads, as the trees became dense. He would stop for supplies and, hopefully, clues, at the next bit of civilization. He thought he should be sad, or at least frustrated, but Russell wasn't. He was in Ontario. The windows were rolled down to the new air, and he breathed it through his mouth, like a dog, alive and moving.

The phone rang. It took Otto four rings to find it, past all the letters and recipes. By the time he got to it, it was too late, the ringing had stopped. He pulled a chair from its place at the table and sat beside it, puzzling over who there was out there who had its number. Did Russell have it? He tried to remember if Russell had ever phoned. He knocked, he shouted, he left notes, but phoning? No, no. Otto was fairly sure he didn't even have a phone. But Etta would know it, surely, her own phone number, of course she would. For most things she would write, had always written, but for an emergency she might try to phone. It must have been Etta. In an emergency. He stayed there, right there by the phone, for eleven minutes, watching it, thinking,

Etta is out of food and money. She is thin, her clothes and her flesh both worn down to near-transparency. It has been three days since her last letter. Three days without eating. She has resorted to chewing grass and drinking dandelion milk, the skin around her lips turned green. Finally, on the outskirts of somewhere—Laclu?—she finds a phone box and digs down to her last quarter, dialing the only number she knows, and listening to it ring and ring and ring and ring and ring and ring and then cut off. No answer. No quarters left, she slumps into the corner of the booth, crumpled, already more ghost than not.

Or,

Etta is walking, striding east with ease, confidence, strong and alert, singing, in an Ontario forest. Just out of sight, off to her right, something else is moving east, along with her, around the trees, the sound of its movement hidden under Etta's footfalls and song.

They continue like this for hours, until the darkness between the trees blurs into one, and Etta stops for the night, laying a bed of clothes in the cavern of a balsam fir's low branches. The cougar waits until she is asleep, regular breathing, then slips in beside her, always noiseless, and lays one heavy paw on her neck. Etta wakes before the claws have a chance to extend, pushing herself backward, away, into the tree's base.

No!

The cougar springs forward, catching some fur in the low needles, back onto Etta's chest.

Yes. You've had a good life, Etta. You're old now. I need this. I need to survive too. The claws tear an even quadruple track down her coat, there is blood.

Not yet, I'm almost there. Not yet. Etta kicks out, into the animal's beautifully soft belly, a female, she realizes, a mother. She rolls left, toward her things, her bag, and beside it Otto's rifle. The cougar catches a leg with its mouth, just below the knee, bites down. The pain bursts through Etta like caffeine, she can reach the gun, she swings it round, firing once, missing, draws back the bolt, automatic, like she's done a thousand times in the yard, with cans or gophers, and fires again, and the cat makes a noise louder than it ever has, louder than it knew it could, hit, in the hip, and flinches back, away, sudden, to the edge of the branch-cave. Looks at Etta, blinks, blinks, confused, afraid, then disappears, away. There is blood all along Etta's side; she doesn't know whose it is. She falls unconscious.

When she wakes she is in the back of a moving vehicle. You're lucky, says someone, a face that's mostly beard poked around from the driver's seat. You are one lucky lady, lady. Lucky for that gun, and lucky it's old enough to be loud enough for me to hear from my place; I got pretty thick walls. Etta's leg is wrapped in plaid cotton. A shirt. Red and green and blue.

It takes them four hours to reach the nearest hospital, over dark, bumping forest roads. Etta tries to stand but the nurses won't let her. They lay her on a stretcher and strap down her arms and legs. They ask, Is there anyone we can call?

Or,

Etta is passing through somewhere, a town, Thunder Bay, and the sun is setting, and she needs to hurry up to be out of town, back in the wild to sleep. The streets are emptying of people, little by little as the dark creeps down and the streetlamps twitch on. Etta tries to increase her pace, bigger strides, more steps, but it's the end of the day and she's been walking since sun-up, since six or so; she's tired. She comes to a split in the road, opening up to a park. She can walk straight through it, the direct route, or keep to the road with the sidewalk, lamps, houses warmly lit, and go around, twice as far. She lifts a metal latch and pulls a gate open toward her, she'll go through the park, be through in five minutes. She straightens up and grips her bag with both hands, as, from somewhere close, a siren sounds.

The adrenaline of the dark revives her legs, and Etta's almost all the way across the park when she notices the small pack with smoke curling from their heads in tendrils like hair extensions. Young. Maybe fifteen or seventeen. Like the students she used to teach, like Otto and Winnie and Russell. There are three boys and one girl, all with cigarettes except one boy, the shortest. They hear Etta before they see her, before she sees them; they're ready. Casually, they open up to form a line, a fence with their bodies across the path. Hey, says one, a boy with a winter hat on, even though it's not winter, What you got in your bag, lady?

Etta, still a teacher, always a teacher, raises an eyebrow. Well, she says, I don't think—

You should show us, says the girl, interrupting, stepping closer.

I don't think—says Etta again, calm, eyes forward, at the not-smoking boy, at his blue fleece hood up around his still pudgy face, that you should be, while reaching around, the rifle, is it too soon for the rifle? They're just kids.

It's late, she says, what about your—

Or, I guess, we could just take a look for ourselves, the first boy again, the winter hat. He lunges forward, grabs, knocks Etta down. The girl follows her down, her face close enough for Etta to smell the beer, cheap. Etta, instinctual, closes her arms around her bag, its socks, crackers, chocolate, writing paper and pens, closes her eyes before the first blow, the girl's smaller fist, into chest, between clavicles. A basketball shoe to her side, and another, and then everything, everywhere, kicking and hitting and harder and harder, her body is made of paper, tearing, and is that blood or spit on her face, and Etta releases her grip, covers her face with her hands, and the bag falls away, is grabbed up before it hits ground. And then they are gone. Crackers, chocolate, writing paper and pens. The rifle still on Etta's back, digging in. She lifts her hands away, off her face. It hurts to breathe. Her ribs won't rise and fall properly. There is a split in her lip that stings with each inhale. The little bits of starlight blur and dance. She turns her head away from them and her spine shoots warnings, don't move, don't move, and there, still just right where he was before, is the boy in the blue fleece hood. He is crying.

Don't cry, says Etta.

Sorry, says the boy. I know I shouldn't.

Your friends are gone.

I know. I should go.

But he doesn't go. He just stays there, just right where he was before.

I bet I could carry you, he says. I have a little brother, I can carry him.

Etta thinks about her back, the rifle. No, she says, you don't need to do that.

I need to do something.

Do you have a phone?

Yes, from my mom, for emergencies.

Maybe we could use that?

Okay.

Thank you . . .

James.

James. Thank you, James.

Or,

Etta has forgotten. She stands in a field, somewhere, stopped. She sits down in the yellow. Spreads her fingers against the sun into her eyes. Russell and Winnie and Amos and the others will be done their chores soon and they'll all meet and walk home together. She sits and waits and watches grasshoppers bound toward her and away. When the sun starts to set she stretches out, puts her hands under her head. She falls asleep thinking,

Any minute now.

When the farmer, a woman, broad and strong and tan with always squinting eyes, finds her two days later, Etta is still like that, smiling, with her hands behind her head. What a beautiful way to go, thinks the farmer. She strokes bits of dust and seed from Etta's hair. She reaches through the old woman's tattered bag, arranging items neatly in piles beside the body, like a shrine, until she finds the bit of paper that says

Home:

and then a phone number.

The phone rang again. Otto jumped. Fumbled, grabbed at it. *Hello?* he said, Yes? Hello?

A moment of silence on the other end, the audible fuzz of distance, and then, Otto? Is that Otto? This is William, your nephew, Harriet's son. Did you know Etta's in the paper?

William. The accountant. Brandon, Manitoba. He was still talking,

She looks good; a little crazy, maybe, but good, as in, healthy. There's a picture, in color. Want me to describe it? Here, I'll describe it: She's walking. She's in a field of grass, it looks like wild grass, like, not a lawn, but tall grass, the kind that sometimes has stripes. And there are trees in the background, big firs or pines. Coniferous for sure. Her hair is longer than I remember. And straighter. It's all out behind her in the wind . . .

And on and on, talking.

William, Otto interrupted, which paper is this?

Oh, um, here, it's the *National. The Canadian National.* It says in the corner, down at the bottom of the article, that it first appeared in the *Kenora Chatter*, but now, this, this is the *National.*

And she's alive and not hurt?

No, no, I mean yes. Yes, she's alive, and, no, she doesn't seem to be hurt. Here, it says, *Moments of fumbling confusion contrasted with moments of startling clarity. A striking presence,* it says. No mention of injury. She looks good, healthy. You know, I thought it was a bit odd, a while back I got letters here addressed to her—I sent them back to you, did you get them?—but it makes sense now, I guess, if she was passing through. Though I didn't see her. I bet she was south of us. Walking . . . do you think it's okay, her doing this walking? I mean, she looks healthy, so I suppose it's fine, but, there are animals and things, right? And people, there are more people out that way, Ontario, Quebec. I could see about getting some time off work, maybe following in the van? Or get one of the kids to do it, Stephen needs a job . . . though Lydia's the better driver . . .

No, said Otto, interrupting again. No thank you, William. She's okay. There's a plan. She'll be okay.

Okay then. Okay. I'm sure you know best, Otto. . . . Hey, I wish Mom could see her, eh? She'd have loved to see that.

Yes, she would have.

Mom would have loved it.

You miss her?

Yes, oh yes.

Me, too.

Once off the phone, Otto got in his truck and drove to the Co-op. He bought eggs, milk, and the shop's entire stack, twelve copies, of *The Canadian National.*

Sixty-six years earlier, all the Vogels lined up at the nearest train station—the one that had brought them Russell—in a line from smallest to tallest. Otto shook their hands and kissed their cheeks. He whispered one thing to each, one secret each. Some whispered back, some didn't. *Thank you*, said Ellie. *I know, I know*, said Amos. *I will*, said Russell. *Please?* said his mother. *Soon enough*, said Winnie.

The train to Regina took no time at all. Otto stayed standing to feel the movement under his feet, moving without moving, one hand on a suitcase borrowed from Russell, unused since the day he arrived, and one hand braced on the window, running over everything they passed.

Dear Miss Kinnick, *

First, thankyou for letting me write to you. I hope it is not too
intruesive. I will try to keep it short. Just long enouf to practice all the
letters and a fair few words. Ready? Ok.

When they sayed I was going to Regina, they lied. This camp is not
in Regina, it is near Regina, in a field. A bunch of low flat buldings
droped in-to a field. Every-thing square. There are about 75 of us here,
now, from all over Sask. We eat to-gether, sleep to-gether, and train to-
gether, which I'm glad for. Its like home. Eccept here were all about the
same age, and all boys.

They have allready given me a gun. A real gun. I know how to
open it and shut it and clean it and dis-arm it and fire it, but not how
to carry it confortably, like Im not carrying a gun. Its the same for most.
So theyre having us practice. Have us walk all the way a-round the
perifary with the guns on our belts, eat dinner with the guns on our
laps, play cards with the guns tucked into our socks, sleep with the guns
beside us. Once we can dance with the guns and run with the guns and
embrace each other with the guns well be ready to go, on a bigger train,
east, to Charlotte-town or Halifax. It wont be long, I think. Some have
allready gone.

Have you been out there, ever?

I hope every-thing is well at home. That the winds arent to
big and the students are behaving them-selves and learnning and
singging. And that your well. What happens if the teacher isnot
well? Please write back soon. You can write about any-thing at all,
I dont mind. About the sun or the dust or your own self. You can mail
it back here, and if I have moved East theyll forwerd it, so dont
worry.

Please send love to all the Vogels and to Russell.

Sinceerly,
Otto.

*This is my first letter. That means it will be the werst, in terms of spelling, neat-ness and all that. It will get better from here.

Etta read the letter on her front step, her legs stretched down the wooden stairs to let the sun catch them. The post date was two and a half weeks ago. Once she got to the end, she put a rock on top of the two sheets of army-issue faded green so they wouldn't blow away, and went inside for pens and paper. When she came back, legs back out, down, she corrected all Otto's errors with her red pen before switching to the black one and starting on her reply.

She'd do the same with the next letter, and the next and the next. Legs stretched down the teacher house's three front steps. She now kept her pens and paper in the mailbox, ready.

Dear Otto,

Thank you for your last letter. They're getting better, they really are. Especially the contractions.

You've been out there, out east, for some time now. I bet you're becoming an excellent swimmer. And eating a lot of fish. What else are they teaching you? What else do you need to know before they let you go all the way over?

As I'm sure you're aware, we said goodbye to Walter and Wiley this week. They stood up in front of the class and sang "I'll Be Seeing You" for us before they went. They even did harmony. I imagine they're in Regina (or just outside it) now, but wouldn't it be nice if you all were together in Halifax? I am hoping, for you.

The weather here is hot. Hot and dry. My Teacher's Daily Diary says it's fall, but I'll believe that when I see it. The school's been back open for weeks and still nothing like a frost. Still sunburns at lunch-hour.

You said it was just your birthday, a day or so before the last letter was sent. It was just my birthday too, a few days before that. Which means we're the same age. Almost exactly. Russell and I, I've discovered, were born in the same year, but you and I are even closer. So, I was thinking, because of this, and because you're not in school anymore, I'd like you to stop calling me Miss Kinnick, and start calling me Etta. Okay? I have told Russell that outside of school, in town or at dances, he's to do the same.

Yours sincerely,
Etta

So, what about the women?

Etta was teaching the class a Brief History of War, at the request of Winnie. They had been acting out Troy. Now most of them were pretend-killed on the schoolroom floor, and it was time for questions.

Women, Winnie? What about them?

Winnie sat up, brushed the chalk and boot-dust off the back of her head. What did they do, to fight, to help? Where were they?

Well, we know about Helen . . .

She doesn't count. Queens don't count. What about the normal ones? What about the sisters of the Greeks?

I bet some of them helped. I bet some were spies.

Like Mata Hari?

Exactly.

But not fighters?

Not fighters.

That's stupid.

There are nurses . . .

In Troy?

Now.

So, women can only be nurses or spies?

Nurses and spies.

9

Russell stopped at the O-K-Kenora Pitstop 'n Shop. He bought more peanuts, water, chocolate, bananas, Ritz crackers, socks, and a newspaper. The cashier was wearing headphones and rocked slowly back and forth while counting out Russell's change. Thank you, said Russell, taking the coins.

The cashier nodded in time with her dance, smiled.

And, also, sorry . . .

She stopped swaying. Tilted her head to one side.

I was wondering if you'd seen . . .

She held up one finger, pointing at the foam circle on one of her ears.

Oh, said Russell. He paused. The cashier swayed. His wallet was still on the counter between them. He picked it up and carefully pulled the photo out from the billfold—Etta and Otto, years ago. He pointed at Etta.

The cashier looked down, at it . . . squinting. Then her eyes opened a bit wider and she nodded. Yes, said her lips, even though no sound came out. Yes, yes. She reached over the counter and pulled the newspaper out from under Russell's arm, excited. She opened it to the fourth page, flipped it around so it was facing him, and pointed. There was Etta, in some tall grass, jack pines in the background, not wearing boots at all; wearing a newish pair of running shoes.

Different treads, different tracks.

What shoes are these? Russell pointed at Etta's feet in the picture. Shoes?

The cashier stepped back and pointed at her own feet. Russell leaned forward to see them. The shoes were a different color, and a smaller size, but had the same logo as Etta's. The cashier took one off, handed it across to Russell. She was wearing red socks. Russell took the shoe—it was so light, he expected such a technical thing to be heavy—and turned it over to examine the treads. Rubber. He ran his fingers over them, memorizing. The cashier swayed, smiled. Russell turned the shoe back over. On the inside tongue someone had written DIANE in blue marker. He handed it back.

Thank you, Diane, he mouthed.

Diane smiled, shrugged, one shoe on, the other in her hand.

It wouldn't take him any time at all to find the tracks, now Russell knew what he was looking for. No time, no time at all. A few hours, maybe before sunset even.

I told you there would be more rocks here.

Yes, you did. And?

And, well, I think you're maybe struggling, now, with that.

James was on top of a low, jagged cliff. Etta was slowly zig-zagging her way up. Across, up, across, up. She was breathing hard.

No, I'm not. Struggling.

James had just jumped. Two jumps, up and up.

Okay, well, if you're going to be a while, I think I'll go smell around this place a bit. Just yell when you get to the top.

I will whistle.

Okay, James said and trotted off, nose to the ground.

There were a lot of these cliffs. A lot of slow zig-zagging for Etta and jumping and smelling for James. After making her way scrupulously up the fifth one that day, Etta whistled, but James did not run up from out of the brush as he usually did. She whistled again, but still no coyote. She sighed and put two fingers in her mouth and whistled shriekingly loud, like calling a lost horse. But no horses came, and no James either. Etta sat down on the plateau. Tired. Her new shoes were all gray-brown with mud and dust. It was very quiet here, when she wasn't whistling. No birds sang in the middle of the day.

You're crazy, she said to herself. You're going crazy. You made him up.

No. I'm not. No, I didn't; I'm just old.

It's the same thing.

It's not.

It is.

She drew a line with the toe of her shoe across the chalky-rock ground, white. That's real, she told herself. I did that, that's real. She ran a fingernail across the skin of her arm, raised white, then red. That's real.

You're confused, you should sleep.

I'm not tired.

You are. You always are, now.

I'm not. I am not.

She stood up. I can walk.

It was almost twenty minutes later, almost a mile, when the quietness of midday gave way to a sound, a new sound, a sound like the wind had made sixty-some years ago through the cracks in her teacher's cottage. But there was no wind here. Etta followed it, the sound of wind with no wind, off her path, through barnyard grass and hogweed and nodding thistle. Seeds and burrs stuck to her legs. She followed the sound down to a curtain of bent leaves, and, under it, a matted bunch of fur and thistle and blood. James. His right front leg in a trap. Making the sound like the wind with each breath.

I was trying to call you, but getting tired.

Goddammit, said Etta.

I did hear your whistle, said James. *That was a good, loud whistle.*

I thought you weren't real, said Etta. I thought I had made you up.

You could have.

But I didn't, did I?

Etta, it could be everything, it could be nothing, what you're making up. You shouldn't let that bother you.

No?

No.

Etta crouched down to James's level and pulled a thistle off his coat. Its needles stuck in her fingers a bit. There, that's real. I feel that.

It's going to hurt you, your leg, she said. When I get you out.

It's okay. Coyotes don't feel pain much, it's okay.

Still, close your eyes.

James closed his eyes, and, before forcing open the trap with a thick branch like she and Alma used to do for the neighborhood cats, Etta stroked his head once, twice, along the fur line, like a dog. Rough, thick fur.

James's leg was busted, broke. The blood crept out of it undramatically, barely noticeable, dropping off in congealed clumps every now and then. Etta set it as best she could with a sock.

Try not to use it, try not to put any weight on it at all.

But for a coyote, always balancing in fours, that was impossible. He would forget, hit a stride, hit the leg, the front-right, and collapse into it, yelping.

Okay, fine, said Etta. How much do you weigh?

James was sitting, licking. *More than a rabbit but less than a horse . . . maybe forty pounds.*

Get in my bag. Don't squish the chocolate.

She wore him across her back, her canvas bag stretching but accepting the weight across her shoulder. Since she couldn't carry the rifle on her back in this configuration, she carried it in front, using it alternatively as a walking stick and as a gun, to kill gophers for James, as he couldn't hunt now, injured. They took the long way around cliffs and large rocks.

You know, said Etta, I'm surprised you don't speak French.

Like the fish skulls, said James, his head bobbing gently against her neck.

Yes, exactly.

I could say the same thing of you.

But I'm not a fish.

But you're not a coyote either.

True, true.

After the local Co-op, Otto drove out to the Co-op in Bladworth and bought all of their *Canadian National* papers too, then on to Kenaston and Hanley and Dundurn, to all the towns along the once-railway and now highway. When it got too late for any of the shops to be open, he continued along the gas stations, which stayed open through the night. He only turned around once today's papers had been replaced with tomorrow's, pulling back into his own driveway in early pastel light. He carried three hundred and twenty-six newspapers into the kitchen over several trips, then went to the bedroom and slept better than he had in weeks, for once not awoken by a pressing bladder or a dry cough or a heartbeat running marathons in his dreams for hours and hours and hours.

When he did wake, it was midafternoon. He cleared a path through the papers into the kitchen and set about cutting while the coffee brewed. He clipped Etta's picture out three hundred and twenty-six times. The first of these he set aside to post to her with his next letter. The next he folded and put in his pocket. The remaining three hundred and twenty-four he stacked into a pile, and put behind the cake stands, cooling racks, muffin tins, bread pans, and cookie trays in the very back of a cupboard.

He replaced everything carefully, perfectly, in front of the clipped pictures, orderly towers of tin and steel. Then he ate a cheese and raisin scone with last season's raspberry jam and wondered what he could or should do with all the remaining newspaper. It was too much of one thing to not use for something. A waste to just throw out or burn. He took a pen and wrote in the white bits of the front-page photo of a man in a suit looking at the sky.

Uses for Newspaper:

1. Burning. (Not very useful unless want/need to make a very big fire.)
2. Gardening. (Formed pots for seeding.)
3. Animal bedding. (Would need animals for this.)
4. Something else. (Art/sculpture/building things, maybe, etc.)

A big fire could be nice, entertaining, but this was dry season, and it could also easily get out of control. And even if it didn't, people might see it from the highway and think there was a real fire, a problem fire, since it was dry season, and call for help. And then there'd be the fire department, a commotion. And, it was too hot for a fire now anyway. The smoke would hang in the heat like mist, over and into everything for days. Otto drew a line through option 1.

It was too late in the season for 2; that option would mean waiting, holding on to all the newspapers until next spring. But Etta would almost certainly be home by then and not wanting a kitchen full of paper, with newsprint stains on the floor, the counters, their hands. Otto drew a line through option 2.

Dear Etta,

Do you remember, five or so months ago, when the neighbor girl from the far side of Russell's came round with her box of little guinea pigs? All the babies that were Just Too Much, according to her parents, according to her, that she tried to give us? I think her name is Kasia. Probably around nine years old, now. I went to visit her this morning. She was still in school, but her parents were around the farm and happy to see me. Yes, they said, yes, oh yes, we still have them. And yes, you're welcome to them. Just one? You sure? Okay. They said I could pick, could go into Kasia's room to where the cage is and pick whichever I liked, but I said, No, I'd really rather not, please. So they picked for me. A mostly brown one. Still small.

So. We've got a guinea pig now. I hope you don't mind. They're nocturnal, and so, it seems, am I these days, so I thought it might work out well. Some motion and noise around the house other than my own. It doesn't have a name yet, but it will. I forgot to ask if it's female or male, so I will choose something unisex.

And corn is looking good this year, and I think they eat corn.

I don't know where you are, exactly, now, but I bet it's close to Kenora. So I'm just putting SOUTHERN ONTARIO on this as a mailing address. It should get that far before it is returned back here. Then I'll put it in a pile with the others. When you get home you can read and read.

Here,
Otto.

P.S. There's a picture in here, of you, for you.

Otto named the guinea pig Oats. Because it liked to eat them and parts of it were the color of them and it was shaped a bit like the word, all round and soft and squat. He ripped up the A and B sections of one *Canadian National* and laid the strips as bedding in a mandarin orange crate left over from Christmas. In the crate he also put a shot glass full of water, a sugar bowl full of oats—it would be a little while yet until the corn was ready—and Oats the guinea pig. It immediately burrowed under the papers. Okay, said Otto. I'll see you later tonight, maybe.

Dear Etta,

Walter and Wiley have arived which is just great. They both look so strange in pressed and matching uniforms and with there hair cut by a real barber. But I suppose so do I. We all went swimming the weekend they arrived, in the Atlantic, and it was so long and wide they could hardly beleive it. Like the sky had droped into the ground said Walter. Yes exactly said Wiley.

But theyve only just arrived, and I'm just about to go. 3 days and 2 nights and then I'm on a boat in the morning. My first boat.

Etta, here's the thing, I'm scared.

I wanted this so much and I still do but, I am. And thats all.

> *My love to Russell.*
> *And all the others.*
> *Otto Vogel.*

P.S. En-closed is a picture. Its me in my uniform. One of the offitcial pictures they take and give us. They give us two. I've already sent one to mother so this one might as well be for you. In case your wondering what I look like without dust every-where.

When Etta replied, she did not say,

You should be scared. If you could see the students I'm getting, the boys coming back, you'd be terrified. Though they're big like men, they're just boys with bits of them missing. Arms or legs or brains or souls. They squeeze into the desks next to the children and recite A–Z or 1–10 because it's all they can do, now. They sit and look so much younger and so much older than they are.

They're usually only back for a few days before their mothers or fathers or wives or sisters bundle them home, where things are more controllable, where it's easier to dim lights and pull up covers; to run half a mile into the fields and open your mouth like an animal and howl and howl.

She did not say,

Only two days ago Thatcher Muldeen stabbed his right hand, between the pointer and middle knuckle, with a pencil during geometry and I try and try but the blood won't come out of his desk's wood finish. And Kevin Leary, back three weeks, used a small knife to cut the braid off the girl in front of him, and now he carries it in his back pocket at all times, ribbon side hanging out.

She did not say,

And yet, they keep going. They keep joining and leaving. All the boys, the men. At the dances it's just the women, the broken returners, and Russell.

She did not say,

And even though he's too young, much, Owen has gone. His fair skin still letting the light through from behind, he's so delicate. His hands shaking at his sides as he asked if I knew which crew you had been grouped with.

And, what's more, she did not say,

The picture is on my table. I bought a frame in town. It's wonderful not to eat alone anymore.

She did not say,

The only other pictures in my house are one of my parents and one of my sister.

She did not say,

You look more real in that photo than I remember you looking in life.

What she said was

Dear Otto,

We're all scared, most of the time. Life would be lifeless if we weren't. Be scared, and then jump into that fear. Again and again. Just remember to hold on to yourself while you do it.

Sincerely,

Etta

P.S. Thank you for the photo. I do recognize you, even without the dust.
I enclose this year's class photo, myself in front of the school with the
students, as a reciprocal gift.

In the photo she is wearing a light dress with short cap sleeves, a
close waist, and a pressed collar. Her best dress. Her smile is the biggest thing in the picture.

The photo was tugging away from Otto's fingers in the wind, so he put it back in his heavy wool pocket. An inside pocket. He gripped the cool metal of the ship's railing and threw up once more over into the gray water. It looked so much less blue now that he was on it. *Jump into that,* he whispered to himself. Left, right, front, and back, everywhere was water and only water. The boat treaded clumsily through it, the proximity of the rising sun the only hint at progress. You all right? said the soldier to his left, also throwing up. A boy from Montreal, a rich hesitance to his English.

Yes, said Otto. Salt and water and wind. Alive. I am Alive.

D'accord, said the soldier. *C'est bon.* Me not so much. His face was the color of the water. He had, Otto saw, taken off his coat and left it on the ship floor, with his gun on top. Otto picked them up, draped the coat over his arm, warmed the cold gun between his hands.

This'll be something, said Otto. I don't know if it'll be good or bad, but it'll be something. He could feel his heart hard and fast like the first time he had coffee. Like this from the moment he stepped aboard. His hands shook.

Oui. Yes, said the gray boy, before bending over the railing again.

When their ship pulled ashore, seven days later, all of Otto's hair had gone white, like the seafoam, like the bones of the fish they had every day for dinner and supper, all of it pure white.

I would do a better job, said Winnie.

It was after school. Today's class had been about cutting; making three-dimensional shapes out of two-dimensional drawings. Now Winnie and Russell were helping Etta clean up the leftover bits of paper littered between the desks.

What makes you think that? said Russell. There were little shards of white and blue paper stuck with static to his shirt. A better job than everyone? Than Otto?

Than most. Maybe Otto, maybe not.

Etta just listened, didn't enter the dialogue. She held out the dustbin for handfuls or skirtfuls of scrap.

Go, then, go be a nurse.

I don't want to be a nurse . . . you want me to go?

I want you to go if you want to go.

It wouldn't make me crazy. I am not as delicate as they are.

Or as me—

Russell, you're hardly delicate, inserted Etta.

Ha! Exactly, said Winnie.

Russell looked up from the floor to Etta. Something there. Hurt? Gratitude?

You know what I mean, he said.

Anyway, said Winnie, being a nurse is not the same. I know where to punch a calf to kill it, if it needs it. And hard enough. One punch.

Etta laughed.

It's true.

I know, I know.

10

Etta was taking the low, longer, easier routes, and Russell was grateful. Almost like she was making accommodations for him, even. He followed her tracks, a half heel in rock dust here, the outside roll of a foot out of a stream there, carefully measured as they became darker and deeper, closer and closer. He whisper-measured seconds and meters like the beats between lightning and thunder, closing the distance between them in both space and time. When the numbers got small enough he took off his shoes and socks, tied them together, and slung them over his neck. He might not be graceful or fast, but Russell knew how to be quiet. He placed his feet in Etta's steps exactly, measuring and counting, stepping and listening, until, in a sweep of white spruce trees where everything smelled like deep, wet, green, after stepping and counting and measuring and listening for just over two hours, Russell looked up from the treads at his feet, through a hundred and fifty meters of white spruce and spiderwebs and sun through the canopy of needles like mirror-ball traces at a dance, and saw, as natural as the trees, the spiders, the sun, Etta. Tiny next to the pack on her back and the trees all around and the land stretching out in front of her. Her hair was out and down like it never was at home. The wind blew it back in waves and Russell imagined it was his hand, not the wind, running through it and down, through and down. He was so close now.

He kept a distance behind, only just close enough to watch and follow, while he decided what to do next. Wait until dusk. Until she stopped for the night. For four hours they moved in an extended tandem, and, then, Etta stopped. She huddled down to take off her pack. Russell ducked behind some trees and took the long, covered, way to her.

When he stepped through from behind the larches, her back was to him. Etta, he said. Etta, it's Russell. I've come to see how you are.

For a second she didn't move. Frozen. Then, slowly, she turned around. She had a long gun, Otto's rifle, in her hands. Up, pointed. Get back, she said. Get away.

There was a coyote, smallish but snarling, at her ankles. It limped.

Etta, Etta, said Russell. It's just me. Russell. It's Russell.

Russell? Ha! Of course not, said Etta. Of! Course! Not! You're old, you're much too old.

But, said Russell, we're the same age.

Oh no, said Etta. Oh no, no, no, we're not. You must be eighty, ninety, maybe. I'm sorry. She lowered the gun right down, so the muzzle was pointing at the ground. She took the hand Russell had outstretched. You must be tired. It's rough out here for someone like you, I'm sure. Why don't you stay and have dinner with us?

Russell flexed his hand in hers. Both their fingers tough and thickened with decades outside. Okay, he said. Okay then. The coyote looked up at him warily as it settled against a nearby rock, licking its leg.

Etta left them there, Russell and the coyote, while she went hunting. She came back with two squirrels. There aren't so many gophers here, she said. She laid the animals on the coyote's rock and carefully felt around the bullet holes in their bodies. Need to get the shot out so he doesn't choke, she said. You can help if you want.

They washed the blood off their hands with water Russell offered from one of his bottles and ate their dinner of Russell's peanuts and crackers and bananas while the coyote ate his. Etta offered her chocolate, but Russell wouldn't take it, so she put it back. They made camp on their coats under needled trees, Etta with the coyote, and Russell one tree over. They could hear a thunderstorm a little ways off, over the lake. You shouldn't stay under a tree if a storm comes, said Russell.

I know that, said Etta. Of course I know that. I'm not looking to get killed.

Russell dreamt of lightning and of electrified wire hair. You don't want to touch that, he said to his barber, just leave it. There's just nothing we can do about it.

James woke first, and went off to try walking a bit. Etta was next, rolling out from under the branches to see Russell under his own tree, still asleep, on his good side, with his plaid fleece over him like a blanket. The same plaid fleece he wore every day, out watching for deer. Russell? she said. Russell Palmer?

He opened one eye, barely, barely. Good morning, Etta, he said. It's really good to see you. I've come to take you home.

Well, that's silly, said Etta. And a lie.

It's not, said Russell, sitting up, brushing needles from his arm.

It is. I'm not going home, Russell. Not yet. And you know it.

It's not safe, Etta. It's not wise. We can walk at home, we can walk every day if you want.

I don't want to walk with you. And I certainly don't want to walk at home. I'm walking here, alone.

You, said Russell, you're not . . . Etta, you know that you—

I always remember to eat and drink and walk. I remember which way is east and how to shoot straight. She sat down next to him. Anyway, Russell, you don't worry about that, about me, because, like I said, you're not actually here to fetch me.

Russell looked sideways at her. At the deep lines sunk across where her dimples had been; they were the deepest lines on her face.

You're here, continued Etta, because it's your turn, finally. It's sad that you felt you needed my permission for that, but, oh well. Go, Russell, go do whatever, wherever. Go do it alone, and now, because you want to and you're allowed to and you can. You always could have if you wanted to enough.

Russell sighed. He put his hands on Etta's sides, against her arms. You're sure you won't come with me?

Of course not.

He leaned into her and kissed the dimple line on each cheek.

Then he hesitated, just long enough for her to inhale, and then he kissed her mouth. She let him. Shifted her weight toward the same red and black plaid fleece. Their lips thin and tight and together.

And they held like that

and held

and held

and then,

You and Otto both, said Russell, as he pulled away.

Yes I know, said Etta.

So much and so different. So so much.

Yes, said Etta.

I'm going to trade my truck for a horse and ride north, said Russell. I'm going to find migrating caribou and follow them.

And I'll meet you back home, after.

And I'll meet you back home, after.

Otto was watching Oats. It was between three and four a.m. and she was awake and chewing on the side of her box. Sometimes Otto would cough and she would stop and look at him, then run to the other side of her box and chew there instead. Back and forth. Otto was awake with a fast heart again. His fifth night up with Oats. She chewed and he drank milk and little bits of rye.

On the sixth night, his cough had eased a little, so Otto carefully and slowly reached into the mandarin box and took Oats in his hand. Hello, he said. Good evening, Oats.

Her body shook like crazy, but she didn't try to get away. She looked up at Otto, then past him to the microwave, then at him, then the microwave. Her eyes were all pupil. Otto turned around to see what she was seeing. There, in the microwave's dark glass door, were their reflections. Oats stared at hers intently. Otto put her down on the counter in front of it, and she walked as close to the microwave door as she could, nose to nose with her reflection, and stared. Just stared. Otto tried to ease her back into his hand, but Oats wouldn't go. She pressed her small claws into the counter and tensed her legs and body and kept staring. So Otto bent down to her level and stared too. The impure glass blurred his features and softened them. He looked younger. I should take a picture for Etta, he thought. Meanwhile, Oats had adjusted herself and was now licking the door. Otto had to put on his gardening gloves to get her back in her box without scratches. I know, I know, he said.

On the seventh night, his heart going and going and going, Otto woke up with an idea. He put on his robe and went to the kitchen. Hello, Oats, he said. Good evening. She was digging in her newspaper, kicking down through it to the box's bottom and then moving to another spot and starting again. Otto got out a mixing bowl and filled it with half a *Canadian National*'s worth of paper strips, then got another and filled it with flour and water. I understand, he said, that I'm not always company enough. So I'm going to try and make you some more.

The layers of papier-mâché dried quickly out on the front steps. Once he had layered enough, in roughly the right shape, Otto found some nonpoisonous animal-marking paint in the shed and drew two dark eyes, a nose, and a mouth. It wasn't an exact likeness, but it wasn't too bad. Better than he'd expected. When the paint was dry and didn't smell anymore, he put the papier-mâché guinea pig in Oats's box, nestled into a corner. There, he said. I hope that helps. Oats stared at the new thing, nose twitching, then walked over and licked the side of its face.

The next day, Otto soaked and washed the large and medium mixing bowls and the collection of spoons that were all still crusted with dried flour paste. He toweled them with a soft cloth and put them away, back in the cupboards and drawers. Outside the sun was white-yellow, and reflected off the backs of the spoons he stacked curve-side up. Oats was sleeping next to papier-mâché-Oats. Otto would leave them in peace, go check the corn, the potatoes, the zucchini. It had been too hot, too dry these days. Everything needing water always. He put on his gardening gloves and went out. He forgot his hat.

After weeding and watering and inspecting leaves for pests and blight, Otto headed across the field to check on Russell's house.

It was fine. It was exactly as it always was, key under the orange kettle at the front door, things and dust in piles inside. Otto sunk into Russell's front-room armchair and fell asleep.

When he woke it was almost dusk. Shadows longer and in different places. Otto checked himself; he hadn't woken from coughing, or from his heart, or from his bladder, it was something else. The tension of movement, of other living things somewhere close. He held his breath and scanned the dark and crowded places in the room. But the motion wasn't in the room, it was outside, just outside the two front windows. There were two deer, right there in Russell's front garden. Eating, standing. Oh, oh. Otto moved slowly so as not to startle them, crawling on his hands and knees over to the windows. He put his head to the bit of window where the glass was lifted and the only barrier was screen-mesh.

You've come, he said. After all that.

The deer did not respond.

He's been waiting for you for ages, you know, for years, he said, a bit louder.

The first deer jerked, alert. It looked at him and blinked.

Do you know if he's okay?

The second deer turned now too. Twitching ears. They both looked at him. Both blinked. Once, twice.

When he got home he took the fresh-cleaned bowls back out of the cupboard and poured more flour into them, and then more water. Then he took three newspapers, shredded them, and set about meticulously crafting two full-size, life-size, deer. For Russell.

My Dear Etta,

These days, we march and march and march and march and march.
Only, always. But we sing as we do it, which reminds me of your class,
which I like. Boots over new soil, under new trees, guns rubbing against
the bare skin of our hips, at odds with our feet warm in socks knit by
nuns.

So far all of this seems to be about moving. Trains, boats, feet. As
long as we keep moving, were making progress. Who-ever stops moving
first loses.

Two days ago a man with a dog dragging a rope leash ran from a
burnt-shell house as we were passing, right up to me, me specificly, and
begged me for carrots. Please, please, he said, I know you have them, I
know you do, please, please, just one or two, or the tops, even, please.
Please! I had a little chocolate in my pocket, and cigerettes, but he didn't
want them. Please! he said. Please! Thats all she needs! Just one! Please!
But I didn't have any carrots, and we had to march on. Once we were
far enogh away I asked Gérald, my marching partner, What was that?
and he said, I think thats only just the beginning.

Tell me about home, please. Tell me about the weather. About the
heat or dust or still-ness. Anything. And tell me about you. I keep your
photo in the pocket on the side without the gun. For balance.

Truly,
Otto.

The letters would arrive in no particular order. Sometimes a disarray of chronology, sometimes nothing for ages and then three together, all stuffed into one army-issue envelope.

Dear Etta K.,

It's been two months since your last letter. I hope you're okay, you're not upset, and that you will keep writing me. It does mean a lot. It does.

O.

Dear E,

Don't get me wrong, there are people everywhere here. We sleep and eat and march side by side by side. We breathe each others' breath and sleep each others' sleep. Its like home like that. But, still, Etta, there is a sort of connectedness that I don't know I need until it's gone. Until the months go by without any letters. A certain layer of loneliness.

I'm sorry to be so earnest, so honest. I hope you understand, forgive me, and write soon.

Yours,
Otto.

Dear Etta,

Nevermind. I recieved your letters, all of them, this morning. Post-marked one a week, like clockwork. Thank you, Etta.

Otto.

Dear Otto,

As you know, I always try my best to correct your letters and return them to you so that you can learn and avoid those particular mistakes in future. But I have an admission to make, something I haven't yet corrected, though maybe I should have. At the end of a letter, after the signature, one does not need punctuation. No full-stop. I guess that's because it's just one's name, usually, and one's name is not, in itself, a full sentence. However, Otto, I like it. I like that you do it. I like the finalness, the confidence. So, please, don't stop.

> *Yours,*
> *Etta.*

Dear Otto,

The school keeps emptying out. Now Winnie's gone too. Do you know where she's gone? Your mother is sick, just sick with it. She came to my house last night to ask if I knew anything.

I hadn't before realized how much she looked like you.

Mrs. Vogel stood awkwardly on the doorstep, unwilling or unable to cross the threshold, to come in.

Are you sure you wouldn't like some coffee? said Etta. I like an excuse to make it. She held her hands behind her back to hide their ink stains.

I don't want to bother you for very long, Etta. Her skin, normally dark from the sun, was gray-white.

No, I mean it, Mrs. Vogel, it's too quiet in here. Too dusty too, but we'll ignore that.

Are you sure?

I'm sure.

Okay then, said Otto's mother, stepping, finally, over the doorsill into the house. And you should call me Grace.

She moved toward the table, but before sitting down, just two feet into the entrance, she tumbled into her questions, like a waterfall: Etta, do you know where she's gone? Did she tell you something? Do you know how?

Etta had retreated to the sink, was washing her hands. I know she wanted to go. I know she felt strongly.

I know. I know that too. They all did. I just don't know why. She sunk, finally, into a kitchen chair. I just thought, with her at least, a girl, my girls, would be safe.

A beat while she sat down, and then, How do you think she did it?

Maybe as a nurse . . . there's a sign-up in town, at the post office.

No. Not as a nurse. The uniform would make her crazy. And I asked them, there, too, to be absolutely sure. She hadn't been by. Not a nurse.

Okay. I'm sorry. Not a nurse.

If you hear anything, Etta.

If I hear anything at all, Grace.

Etta made the coffee as loudly as she could to fill the silence that expanded between them. She laid the table: cream jug, milk jug, sugar bowl, sugar spoon, saucers, cups, coffee. Grace Vogel circled her hands around her coffee-warm cup like it was winter, although the heat was still close and heavy. You can never stop, Etta, she said. You can never stop being a mother. Never, never, never.

I mean, I suppose you do all look like each other to some extent, but she and you especially. The long oval face, the high forehead, the lean build.

I told her what I could, which was not much. I know your sister was restless and didn't want to be a nurse. I couldn't tell her anything she didn't already know.

So my class gets smaller and smaller. Five regular girls, a small coming and going of men and boys, and Russell, who keeps showing up occasionally even though he made it through all the material long ago. I'm glad for it. He helps me with whatever needs helping with, and, besides that, it's just nice to have a friend around, someone on the same level, now you and Walter and Wiley, and Winnie, are gone.

He talks about getting a farm of his own, as so many are going cheap with the farmers gone away or killed. He talks, sometimes, about running it with you, someday, once you've finished marching and marching and marching.

Etta.

Etta,

We've stopped. The marching, the jeeps, the singing, stopped. We're in a
___ just outside ___ where the buildings are mostly stone and old and
damp and cold. We're camped in a crumbling old house. I don't know
who normally lives here or where they are, but they've left all their
things. Jackets and trousers still in the closets. Not my size. We're all in
buildings like this around town, __ men here, __ men there, all tucked
up inside these places like locals. The jeeps are parked _____, so
when we're all inside you'd never know we were here. We wear this
town as camouflage.

    We are here, they say, to hold the town. I like the idea of that. Like
a kite.

    There are a few residents still around, but not many. They seem to
be overwhelmingly old and quiet. They pass us in the streets with eyes
round and staring. Last time ___ and I were in ___ I bought some
candy for any children we might come across, but there don't seem to be
any here, anywhere.

    _____ ___ __ _____ if I see her. I
am hoping.

                        Yours sincerely,
                        Otto.

This was when Otto's letters started to come with windows. Little rectangles cut out so that Etta could see her fingers underneath, holding the paper. People, places, and numbers, mostly, had been extracted, carefully cut and kept somewhere else. An office, Etta imagined, in England, stuffed full of these people and places and numbers on their original little rectangles of paper. Passers-by could pay five pence each to stick a hand into the letter slot, rustle about, and pull out

Helsinki

or

Mozambique

or

Sgt. Andrews

or

Carla

or

Seven

or

Five thousand, nine hundred and twelve.

11

James was able to walk again. Which was good because Ontario was proving itself to be huge, twice the length of Manitoba, and then twice that again, with all the ducking and dodging around rocks and lakes.

I had always thought, said Etta, that Ontario was full of people. People and towns and cars and businesses everywhere.

Well, they're certainly not here.

No. Not unless they've been turned to stone.

That's a possibility.

It was longer now, between towns. Longer and longer. Etta was eating more berries and dandelions. Rationing. She was hungry all the time.

That's what it's like, said James, *to be a coyote.*

Being hungry all the time?

Yes, either hungry or sleeping. But, mostly hungry. That's why we're able to kill so easily, and why humans aren't.

Because we're not hungry enough?

Exactly.

That evening Etta got to her final piece of chocolate and her last chunk of bread. She ate the chocolate and held the bread in her hands, looking at it.

If you have food, you should eat it, said James.

No, said Etta.

No?

No, if you have food, you should use it, corrected Etta, to get more food.

She went through her bag until she found the map-in-a-plastic-bag. With James to help navigate she hadn't been using it much; it was squished down under her clothes. She took the map out of the bag and rewrapped it in socks. Then she took the plastic bag and the remaining bread and started through the trees, toward the nearest lake.

Where are you going?

Being hungry makes you empty enough to kill small animals and it makes me empty enough to eat fish.

Her plan was: take off shoes and socks, roll up skirt, and wade into the lake. Hold the plastic bag open half under the water so it filled. Hold it steady. Break off a few crumbs of bread and scatter them in the vicinity of the bag. Break off one or two crumbs to float in the water in the bag. Hold everything steady and still. Don't move. Wait.

There were small gray-black fish here, around the size of Etta's finger, some a little bit bigger, up to two fingers long. Etta was a statue. The water pushed up and back against her knees, up and back. The crumbs she had scattered pushed up and back, up and back, slowly dispersing themselves further and further from her and her bag. Eventually, the fish she had scattered when she first stepped into the water returned, cautious, sniffing the water before and around them with their mouths, unblinking. They ate some of the scattered crumbs, swam in closer, ate more crumbs, swam in closer, until all the bread bits outside of the bag were gone. They sucked and sniffed and swam closer to the bag, and closer. They looked anything but edible, metallic and wet and alien, eyes always open. One of them was at the edge of the bag now, long as a pointer-finger, its head was just inside, mouth opening-closing, opening-closing. Etta tensed, inhaled, and scooped the bag up around it, as fast as she could.

Which was not very fast. The bag dragged in the water, and the fish zipped away like a pencil line long before Etta got the makeshift net to the surface. So, she tried again. And again, and again. The fish would swim off in a frenzied cloud at her movement, then edge back little by little to the crumbs and bag, then away again, then back, again and again, until it was too dark and too cold to be standing in a lake.

Etta waded back out to the shore with no fish and half as much bread as she'd started with. She ate some dandelions and some half-ripe blueberries and went to bed with the tingling tiredness of hunger sparkling through her legs, belly, and head.

You should eat the bread, said James the next morning as they were getting up.

No, said Etta. I have a new plan.

She took a pen and stabbed the bottom of the plastic bag, one, two, three, four, five, six, seven, eight, nine, ten times. More like a net, she said. Faster. She walked down to the lake, took off her shoes and socks, rolled up her skirt, and tried again. James watched from the shore. Silent. The fish edged toward Etta little by little, eating the crumbs around the bag, carefully, carefully, slowly, slowly, creeping into the bag and then—faster than anything, Etta was sure, faster than anything on land, at least—streaming effortlessly away as she tried to scoop them up. Again and again. Even now that the bag was faster, it wasn't anything near as fast as a fish. Etta waded back out of the water. Sat on the rock-beach. Tired. Her bare feet and legs dripped dark patterns onto the rocks. Even when I was young, she said to James, who sat ten meters up, behind her, I could not move fast enough for that.

It's to be expected, Etta; they know water better than you. James scampered down next to her, favoring his hurt leg on the slippery, uneven stones. He laid a gray squirrel on the rock between them. Bleeding and still kicking a little. *Eat this.*

Isn't it yours? What will you eat?

I already ate. A ground-dove. You eat this.

But I thought you were always hungry.

I am.

And I thought animals weren't susceptible to sympathetic or altruistic whims.

Aren't you an animal too?

True. Still.

Eat it. We need to keep moving.

I don't know how.

You don't know how?

Yes. Skinning and deboning and all that. I don't know how.

Why don't you just take a bite?

The squirrel had stopped moving. It was on its back. I should have brought a knife, said Etta. I don't have a knife. She scanned the rocks around them until she found a small, sharpish one, and picked it up. Okay, she said. Tell me, is the tail worth doing, or should I start with the body?

She washed her hands in the lake afterward, the squirrel blood spiraling away in tendrils, her own blood moving again, awake. Thank you, she said to James. They walked all day.

Then another lake, another plan. Etta didn't want to take James's food any more than she had to, and only had three bullets left for the rifle. She took out her two water bottles, clear, hard plastic, one big, one smaller. The small one was still full, the big one was three-quarters empty. She tested the firmness of the sides, pinching with thumb and forefinger. The smaller once bounced back more quickly, so she poured all the water from it into the big one.

I'm going hunting, said James. *Are you sure you don't want anything?*

Feed yourself, James. I'll be fine.

Okay. But if you—

I'll be fine. I have a plan.

She took the dry half-handful of remaining bread, the plastic bag, and the smaller bottle and headed for the lake. Removed shoes, socks, rolled skirt. She sprinkled some crumbs around, squeezed the bottle in on itself, thumb and forefinger almost touching through the sides, submerged it, and waited. Two minutes later the cautious fish returned, sucking down the crumbs on the furthest periphery, then closer and closer toward the bottle. One just the size of her pinkie swam in twitching jerks up to the bottle's mouth. Just as it had its nose to the lip, Etta released her grip. A gasp of water sucked in and, with it, the fish. Whoosh, whispered Etta. The fish swam in a disoriented flurry, all right angles inside the bottle. Well, said Etta. That's one.

She caught six fish this way, whooshing them in an unexpected and distressing ambush of current into her bottle. Each time she caught one she would wait until it calmed down a little bit, swimming in slower and slower angles and finally settling into stillness, and then she'd put it in the fishery cage she'd made of the map-bag suspended taut from an overhanging branch into a rock pool. The smallest fish swam away through one of the holes, but all the others remained, gray and black and marble-eyed, glistening in torpedo shapes, looking thoroughly inedible.

Like she had yesterday, for the squirrel, Etta used a lighter the reporter woman had given her to start a fire. James hated it. He stayed back, far back, in the direction of the lake; he stayed standing, ready.

It's okay. I built a stone circle. Etta was jabbing the fish one at a time onto a pointed branch. One, two, three, stab. The wet rubber texture of fish skin. Horrible. And again, one, two, three, stab.

It's still dangerous.

Not always. Now all five non-escaped fish were on the one branch, in a slick, shining row. Their scales made Etta think of insects.

You can't trust it. Always. And isn't something you can never trust dangerous, always?

No, said Etta. And then, I don't know, maybe. She held the skewer over the fire. Hissing, popping, spitting. It's a good thing I'm so hungry, she said. And then, do you eat the eyes? I wonder.

I usually do.

Etta didn't eat the eyes. Instead, after dinner, she went back down to the lake once more and rubbed and rinsed off the skeletons, clearing away the face and eyes and the bits of meat she hadn't been able to get at herself. More little fish came along and ate them, swallowing up the eyeballs in easy mouthfuls. Etta let the spines and tails break off and float away, but she kept the skulls, smaller and softer than the one she already had. I'm sorry, she said. I am just so hungry.

Il faut manger, they said, one at a time, over and over.

It's a long long way to go still, isn't it?

Oui oui oui oui oui.

It took more than a week for Otto to finish the deer. At first the legs wouldn't support the bodies, and then the necks wouldn't support the heads. He would work meticulously through the night, only to find crumbled piles of paper and paste in the morning. Oats would watch him, quietly chewing on her papier-mâché friend.

When he did finish, at last, and the deer could stand up on their own, he carried them, one at a time, over to Russell's. He put them in the front yard, just where the other two had been.

There, he said.

Then he walked back home and got to work sketching and planning. Calculating dimensions in advance, this time. An owl for himself, a swallow for Etta.

The next day, Otto received a postcard in the mail. It had a narwhal on it and was postmarked Rankin Inlet. It said,

I've changed directions.

Russell.

A narwhal, thought Otto. That can be next. He still had plenty of newspaper.

Otto was sleeping in the town and the town was sleeping around Otto. All quiet, all dark. Gérald and Alistair and him in the one crumbling old house, dreaming of maple syrup, of shortbread, of cinnamon, and of women who smelled like these things. Soldiers in houses all up and down the two streets that made up the town were all sleeping in their brightly colored and unmatched socks, black boots lined up and ready. The town's remaining residents, in once-white bedclothes, staring straight up or out, were sleeping with eyes open as they had for years now. Their dogs the same way.

The only ones awake were Michele and Gustav, from Trois-Rivières and Selkirk, respectively, who walked up and down, one street each, looking and listening. Michele, who had so much hair, dark, and Gustav, who had just a little, light and short. They'd walk their streets twenty-five times, then meet at the junction and swap, to keep things interesting. When they met they couldn't speak or make any noise, so they would just shake hands, silent, formal, and then turn and walk off in their new directions.

It was Gustav who heard something. Something apart from the regular crescendo and decrescendo of Michele's boots coming and going. Something like a drawing in of breath, but of more breath than natural, like all the breath you could fit in you, all at once, and then a faraway crack, like the baseballs he used to throw against the wall of his school. Then nothing. He started to sweat. He listened for Michele's boots. Nothing. He sat down on the curb, sweating and sweating, his hands slipping as he fumbled off his boots. He left them by a lamp-post and ran in stocking feet, soundless, yellow and orange, to the junction.

Michele was there, on the ground, in the middle of the street. His dark hair was getting darker and thicker from the blood pooling up into it, out from his throat on both sides. The wound hung open like Michele's mouth and eyes.

Gustav moved toward him, then caught himself and turned back again, away, toward the old city hall, where the generals slept, he opened his own mouth to shout to scream, despite what he'd been taught, and the bullet that rang through it and out the back of his skull woke everyone and everything.

Dear Etta,

Everything has gone from all quiet to all loud. _____ ago we were hit in the night, which I knew could happen, of course, had been trained for, but, still, felt against the rules, cheap. I know no-one ever said their were rules, but, still, it feels like their are, underneath everything, always.

So we lost our hold on ____ and with it ____ and _____ and _____ and _____ and _____. We have moved back to ____ and no one can sleep. The thing is: it was horrible. But, the thing is, through all that, all the horror and un-naturalness of it, there was this serge, of being here and doing this thing, this Right Thing, with everyone. All us boys here, and beyond that all the boys all over this country, and this continent, and stretching all the way back over to home, too, to you and everyone.

All moving together, all fighting together. And even though everything was horrible, that thing, that connectness, was wonderful.

I am fine, don't worry.

I know it won't be for some time, a lot of time still, but I am told that eventually, they will give me time to come back home for a few days, I do look forward to seeing you, then.

Truly
Otto.

P.S. Still no word from _____, but my ears are open, always.

Dear Etta,

Its always new towns now. Back to always moving. Move and hide and wait. Play cards. Listen in every direction. Then move, hide, wait, again. We wear each town as a new disguise, and they do too. And sometimes we choose the same towns as they do and stain the gutters and grass and front steps, until they go on to another town, and we stay, or we go and they stay. Either way, soon enough, it all starts again.

I have used my gun now, and my arms and hands and fingernails and teeth. I have never felt so much in my own body.

There is word that their going to send us some new boys, to accommadate for those lost, more and more. I have only _____ as roommate now.

I'm glad to hear there are still dances up in town, even if there is almost no one to dance with. If it's any consolation, we too have no one to dance with but each other. Still, sometimes we find old records and players abandoned in these towns and play them with the volume low. Although its almost as quiet as nothing, the few phantom residents always hear and come out into the streets toward it, swaying and smiling with cracking faces, like they haven't heard music in a million years.

When I come home,
I will dance with you.
Otto.

Etta put the letter down on her table, put one hand on it. The textured scratching of ink not at all like skin, but close enough. Then she drank the rest of her milk and went to open the school.

Ten minutes after the scheduled start of the day, there was only just Etta at the front, behind her desk, and six-year-old Lucy Perkins opposite, at hers.

Well, said Etta. I guess it's just us.

Yep, said Lucy Perkins. She was holding her pencil, ready.

Where are the girls?

Farms. They're needed, now.

But not you?

My mom's selling the farm.

Oh. I'm sorry. Well. What would you most like to learn about, Lucy Perkins?

I like singing. And cats.

Okay. Today will be Singing and Cats Day. Lucy Perkins Day.

One week later, Willard Godfree, larger area super-intendent of the civic and meta-civic bureau office came to see Etta during school hours. She and Lucy Perkins were drawing a chart of cats by size, from the African black-footed cat up to Siberian and Bengal tigers.

I am sorry to interrupt, said Willard Godfree, wiping his boots on the front doormat, still holding the door open.

It's fine, of course, said Etta. Good to see you, Mr. Godfree. Though, in fact, it wasn't.

Would you like to finish this lesson? I can wait in a desk at the back.

Yes, thank you.

She and Lucy drew a domestic cat, a Canadian lynx, an ocelot, a puma, a Chinese mountain cat, a caracal, an Asian golden cat, a cheetah, a snow leopard, a lion, and four types of tiger. Then Etta left Lucy to do the coloring and walked back to where Willard Godfree was sitting, hands intertwined and resting on the tiny desk in front of him. Okay, she said. How can I help you?

They let her keep the house.

No other use for it, right now, so you might as well, I mean, it's the least we can do.

There was a possibility that, come winter, when the farms were quieter, they might start the school up again. Or when things quieted down and everyone came home. But for now, Lucy Perkins and any others would get folded into the school in town, and Etta's school would be closed. A bus or horse would be sent round mornings and afternoons for Lucy. You can ride it too, if you like, if that helps.

Willard Godfree was not at all a bad man. He felt terrible about what he was doing.

I feel terrible about what I'm doing, he said. He took his glasses off and rubbed the place where they sat on his nose. He was old. Too old to fight.

Okay, said Etta.

Once he had gone, she finished the day with Lucy. They made their cats into a poster, a giant, colorful, breathtaking poster. Give it to your mother, said Etta.

I want you to have it, said Lucy. It's for you. When the kids come back you can show them.

Thank you, Lucy. Do you want me to walk you home?

Oh no, it's easy. I do it all the time.

Still, Etta walked her most of the way. Until she could see the sagging cream-and-blue of the Perkinses' farmhouse. Lucy cut through the pasture, past a scattering of lowing Charolais, made huge in comparison as she ran by.

Etta put the poster up in her kitchen, then mentally laid her options out before her on the table. In one pile:

She could go back to her parents. Back to town. Spend time there, reorienting. It would feel good to just be in the same place as them again. To belong in that easy way.

In another pile:

She could try to buy the Perkinses' farm. She belonged here now. Could stay close. Could learn about cows and chickens and grain. It would feel good to get her hands dirty. To be in her body like Otto described being in his. And maybe Russell would help.

In another pile:

She could get a job. Something to Help. In a factory, say, making things that were needed. Wear coveralls and heavy boots like a man. Use herself to ripple outward into the world.

Well, she said to the table, to the three piles, I guess the choice is easy then.

That night she stayed up late, waiting until the air got cool so the oven could be used without stifling the whole house, and made oatmeal-raisin cookies and date squares.

Dear Otto,

I don't know if this works, sending food. I'm somewhat skeptical, as I know our correspondence travels past many hands and eyes on its way from me to you, or you to me. (Your letters are like clumsy snowflakes, with all the different patterns of holes.) But, in the off chance that it does work, you should find a small selection of things here for you. I made them just last night, so you can take comfort in the fact that they were fresh, once. (Growing up, my older sister, Alma, could do most things better than me, but not bake. She would labor away at the same recipe again and again, bringing in my mother for help, sending her away, and always ending up with a too-dry cookie, a raw-in-the-middle cake, bread like worn rubber. It was never hard for me, though, I could feel through the spoon what the consistency, balance needed to be, like knowing if a song is in tune or if something is red or green.)

So, if you cannot find comfort in sleeping or security, find it here, (hopefully) in butter, sugar, flour, fruit. And if this little bit of extra energy lets you move that tiny bit faster or think that little bit sharper to keep yourself safe, well, that's good too.

Etta.

P.S. They've gone and closed the school now, on account of having no students. But don't worry, I've got a plan.
P.P.S. My mailing address will remain the same.

The next morning she caught the bus with Lucy into town.

This is great! said Lucy. We can still be friends, on the bus.

The bus dropped them off at the town's bigger, squarer school, and Etta walked from there to the post office, and then to the Citizen Women's Recruitment Center, which had been set up in the back room of Virginia Blanchford's house. To get to it Etta followed signs through the front yard, around and past windows in which she could see beds and children's things, into the backyard, and up three steps to the back door, where there was a final sign, in official government font:

CITIZEN WOMEN'S RECRUITMENT CENTER—HERE!

Etta could see bits of the dotted line along which you were supposed to cut on its bottom and sides.

Virginia Blanchford was inside. She had a baby at her breast and two toddlers asleep on a blanket by her feet. Welcome! she whispered as Etta stepped in, to your chance to make a difference! She smiled. Etta smiled. She handed Etta a form. It said,

FAMILY NAME?

CHRISTIAN/GIVEN NAME?

BIRTH DATE?

POSTING ADDRESS?

OPPORTUNITIES IN YOUR AREA (PLEASE TICK PREFERRED):

1. *Munitions Factory Work*

Have you got a pen I could borrow? whispered Etta.

Of course . . . yes, somewhere. Ah! There. She pointed over

both of their heads to a tin with a number of sharpened pencils in it perched on the top of a bookshelf. Safer up there, she whispered. Etta reached up and took one.

It's just the one option? she said.

It's a good option. It's right in town.

Okay, said Etta. And she put a tick beside

1.   *Munitions Factory Work*

What happens now?

You give that form to me, and report to the factory. You know where? East edge of town? Past the elevators? Tomorrow morning, eight-thirty a.m. You can go pick up your uniform today though, if you want. It might need a bit of mending, so you might want to get it in advance. Any time before six-thirty p.m. tonight.

It was still early, so, before going to the factory, Etta walked the long way to her parents' house. She helped her mother with chores until her father got home for lunch, and then they all ate together.

They're trying to get us to buy a farm, you know, said her father. Like I could do much farming, almost sixty years old.

I don't mind the idea, said her mother. I think I can still lift and carry. They're offering a heavy subsidy on the land.

And when the original farmer comes back? Her father.

They know which ones aren't coming back. Her mother.

And sell their stuff cheap.

Sell their land. So we can all eat.

On Etta's father's plate was a white bun with butter. Carrots. He had not yet taken any ham.

I don't want you to go to any special trouble because I'm here, Etta had said.

It's no trouble, her mother had said.

Anyway, we don't want to leave this house. I don't want to leave my job. Who's going to edit the newspapers if all the editors become farmers? said her father.

Hm. I suppose if we're going to starve we might as well be able to read about it, said her mother.

I like this house too, said Etta. And I know someone who might be keen on your farm offer.

You? said her father, looking concerned.

You? said her mother, looking excited.

No, said Etta. Not me. A boy I know. A former pupil. A friend.

She picked up her uniform after the dishes were done, and rode home again with Lucy on the school bus.

How was your day?

There were so many people. I got lost.

But was it nice too? An adventure?

Yes . . . there's two other girls with my name, so we're all twins. That's nice.

Good, said Etta.

The uniform, full navy coveralls with matching head scarf, had holes in the elbows and a crumpled tissue in one of the pockets. Etta mended the holes, threw away the tissue, and then put it on over her dress to walk over to the Vogels'. Mrs. Vogel, out picking rocks in the barley with one of the younger boys, saw her first. She waved at her. Come to help us with rocks, Etta? You look ready for it.

Nope, sorry, Mrs. Vogel. I'm looking for Russell. And, hello, Emmett. That's some good lifting.

He's back at his aunt's. She needs the help now his uncle is gone.

Oh. Okay, thanks. Hopefully I can come help you out another time.

*　　*　　*

She found Russell in his aunt's barn, singing lowly at the cows while he checked their eyes and tongues.

You! she said.

He snapped around, hadn't heard her come in. Shhhh! The cows! And then, correcting himself, quieter, The cows.

You! said Etta again, quieter this time, a hissed whisper, didn't tell me your uncle had gone. Why didn't you tell me?

Why would I have told you?

Because I'm your friend, Russell. Because that is a big thing. Because you can, no, you should tell me about the big things.

It's not such a big thing; all the men are going, or gone.

You're not.

No. I'm not.

One of the cows sighed, a heavy sigh with the weight of a cow. Russell stepped over and ran a hand along its back. Etta, he said, you're wearing strange clothes.

Oh yeah, said Etta. I wanted to show you. My new uniform. It was hot in with all the animals, thick with close air.

You're a factory girl now?

A factory *worker*. As of tomorrow. Since they've closed the school for lack of students . . .

Oh, I didn't realize. Oh damn. I'm so sorry. The Vogels needed me, and then my aunt, I would have come, if I had known . . .

It's okay, Russell, really. Not your fault. All the students are in the same position. Well, except Lucy Perkins.

Her mom's selling the farm, I heard. He stroked the cow along the grain of her short, dense fur.

Yeah, I heard too. Which is why I came to see you, sort of.

Not just to show me your uniform and yell at me about my uncle?

Not just that. Besides, I only heard about your uncle from Mrs. Vogel, twenty minutes ago. No, it's because they're trying to get my parents to take one of the lost farms. But my parents don't want to. Well, my father doesn't, at least, which means they won't be taking it. So, I was thinking, you should.

I should take it?

You should take it! A farm! Your own! You're old enough, you're here! You want one! And it's in the area, so you could still help your aunt, the Vogels. You could plant and farm strategically for that.

I could take it.

Yes!

But what about Lucy Perkins's mother?

What about her? She doesn't want it, I'm sure.

Yes, but if they're giving away land, how's she going to sell hers?

Well . . . I don't know. But that's not your fault, or your responsibility.

Still. We are all spreading ourselves so thin, now.

Just for now, Russell. Otto and Winnie and your uncle and everyone will come home soon enough and fill in the land again. It's just for now. And that means there's only a free farm here for you right now, Russell. You have to take it.

I guess I do.

You do.

Okay, I will.

Of course you will! She was smiling big now, all teeth. It's exciting, Russell!

I suppose it is. Her smile so big and so real. He stepped away from the sighing cow and toward Etta in his clumsy, unsubtle steps. But why don't you take it?

I'm not a farmer, Russell. I'm a teacher. And a factory worker now, look at me.

You could be, though.

I don't think so. She put a hand on his shoulder, not heavy or light, just her hand, and Russell, without thinking, closed his eyes. But you'll be great, she said. She squeezed his shoulder a little bit and he opened his eyes again. Etta's other hand was on the back of the caramel freemartin; she bridged the three of them. And I'll help you, if you need it. Letting both hands fall back to her sides. The sun in the barn like a solid thing, solid bronze.

Okay, said Russell, as Etta made her way back to the barn door, home to prepare and sleep for work tomorrow. He had his own hand up to his shoulder, where hers had been. Thanks, Etta.

You're happy, I'm happy, Russell, she said.

From then on, each morning, Etta and Lucy Perkins caught the bus together into town.

I like your pants, said Lucy. I wish I had pants.

Thanks, said Etta. She wore the coveralls every day, itching and bunching and a little small on her ankles and wrists, but a part of her, more and more, like a shell. You might, one day.

Yeah. I hope.

They'd part ways at the school and Etta would walk twenty-five minutes to the east side of town, past the grain elevators, to the factory. And each morning, as she walked, other women would join her, walking in the same direction, in the same navy coveralls. The closer they got to the factory, the more they amassed, until they all convened and collected, bottlenecking in the clocking-in and jewelry-removal station like water at a low point. Each morning, when it was Etta's turn at the station, she would stamp her name card, and Thomas, the security man with eyebrows like icicles, would ask, Wedding ring? and Etta would spread her fingers before him, clean, bare, and he would wave her through to the giant rooms that smelled of icy copper.

In the evenings after her shift, at home next to the locked-up school, Etta would bake. Things for her and the other workers, for Russell and for Lucy Perkins and her mother, and for wrapping up in brown paper and rough twine and sending miles and miles away to Otto. She would sing to herself while her hair slowly let go of its metal smell and soaked up the cinnamon, the nutmeg, the vanilla. Her hands went up and down in the dough, up and down, press and lift, bringing air, crushing it out; while Otto's feet went up and down in his boots, up and down, press and lift, bringing space, crushing it out.

Russell walked with Glenda Hubert out across an obstacle course of rocks and holes and weeds and dirt. She was the wife of Rory Hubert, former-farmer, now soldier; the mother of five grown children, two here, three away; the grandmother of fifteen, ages zero through twelve; and, as of one year ago, the head of the Gopherlands Regional Farm Revival Project Committee. Her gray coveralls had G.R.F.R.P.C. hand-monogrammed across the back, with the letters getting smaller where she had started to run out of space. Watch your feet, she said, this place is a veritable quicksand of gopher cave-ins.

Okay, said Russell. Thanks.

They walked for twenty-five minutes, in a wobbly square. All right, said Glenda, that's it. You'll take it?

Russell righted himself after almost tripping over a rock the size of a small sheep. Yes, he said, I will.

You'll have to promise to fix it up and live on it and get it producing again within the year. You'll have to sign things. You'll be able to do that?

Russell looked out over Glenda's gray coveralled shoulder to the west; there was nothing but dirt and weed and rock for miles and miles and miles. Yes, he said. Yes, I will. The almost-setting sun lighting it all up in caramel and orange and gold.

12

And Etta walked and walked and James walked too, sometimes running up front, sometimes sniffing behind, sometimes just at her side. Rocks, lakes, trees. Rocks, lakes, trees.

And Otto stayed awake and made and made. An owl, a swallow, a narwhal, a gopher, a pair of raccoons, a fox, a goose, a squirrel, a rattlesnake, a bison that took him nights and nights, a lynx, a chicken, a coyote, a wolf, a collection of the smallest, most delicate grasshoppers.

And Russell was somewhere in the North and nobody knew where except him.

Winnie was dead now, but not so long ago she wasn't. She had called them, Otto and Etta, on a long-distance call from the government home in Paris, for Otto's birthday.

Will you come home? he had asked, like he always asked.

This is my home, she said, like she always said, voice deep within the grooves of an accent that fell away the longer she spoke to him.

Okay, said Otto. Just worth checking again, just in case.

Ha! In the background the foreignness of language he couldn't understand.

Sixty-five years, Winnie. Did you think that, when you went?

Yes, I think I did.

Hm . . .

Hey, Otto, how is Etta?

She is . . . good most of the time. Most of the time she's just fine.

Okay. Otto?

Yes?

If you need me back there, you know I'll come. I'll come home.

I know, thank you, Winnie. And thank you for the gift, the globe.

It arrived on time? Not broken?

It arrived perfect. Beautiful. Thank you.

De rien. Joyeux anniversaire, mon vieux.

Dear Etta Gloria Kinnick,

I look at each bullet now and wonder if you've looked at it too.

Not often, but occasionally, Otto would find himself with an evening off in a place big and resilient enough to still have bars and music and women. Though at home he'd only drunk beer and rye whiskey, here Otto would drink wine, staining his tongue and lips deep red. The drinks were always free for soldiers.

There was a woman called Gisèlle who was often around. The town or city would be different, but Gisèlle would be there, the same Gisèlle. Her hair was short and dark and she would always find Otto before he found her.

My favorite, she'd say. The boy with the white hair. Are you ready to dance?

Who do you dance with when I'm not here? asked Otto, against accordion and clarinets.

You're not my only favorite, said Gisèlle. One hand pressed around on his back, one in his hair.

Etta,

_____ ___ ____ ___ so we thought we were catching up with them, but, really, they were catching up with us, and _____ _____
_____ _____ _____ _____ _____ and I ran, not chasing,

not escaping, just running until I found myself _____ ___ and it was
dark and closed, but we've been in the dark so much that we can see
everything, and I could see him, this _____ in the back, against the
wall, breathing like he'd just been running too, and I knew he could
see me. His hand at his right side and mine at mine. I wanted to say
something but we didn't know the same words. Then a ____ ____ and
he started, jumped, and reached quickly down and I ducked behind a
bookcase and reached my arm around and shot and shot. All in one
movement, like one breath, one word. And then I jumped up and out,
out of ____ ___ out of there and started to run again and ran and ran
and the thought that pulsed in my head was Write It Down, Write It
Down and I knew that if I kept that thought in front of all the other
thoughts then I would have to be okay because I'd have to stay safe in
my body and mind long enough to get back to my pen and paper, to this.

And dancing with Gisèlle, whose hair curled into her face just so, and who smelled of perfume, the sweetness of flowers edged with the sharpness of alcohol that led his nose and mouth to the places she'd dabbed it, inside her wrists, behind her ears, between her breasts, up the guiding lines of her stockings.

Dear Etta,

Each time, each thing hits you like water in the face, like gin in
the throat, saying This is Real This is Real This is Real. As though
everything back home, and even Regina, and Halifax, and the train,
all of that was just a set-up on a stage and when you look behind it,
open it up, you see it was just a façade, and that the real thing is this,
always this, only this.

It won't be too long until my first year is up and they send me home for my few days and, Etta, I'm not even sure I want to go. Not sure I'll be able to merge that with this, that that's even possible.

I have been re-reading your letters and looking a lot at the picture of the school and the kids and you. These threads that connect this to that. Reminding myself that there is that and that that is still something.

Etta,

I will be off for home leave in ten days. The year so big until its over, like walking across a full-height wheat field. It will take me another ___ _____ for the crossing, then three days for the train, so I should be there ____ _____. I would like it if it was only you at the station. Just for that moment, stepping back into home. My mother and father and Russell and sisters and brothers are so much; I'm afraid at what I might feel or do. Do you understand? I will look for you there.

                            Sincerely,
                            Otto.

How long does a crossing take? Etta had brought shortbread over to Russell's new farm. He was outside repainting the new old house. White. The sun was nearly setting.

Um, I think it took Otto seven days when he went over. But it can be faster. I think my uncle was only four days. . . . Between four and eight, I'd say. He was up on a ladder, calling down. Why?

Just curious. She put the plate of cookies off to the side, away from the ladder and the drips. I'm going to leave these here, okay?

Okay, thanks. I'll run the plate back over to your place when I'm done with it.

Maybe let me come and get it, my factory shifts are going to be a bit unpredictable for a while, I think.

Okay.

Okay, good night, Russell, don't work too hard.

He watched her go, a good view from up on the ladder, all the way across the field. Once she was out of sight, he climbed down and took a cookie. He ate it with his paint-spattered hands.

There was only one train a day into town, and usually nobody got on or off; it was a request stop, usually the cars just passed noisily through, between two-thirteen and two-fourteen every day except Sunday. But on any given day somebody could get off, there was always the possibility. And, so, Etta did the math, and figured: Otto could be coming home any time between next Thursday and the one after. Any time except Sunday. She asked at the factory if she could be switched to nights.

Just for the one week?

One week and one day, please.

She stayed with her parents so she could walk to the factory, since the school bus didn't do a night-shift run. She told them, just,

I'm working nights at the factory.

Which wasn't a lie. They didn't ask why, or if that kind of swapping was normal, if they should expect her to need them often, if they should keep her old bed made up. They just did, just in case.

And she told Lucy Perkins, the Wednesday before, on their way home, bumping next to each other on the gravel, in their regular seats,

I won't be on the bus for a while.

For how long?

For eight days.

Are you going to fight?

No, no.

Okay good. I'll save your seat.

So, starting that first Thursday, Etta began a new sort of ritual, putting on her light blue dress with the cap sleeves, the close waist, and the pressed collar at one-forty-five in the afternoon, walking over to the station in time to be there just after two, standing on the platform and waiting for twelve minutes, the adrenaline mounting in her parallel to the sound of the train approaching, discernible from miles away, and watching with breath held as it pushed past her. Then she'd wipe the dust the train had thrown up off of her face and dress, and, between two-fourteen and two-sixteen, would walk back to her parents' house, take off the dress, and go back to sleeping or reading, or helping her mother or talking to her father until it was time to put on her coveralls and walk to work with the setting sun.

The night shift girls were different. When Etta showed up for the first time, one of them, who had swapped her issued navy head scarf for a green one with yellow dots, said,

New girl, someone bite her.

And another girl, in the regular head scarf but with bright red lipstick, grabbed Etta's arm, brought it to her mouth, and gently nipped her wrist, leaving faint teeth marks and pronounced lip marks. We're vampires, see, we night girls. So we had to make you one of us.

More of this, and more talking, was allowed on the night shift. It kept everyone from falling asleep.

How come you swapped? said green with yellow dots.

Just wanted to try it, said Etta.

Really? said lipstick. She raised one eyebrow. Practiced, acute.

On the first Thursday nobody got on or off the train and it just clicked by, steady, rhythmic, not-gonna-stop-not-gonna-stop.

Friday was the same.

Saturday, Etta could hear the train's wheezing ritardando from two-ten p.m. She held her hands behind her back, clenched. She breathed in deep gulps of the thrown-up dust. At two-eleven a woman ran up onto the platform, panting, holding two small brown cases with silver buckles. She smiled at Etta, wiped a hand across her brow dramatically. At two-thirteen she stepped up the train's three metal steps. At two-fifteen the train picked itself up again and pulled away, laboring at first, then more and more at ease as it drew further and further away.

Sunday, Etta borrowed her father's car to go home to her teacher's cottage, where she watered and weeded her garden, dusted away all the bits of prairie that had settled on the surfaces and broader objects, and struggled with her body to know when to sleep.

Monday nobody got on or off the train, rhythmic, not-gonna-stop-not-gonna-stop.

Tuesday, Etta could hear the train's wheezing ritardando from two-oh-seven p.m. She held her hands behind her back, clenched. She breathed in deep gulps of the thrown-up dust. No one else on the platform at two-ten or at two-eleven. Etta reminded herself to blink. Ran a hand over her hair. She could see the train windows now, they could see her.

At two-twelve the train stopped. At two-thirteen the doors of the third carriage opened and Otto stepped down the three metal stairs, one, two, three. His hair was as white as the dust.

He only had one bag, green, soft. He dropped it on the platform as he walked to Etta.

Otto, she said, your hair,

He put his hands on her arms, above the elbow, held them in, and kissed her mouth and kissed her and kissed so that neither of them could breathe and neither of them wanted to.

13

Dear Etta,

I have made you some things, for when you get back. I understand now, all the baking you sent me, stale and crumbled in brown paper and rough twine. Now you're away and I am here. So I will make and make until you get back to remind you, and myself: there are reasons to come home.

People started to notice Otto's collection. Driving by, you could see it spilling away from the house like a stretched-out garage sale. What's that? said the neighbor girl, passing by with her parents on their way to swimming lessons.

It looks like . . . a wolf? said her father.

Oh, and a bison! said her mother, pointing, and . . . I can't tell, is that a cat?

A skunk?

I think those are rabbits.
Are they real?
Can we not go to swimming?
We have to go to swimming.
I thought you liked swimming?
I do, but . . .
Is that a whale?

During daylight hours, traffic grew thick along the single-track road, crawling like a parade, with Otto's animals, all matching in their off-white of flour and water and newsprint, like a frozen audience. But Otto never noticed the parade, sleeping every day now through the sun.

After five days of fish, James and Etta came to the outskirts of a town.

I'll go around and meet you on the other side, said James, who didn't like towns. *I'll smell for you there.*

Okay, said Etta, for whom the prospect of bread and sugar and butter was more immediately pressing than companionship. There should be a grocery store in these suburbs, I shouldn't be too long.

She stopped at the first store she came across, a gas station. She bought sugar-buns wrapped in plastic and three packets of almonds and a liter of orange juice and six pieces of twisting red licorice and a cheese sandwich. As she lay it out item by item on the counter for the attendant she asked,

Is there a grocery store nearby?

And the attendant cocked his head and pointed at a sign taped to the cash register that read,

EN FRANÇAIS, S'IL VOUS PLAÎT.

Which was how Etta realized she had made it to Québec.

Right, said Etta. Okay. Um . . . *pouvez vous dire moi où je trou- verais une shoppe de grocerie?*

That's better, said the attendant, in English. I just like a little ef- fort, you know? So close to the border, it's easy to feel forgotten, you know? So, thank you, Etta. And, as it happens, there's a grocery store not more than six blocks from here. Two blocks that way, he pointed across the store, toward the Popsicles and frozen entrées, and then four blocks that way, he pointed through Etta, out the back of the store. It's got a big red sign. It's called BOUFFE-BONNE. They've got beautiful tomatoes.

It was not until Etta was outside on a square of grass between two identical houses, eating her sandwich and sugar-buns and drink- ing her juice, that she grasped what had bothered her about the man in the gas station. He had called her Etta. But she had never met him before; she did not know his name. She tried to recall his face, his features, but could only remember his hand pointing this way and that way. She pulled a piece of carefully folded paper out of her pocket:

Family:
Marta Gloria Kinnick. Mother. Housewife. (Deceased)
Raymond Peter Kinnick. Father. Editor. (Deceased)
Alma Gabrielle Kinnick. Sister. Nun. (Deceased)
James Peter Kinnick. Nephew. Child. (Never lived)
Otto Vogel. Husband. Soldier/Farmer. (Living)

None of these would make sense. But Russell wasn't on this list, and she knew she knew Russell. She took out a pen and wrote in:

Russell Palmer. Friend. Farmer/Explorer. (Living)

under Otto's entry. But no, no, this boy wasn't Russell. But there were others. Others missing. Cousins? Brothers- and sisters-in-law? Friends? Others? She wished James were there.

BOUFFE-BONNE was not hard to find, it was just as the man had said, two blocks across, four blocks up. So, thought Etta, he's not a liar, at least.

She filled her bag completely, and then took five of the store's plastic bags, filled one, and tucked the other four away for fishing and other emergencies. This was, she figured, as much as she could comfortably carry.

She took it all up to checkout counter number four, staffed by a teenage boy whose uniform hung off him. *Bonjour,* she said.

Etta! he said.

Etta stopped unloading her bags onto the conveyor. This boy too. This skinny young stranger. She pulled at her thoughts, tried to collect, organize. Friend? Uncle? Nephew? She squinted her eyes for focus, to remember. She looked down at her groceries. Why did she have so much? And these kinds of foods? Did she eat these kinds of foods?

Etta, continued the boy, stretching over his syllables, Et-Ta. I really think that you are amazing. I really wanted to say that. You really really are. His voice struggling to say so much, so fast, in a language not his own. You know what? I'm going to see if maybe we can get these foods for free, for you. Really, we should be able to do that. Yes? No? Don't worry, it is no trouble. Wait here, I will be right back.

Etta squeezed and squeezed her thoughts. Nothing, nothing. She looked around for clues, now that the boy was gone. The cash register, her food, the other shoppers, the aisles of food in boxes and bags stacked and labeled in two languages. English-French. français-anglais. She knew these things. The wall beyond the cash registers was mostly windows looking out into the parking lot. Windows and bulletin boards labeled with things like LES ANNONCES LOCALES and CHOSES PERDUE and, the furthest one along, right by the automatic doors that opened-closed in hisses whenever anyone walked past, HÉROS D'ICI. And, there, on the left-hand side of HÉROS D'ICI, between a picture of a golden retriever and a family in bathing suits, was Etta. The picture cut from a newspaper and with a little article and a map alongside it.

Really good news! The boy was marching back. He rolled up his flopping sleeves as he approached. My manager says, All free!

Marching behind him was a smiling woman with frizzy gray curls. *Oui! C'est vrai!* she said.

Where did you find that picture?

The cashier and the manager stopped their marching and turned to the HÉROS D'ICI board. It was in all the papers, Etta. And the article too. And now the *National* publish that little map each day, in the back of the Life & Times section, guessing about where you are. We cut it out and pin it up every day. Well, Janiel here does. He's one of your biggest fans.

Janiel blushed. Well, he said, it's just that, it's really great, right? I think—

Oh! And that means, interrupted the manager, that we can call in a spotting! We've spotted you all right! And they'll thank us on the next map update!

So they didn't know Etta at all. So she hadn't forgotten them. Okay. Okay. But now this. She took a breath. It's just, she said,

They both turned around, away from the board, back to her, eager.

—not supposed to be a very big thing. It's just meant to be . . . quiet.

Of course, said the manager, lowering her voice.

Of course, said Janiel.

That's why we're all so excited.

They helped Etta repack her free groceries. Have there been many . . . spottings reported? asked Etta, slipping carrots down the sides of the bags where she could find spaces.

Oh yeah, loads. But lots of them are made up. Like, this guy in Vancouver said he saw you in the big park there.

And that lady in Nebraska.

And that guy from up north, the elk herder guy.

Russell? said Etta.

They don't always leave their names, said Janiel.

Now the groceries were all packed and Etta was ready to go, wanting to go, to find James and see what he thought about this and what he knew about this.

So, with that in mind, said the manager, would it be okay if we took a picture with you? We can get one of the other customers to take it.

Etta stood surrounded by a small crowd of cashiers in matching red BOUFFE-BONNE uniforms, with the smiling manager next to her, in the middle. The customer-photographer grinned exaggeratedly and said, *Pret? Un, deux, trois . . .*

After the manager and all the other cashiers had gone back to work, Janiel walked with Etta out to the parking lot. He reached into a pocket. Etta, he said, would you take this with you? He held a paper crane, only the size of a nickel and a little squashed from being in his pocket. Tiny in his long hand. Yes, of course, said Etta, taking it from his hand and putting it in her own pocket.

She met James again on the east side of town, just where the suburbs trailed into wilderness.

That took a while.

It's all very strange, James. People are strange animals.

I haven't smelled anyone too close, said James, once she'd told him about Janiel and the manager and the spottings. *But I'll pay more attention now.*

I want to be completely away from all that, said Etta.

You never can be, said James, *but you can be far enough to pretend.*

What about you? What about with coyotes?

It's the same for coyotes, even.

They walked as far from town as they could before even the dusk light was gone and it was all dark and they had to make camp. Do you smell anything? asked Etta.

No. Nothing, said James. *No-one.*

The train had pulled away without them noticing, and they were alone on the platform. Well, said Etta. Otto's hands still on her arms, his body still needing and pulling toward her. Welcome home.

Yes, said Otto. Thanks. He inhaled and looked around. The dry texture of the wood under their feet, the smell of the thin, bright air, the schedule and track safety notice on the station wall, Etta's hair and clothes, like the hair and clothes of everyone here, all pulsed: Remember? Remember? Remember? He closed his eyes. Pulled Etta to him again. Just this one thing. Can we go to your house? he said.

Otto waited on the platform while Etta called for a taxi. Please be sure the driver's not Robert or David McNally, he told her. They're friends of Amos, they know my mother.

All the taxi drivers are women now, said Etta. But I'll make sure, just in case.

The driver was a woman neither of them knew. She said nothing as she drove and they said nothing either, hands held, sticky with sweat.

The taxi driver would not accept payment once they reached the teacher's cottage, putting both her hands forward as though holding Otto and Etta, and their money, away. No, no, she said. I would never.

They stumbled up the front walk, past the school, aching with familiarity. Otto breathed it in with the dust, remember, remember, and he held Etta's hand tighter as she fumbled with the other one for her front door key. He kissed her arm and shoulder and neck as she pushed the door open and pulled him in with her.

They fell onto the sofa in the front room; did not even make it to the bedroom, did not even shut the front door. Please, said Etta, remember,

Yes, said Otto, eyes still closed. Yes, yes.

Please, said Etta, please, please.

Otto looked up at the beams in the ceiling above the couch, counting them in one direction: one, two, three, four, five, and then in the other: one, two, three, four, five. Etta was sleeping or mimicking sleep, her breathing regular and rhythmic, her powder-blue dress pushed up and crumpled, but still on. Are there those same beams in the schoolrooms? he said to himself or to her. I never noticed those beams before.

Otto, said Etta, her voice light with near sleep. Do you want to talk about things?

Not yet, said Otto.

So they lay, not comfortable, not uncomfortable, just there, together, until it was time for Etta to put on her coveralls and head scarf and go to the factory. Is it okay if I stay here until you get back? said Otto. I'll sleep. I won't touch anything.

What about your family?

Tomorrow.

Okay. Of course, of course that's fine.

He walked Etta to the door, kissed her forehead and then mouth, the dust on her lips. On mine too, he thought. Then he went back and sat on the sofa with his head pushed back, and counted the beams, again, and again.

The next morning when Etta got home, she pulled him from the couch where he had slept, to her bed, in her room. She unbuttoned his dust-brown officer's shirt and pulled his arms out of the sleeves. She rolled down and off his socks, and lifted his undershirt off his torso, over his head. She kissed his chest before pulling off her own coveralls and letting her hair fall down from under its scarf.

What happened to your hair, Otto?

I was scared. On the boat.

I think it's good, said Etta. I think it's good that you look a bit different, now.

They ate in bed. Her dinner, his breakfast. Then Otto washed and Etta fell asleep. In the bath he counted his fingers and toes, ten each, the same, the same as always, and prepared to go to his family's farm. To go home.

Grace Vogel had always been proud of her eyesight. She wasn't proud about much, and certainly not by nature, but mention anything about your eyes and she'd challenge you. Right then, she'd say, what color's that ribbon on the neighbor's cat, or, tell me what it says on the front of that newspaper out the door, down the hall, and off to the side, or, how many cookies in that child's hand, there, running down the road. She never got it wrong. Grace Vogel's eyes were sharp and long and true and had always been that way. Which is how she knew, even from a mile and a half across the fields, even with his hair all turned, that her son Otto had come home. She saw him long before he saw her. She nearly knocked him over, running at him.

When she reached him she opened her arms wide and scooped him into them. She didn't say,

Why didn't you tell us you were coming?

And she didn't say,

What happened to your beautiful hair?

She said, releasing her embrace,

Dinner is almost ready. Come along and help.

Otto and his mother were quiet as they walked toward the house. But every ten steps or so she would glance over at him, just to check that he was there. When they had almost reached the house, still quiet, still just the two of them, Otto said,

Where is everyone?

His mother didn't stop walking. Didn't look over. Walter and Wiley have gone over, you know that. And Gus is in Halifax now. And Marie has gone to Clara's, since her husband's gone. And Amos is working the camp in Lethbridge. And Russell's got his own farm. And Winnie's . . .

Somewhere safe.

You know?

No. But still.

And Winnie's somewhere.

They walked up the house's front steps, two big and one, the last one, shallow, then stepped over the raised sill of the front door, then turned left into the kitchen, into the clout of dry oven heat and the smell of siblings' hot dusty hair and breath. Otto saw Harriet first. Harriet with her back to them, checking the hands of his littlest brothers and sisters, lined up, small to smaller.

Harriet, said their mother.

Oh! Oh! Oh! said six-year-old Josie, near the end of the line, hands filthy. *Otto!*

Harriet turned. You . . . You son of a bitch, she said.

Harriet! said their mother.

Otto! said Emmett, eight years old, breaking out of the line toward him.

You never even said . . . Wiley and Walter have us counting down days, but you never even said. Harriet stepped around, past Emmett.

Ot-to! Ot-to! said Ellie and Benji, twins, nine years old, hopping.

Back in line if you want to eat, said their mother.

I just wish you would have said, said Harriet, arms over Otto's shoulders—she was easily half a foot taller—pulling her brother roughly to her.

At the very end of the line, Ted, five years old, was crying.

Hey! Stop that! said Josie, beside him.

Don't cry, Ted, said Harriet.

Ot-to! Ot-to! said Ellie and Benji, hopping.

You're crying too, said Ted. That's why I am.

Where's Dad? said Otto.

Upstairs, said Emmett.

Not now, said his mother.

Ot-to! Ot-to! said Ellie and Benji, hopping.

Dinner, when they got to it, was flour-dumpling soup, and even though it was something that Otto had had many times before, this time the sameness of it tasted different, better.

After dinner, Otto went upstairs. All the doors were closed. The parents' room. The little kids' room. The big girls' room. The big boys' room. Otto knocked on this one. Dad?

Otto. Yes, come in. Sounding normal, himself through the wood.

Otto opened the door, his wrist lifting it instinctively across the place where the floor warped.

Look at you, would you, in those clothes. Would you look at you. No dirt, even.

Otto's father was tucked into Wiley's old bed. Only his neck and head above the covers. His hair totally white.

Did I wake you? I can come back later.

No! No. Come here, come closer. Just let me turn this off. Otto's father looked across to the radio on an upturned box near the bed. Otto hadn't even noticed its steady murmuring.

I'll get it, let me.

Then I don't know what we should expect— said the radio.

I wasn't really listening anyway, said his father.

Well, hunger— said the radio before Otto switched it off. He didn't know if he should hug his father or shake his hand. Kneel down to his level or stand over him in his teenager's bed. He knelt. Put one hand near where he hoped his father's would be, through the quilt.

I should have warned you about the hair thing, said his father. It's hereditary. You do look great in that uniform, though, still.

Thanks, said Otto.

Did you kill anyone?

I don't know.

Okay. Otto's father closed his eyes. It's okay one way or another, he said. Apart from his eyes and mouth, he didn't move the whole time they were speaking. I'm not sleeping, he said. Don't worry. My eyes just get tired of looking in the same direction all the time.

Okay, said Otto.

You can look, if you want to.

Under the blankets?

Yes.

I don't need to.

Go on. It's not so bad. You'll feel better after you do.

You're sure?

Yes.

Okay. Otto folded the quilt and the sheet back as far as his father's waist. He was in his pajamas. His arms were strapped to his sides with heavy leather belts. Amos's or Walter's.

It's the same with the legs, he said. You'd think it'd be uncomfortable, but I don't even notice.

One day, a few months earlier, Otto's mother had found his father pressed up against the slated side of the chicken coop, the pattern of it indented onto his face and hands. I didn't want to be here, he said, my legs just went and wouldn't stop.

The next day the twins found him up in one of the wind-break trees, the one with the thickest branches, the densest leaves. They only found him because he shouted as his arms climbed without his permission, and they'd been close by, in Rocksvalley.

No matter how hard he tried, his body no longer paid attention to his commands, had its own will. He discussed it with his wife whilst lying on the kitchen floor, where his body had him down on his side.

You must try very, very hard, she said. Try to lift your arm.

He tried, but his arm stayed limp against his side.

Try, she said. Try harder. Close your eyes and try. Squeeze them closed and try.

He closed his eyes—he could still control his eyes and mouth and nose, those were his, still—squeezed them, and tried to lift his arm. He thought of his wife and of Otto and Wiley and Walter and Winnie and Harriet and Amos and Ted and Emmett and Josie and Ellie and Benji and Clara and Marie and Gus and Addie and tried and tried, but his arm didn't move. Instead, his legs began to kick out in slow motion, like he was swimming.

Okay. Never mind, said Grace Vogel. We'll try again tomorrow.

Is Dad seizuring? Ted and Josie had come into the kitchen. Josie was holding a day-old chick that kept trying to jump out of her hands.

No, said their mother.

No, said their father. Don't worry. Just seeing what it's like for the mice, being down here. Ted, can you go find Harriet? Josie, let's see that chick.

Harriet and her mother had managed, together, to get Rupert Vogel back up onto his legs, and half-guided, half-carried him up the stairs to the big boys' room. I'm sorry, he said.

It's nothing, said Grace. You're not so heavy. I've carried calves heavier.

Though it was difficult to hear much of anything because Mr. Vogel's fingers had started snapping over and over, fast and loud.

He still did what he could. A wandering body was no excuse for not pulling his weight. During the day, Mr. Vogel listened to the news reports on the radio, to each and every one, all day, listening for anything that they all should know, or any names they all already knew. And at night he had his wife and Harriet bring him down and prop him on a chair beside the chicken coop. Because he was in bed all day, staring at the same bits of the room, he had no problem staying awake and watching for foxes or coyotes. With his arms and legs belted to the chair, his eyes looked all over, back and forth and back and forth, up and down and up and down, taking in as much as they possibly possibly could.

Otto walked up the drive to Russell's new house. He knocked on the front door in a quick rhythm, then waited. Then he knocked again. Then waited. And one more knock, one more rhythm. Then a count up to thirty and back down again. Then he went to check the barn.

The main door was on the other side of some barbed cattle wire, so Otto climbed up through a window instead, propping himself on his elbows and calling into the stifled air inside. Russell! Russell? The few cows who had wandered in for shade eyed him lazily, their jaws going round and round. Russell was not there.

Otto let his elbows relax and pushed himself back down away

from the barn. He looked around. Some shovels, a pile of rocks, a horse at pasture, more cows, and a cat trotting up to him. Black with white feet. You know Russell? asked Otto.

The cat didn't respond. It trotted past him and beyond, around the side of the house. Otto followed it. It continued around to the back of the building, past some swings made from tires and rope, untied and in a stack, to an old tractor with peeling paint, rusted edges, and the hood up. The cat hopped up into its seat.

That's the warmest place. She'll sit there all day.

I didn't know you knew mechanics.

I'm learning. A lot. Russell pulled himself out from behind the hood, wiping his hands on his overalls. His shirt was red and black plaid flannel, too hot for today, rolled up at both sleeves. Otto, he said, stepping around the tractor, you're a son of a bitch for being a sneak about the whole thing, for sneaking back here all quiet like a fox, but, goddamn it is good to see you. He opened his arms and took Otto in. He felt bigger, stronger, than Otto remembered him and smelled of white soap, dust, animals, grain. Familiar. Like me, Otto realized. Like I used to.

How often do you think about dying?

They were walking around the periphery of Russell's land, Otto was getting a tour.

You mean over there? said Otto, picking up a rock just bigger than his fist and tossing it out of the field. I think about living more. I think about living as hard as I can. You should see the dances, Russell. The women.

There are dances here too.

Yes, of course. There's just . . . less contrast.

They fell silent, reached the far edge of the rye and turned ninety degrees. This is real impressive, said Otto, what you've got here. This whole farm, just yours, that's really something.

Thanks, said Russell. It's small. A farm you can walk around in twenty minutes. But I'm going to buy Perkinses' too, once I've got money.

Be sure you save some land for me, for when I'm back.

You're coming back? Russell caught himself, corrected, I mean, I don't mean like that. I mean, you're not going to stay there, once it's over?

Once it's over, I'm coming home, Russell.

Okay. Okay good. I just wasn't sure. It's hard to know, from here.

They reached another corner and turned another ninety degrees. Otto started to speak and stopped himself. Took a breath and started again. I wasn't sure, Russell, he said. When I was over there, I wasn't sure I could, I mean, I wasn't sure I could come home. Not really. Thought maybe all that would superimpose over all this and nothing would make sense, and would be empty, just empty. Like holding on to a ghost. Hollow.

But it's not.

But mostly it's not.

When Etta woke up Otto was gone. She lay in bed and thought through each part of her body, checking to see if they felt different. Warmer, maybe, from the inside. She wanted to talk to Russell. But she didn't, couldn't. Russell might not even know that Otto was home yet. And she wanted to talk to her sister, Alma. She wanted to take her to the Holdfast café and pay for both their pies and have her listen coolly and quietly, like she did, and then respond with composed, simple advice. Etta pushed her sheets away and sat up, legs swung over the side of her bed. The worst thing about night shifts was having to try and sleep during hottest parts of the day. She stepped over her coveralls, discarded on the floor, opened her second-to-top drawer, and felt around through layers of stockings until her fingers closed on something cool and solid and sharp. She lifted it through the stockings and up to her ear and whispered, Is this good?

Oui, oui, oui, it whispered back.

Etta brought pinwheel cookies, dusted in sugar and light like lace, to her last night shift.

Those are awful hard to make, said the girl in the spotted head scarf, picking up a bullet, holding it close to her face, closing one eye and squinting. You shouldn't waste them on us.

It's my last night, said Etta, trying to hold her hand steady, always steady, like the woman had chanted at them in training, always steady, only steady. I thought we should mark it somehow.

What? Already? That was brief. So you're leaving us. You don't like us? The girl's reflection distorted in the casing.

It doesn't matter if I do or not; it's for the bus. The bus only runs for the day shifts.

So how'd you get here today? Yesterday?

A horse. I borrowed a horse. I tie it up behind the parking, in Mickleburgh's field.

Oh . . . I don't think you're supposed to do that.

No, I'm not.

I've never been on a horse. This was from the girl with bright red lipstick, further down the line, joining the conversation.

Never?

Never?

I'm from town. I take the tram. Or walk.

Then Etta will have to take you on hers.

It's not mine, actually.

Still.

I'm afraid of animals.

All animals?

Yes. Especially ones bigger than me.

I'm returning the horse in the morning, said Etta. Tonight's your only chance.

How do you know for sure you're afraid of horses until you've been on one? said yellow dots. Your whole life, maybe, you've been wrong.

I don't think I am, said bright red lipstick. Pretty sure I'll faint as soon as I see the thing.

It's tonight or never, said Etta.

Break's in fifteen minutes, said yellow dots.

Tonight or never, said red lipstick, almost whispering.

14

Etta walked and her legs did not get tired and her feet did not get tired and her back did not get sore. She closed her eyes and saw herself in the red and white uniform of a sprinter, in the long black lines of a cross-country skier, in the green and gray uniform of Otto's regiment. These are good boots, she said to James.

Shoes, said James. *Yes, they are excellent shoes.*

She wrote a letter,

My Dear Etta,

These days, we march and march and march and march and march. Only, always. But we sing as we do it, which reminds me of your class, which I like. Boots over new soil, under new trees, guns rubbing against the bare skin of our hips, at odds with our feet warm in socks knit by nuns.

*   *   *

James pulled it from her bag while she slept and dropped it into a lake. The pen-dark ink bled into the night-dark water and caused the fish to swim into each other until it diluted and cleared.

In the morning he said, *Good morning, Etta.*

And she said, Good morning, James.

And they kept walking; singing and keeping away from towns while their supplies were still good.

Eventually, however, they ran low again. Etta caught fish and boiled water.

We're close to a city now, said James, *I can smell it. All the people and all the cars.*

I'm going to have to stop, said Etta.

I know, said James.

So they altered their course slightly, down, toward the city.

It's hot.

I think I see her!

Wouldn't it be too soon?

Oh, it's not her. It's a motorcycle.

It *is* hot.

Didn't you bring water?

Yes, but not for us. For her.

How much?

It's not for us.

It's hot.

I think that's really her now!

I can't see! Get the dog out of the way.

Oh wow oh wow

Get the camera!

And the water!

Do you think she'll stop?

She rarely stops.

The banner!

The banner!

The banner!

Almost forgot, get it out, hurry!

My hands are slipping, they're sweaty.

Hold it higher!

Here, let me.

It's blocking my face!

Hold it higher!

Etta!

It's her!

Etta!

Etta!

Etta!

Etta motioned for James to get behind her, safer on the other side of her legs. She held up one hand, Hello. Hello, hello, hello, hello. One for each face she counted. I can't stop, I'm sorry. She shouted out in front of her, like a shield.

Oh we know.

That's okay.

We've got water!

(Where's the water?)

(*Did you drink it?*)

Here, some water!

Thank you, said Etta. A camera flash as she reached out for the bottle. Then another and another.

Etta, said a woman with two strollers, one child asleep, one awake, would you take this? She stretched her hand out to Etta, in it a bobby-pin with a tiny opalescent green star on the end. Etta took it, squeezed the woman's hand, and tucked the pin into her hair behind her right ear.

Etta! called a man on the other side of her, young, business-suited, perfectly shining black shoes. Please, he said. He gave her a nickel. It's from the year I was born, he said.

The whole time Etta did not stop walking, moving through the crowd like swimming as it shifted and merged around her.

And then she was out again, on the far side, with the chant,

Etta!

Etta!

Etta!

fading behind her. She had food and water and a bobby pin, a nickel, a green ribbon, a locket, a small plastic soldier, and a perfectly round pebble. She tied the ribbon around James's neck and put the other things in her pocket. Is anybody following us? she asked James.

No, he said.

And they made their way back out to the fields, lakes, trees.

Otto cleared a space in between all the flour bowls, newspapers, and tools on one side of the table and all the letters and recipes on the other side. He got out one of his better, smoother black pens and some off-white paper. Oats rolled her glassy marble eyes up toward him, but stayed silent. She licked the side of her box.

Dear Etta,

he wrote,

> *I have been offered some money, a fair amount of money, for my*
> *collection. The things I'm making to pass the time until you come back.*
> *A woman with mixed brown and gray hair all pulled back sharply*
> *came by the house. She came during the day but I was sleeping. She*
> *saw me, she said, with my head on the table, so she waited in the yard,*
> *wandering between the animals until the sun had gone down and I*
> *was awake. Once she saw through the window that my head was no*
> *longer on the table, she knocked and I let her in and gave her coffee and*
> *squares and she said, It might rain.*
>
> > *And I stirred my coffee and offered her a spoon and she said, No,*
> *really, Otto, it might rain. It's summer now, but it won't be forever,*
> *and then it might rain and it will certainly snow, eventually, and*
> *everything will be ruined. We would take care of your collection, in the*
> *gallery, we could even paint the walls and everything to make it look*
> *just like out here.*
>
> > *And I said, by the time it rains, Etta will be home. Certainly by*
> *the time it snows. So it'll be okay if they melt.*
>
> > *It won't be okay, she said.*
>
> > *It will.*

She gave me her card, in case I change my mind. I'm including it here.

And that's all, here.

I wish I knew where you were. I wish I knew how much farther and how much longer. The yard is filling up, and Russell's too. I'm tired and old. I just wish I knew how much longer.

Yours,
Otto.

In the mornings, Otto helped his mother and Harriet. Lifting, carrying, pulling, walking, calling, holding. It felt good, felt necessary, to be using his body like this. Afternoons he went to Russell's and did the same. He felt sorry for the soldiers who had gone home to quiet, still places in towns and cities, legs twitching on sofas in sitting rooms.

After Russell's, he went to the teacher's cottage. To Etta. Either just after she'd changed out of her coveralls, or just before. As they met they'd hold up their right hands with some number of fingers showing, five for five days left, then four, then three, pressing them together before they fell into each other. Apart from this, they did not mention the inevitable winding down of days.

Until the day of just two fingers, when they were lying together just before sunset in the field behind the school, on land that was technically Perkinses' and was growing too fast and too wild, when Etta said,

I think we should also be counting up.

Their discarded clothes made a trail back to the cottage's front door. Etta's bare feet reached down past Otto's, still in socks.

Up?

Yes. We're counting down each day, but I think we should also be counting up, making a tally of how many days we've gotten to spend together. Counting up.

Otto considered, then lifted his hands above them so they blocked the setting sun, holding up two fingers in one and three in the other. Etta did the same, lining her hands up with his so they superimposed.

The next day it was one finger and four. Otto brought over all his letters. The ones he had written from away that Etta had sent back to him with her corrections. In chronological order, he unfolded each one and read them aloud. After each, he would hand the paper over to Etta, who put the letters in the drawer of the small table next to her bed, one by one. When he got to the end, to the last one, she said,

Keep going.

So he did, reading out letters to her he hadn't yet written down, as she read him her not-written-down replies.

It was windy outside and the wind blew dust up against the windows, coating them thick so all you could see from inside was the glow of late-day sun. From there, they could pretend they didn't notice it dimming.

The next day Etta took her lunch an hour earlier than usual, arriving at the station just in time to join the lineup of siblings, parents, and Russell, who squeezed up to Harriet so she could fit in. They'd arranged themselves so as to have a bench at one end, where Otto's father could sit, legs and arms strapped. Grace Vogel's eyes darted to and from Etta as she slipped in, but she said nothing.

I'll be back soon, I know, said Otto. I'll see each one of you soon, I know.

Be bravest, said Ted.

Don't cry, I'm not crying, you don't cry, I'm not crying, you cry every time, I do not, you do, said Ellie and Benji.

It's stupid that you all go, said Emmett.

Be careful, said Harriet.

Be very careful, said Clara.

Try to stay kind, said Marie.

I love you, said Etta, so quiet Otto only half-heard.

Remember us, said Russell.

Remember what I said, said Harriet.

Please, said his mother.

Don't lose yourself, said his father.

And Otto kissed each one on the left cheek, only hesitating a second to squeeze Etta's hand, and his mother's, then took his bag from Harriet and got on the train that was waiting for him, its only passenger from this stop. On board, just before pulling away, he wrote

Your

Otto.

backward on the window in the dust and grease.

They stayed in that formation, all lined up, after the train had left, watching the space where it had been until Otto's father, from his spot on the bench, said, Right. Back to work now, everyone. Then they dispersed, Russell giving a ride to Ellie and Benji on his horse, while the other Vogels crowded into the truck, smaller children inside the cab, bigger ones with their father in the back, with Grace Vogel at the wheel. Etta walked by herself back to the factory, pulling her hair up under its scarf as she went. You wait and you work, she whispered to herself, you wait, and you work. Her stomach turned backflips, stitched, kicked.

15

Etta and James walked along the river, and there were more and more towns and crowds. Etta took the things they asked her to, a button, a photograph, an arrowhead, a ring, and, once they were through, always asked James the same thing,

Is anybody following us?

And he always answered the same way,

No.

And they'd make their way back somewhere wild to sleep.

We're going to have to cross this river soon. It's widening, becoming ocean.

I know, said Etta. I'm just waiting for the right bridge. The bridges so far had all been concrete and steel and full of cars. That's no way to cross water.

We could swim, said James.

But the banks were high and steep. The current unknown. *I could get down there*, said James, *I could help you.*

Two more days, said Etta, glancing down the sheer drop. If there's no good bridge in two days.

But there was a bridge, the right sort of bridge, by the end of the first day. Dark wood in a latticework of beams all around, covered, so the inside was shadowed and damp. An old railroad bridge, said Etta. This will do.

I don't know, said James. *I don't like it.*

It's beautiful, said Etta. It's good.

No, said James. *You can't see all the way through it, there's darkness in the middle. No.*

We have to, said Etta.

I'll swim, said James.

Down there?

Yes. It's easy, for me.

And I'll meet you on the other side.

Yes. I'll smell for you on the other side. James tripped lightly away, back and forth in a wide crisscross into the gorge, knocking small rocks and flower petals down into the water as he went. Etta tapped one foot on the bridge's first plank, to test for rot, then stepped onto it.

She proceeded like this, slow and careful, testing then stepping, further and further along toward the bridge's dark midpoint, as James zig-zagged below. She kept her left hand out, moving it along the planks that made up the bridge's wall. She wondered if her grasp could possibly be firm enough to hold, should her feet give way. Grasp, test, step, grasp, test, step, to the middle of the bridge, where it was completely dark. Grasp, test, step. Grasp, stop. Her left hand hadn't hit the cool grain of wood this time, but, instead, something warm and soft and regularly textured. Wool. Moving up and down ever so slightly. Breathing. A shoulder.

Etta, it said.

Jesus! said Etta.

I'm sorry.

Christ!

Don't be scared, it's just me.

Just who?

Me, Bryony.

Even though it was already pitch-black, Etta closed her eyes. Bryony. Was this a name? Was this a familiar name? James? she said.

No, Bryony. The shoulder moved. A hand placed on Etta's outstretched arm. The reporter, from before. Do you remember?

The feel of the shoulder was the pressed wool of a burgundy business suit. Yes, said Etta. Of course I do. Bryony. Are you here for another interview?

No, said Bryony.

Are you from here?

This bridge?

Well, maybe. This area.

No, I can hardly speak French at all. I'm here because, well, I've been following the story. And the crowds. I've been in the crowds, each time, just in the back.

You never said hello, said Etta.

I'm sorry, said Bryony. I was gathering courage.

Did you want to give me something to carry with me? asked Etta.

Yes, said the reporter, that's it, exactly. I do. She paused. The pressed-wool shoulder lifted up and down in a sigh. Etta, she said, I'm so sick of everybody else's stories.

Have you brought me stories?

No, myself.

Yourself?

I've brought you myself. I'm ready to come with you.

Oh.

Okay?

Okay.

The reporter Bryony walked along the right-hand side of the bridge, with her right hand along the wall, and Etta continued along the left. They held hands across the center. Do you think you could hold, asked Bryony, if one of my boards gave way and you had me in your hand?

Probably not, said Etta. But they continued like this anyway, all the way across the bridge and into the squinting sunlight on the other side.

They mostly walked without talking. There were fewer towns on this side of the water and things were quieter. Every time they reached a turning point, a lake or road or diversion, Etta would stop, look around, then spit on the ground and rub the saliva into the dirt with her shoe. The third time, before a ridge they'd have to go around one way or another, Bryony said, Why do you do that?

For James, said Etta. So he can find us.

But, three hours after they'd crossed the bridge, there was still no sign of him. Etta, who had been counting seconds under her breath, stopped again. Do you think the river current is very strong, back there? she asked.

The river we crossed? The Saint-Laurent?

Yes.

I don't know. It's very big.

And deep?

And deep.

Okay, said Etta. And they kept walking.

Before they camped that night, Bryony wanted to make a fire.

We can't, said Etta.

Why not? It will be cold at night. If not now, soon.

James doesn't like them. He's afraid.

Oh, said Bryony. Okay.

Etta tore up wide strips of moss and laid them green side down over the reporter to keep her warm instead of having a fire. Before falling asleep, swathed in the heavy green scent, Bryony said, It would be impossible, Etta, for you to get down there, even if we did go back.

I know, said Etta.

You shouldn't feel bad, said Bryony.

I know.

Okay.

Dear Otto,

*I've enclosed some caribou fur here. Feel it, just feel it. Isn't that
something? Isn't that different from a horse or cow or cat or dog even?
Isn't it the greatest thing you've felt in a while?*

   *It's starting to get colder up here. I'm thinking about making a
coat. A Netsilik woman has already made me a hat. She does that.
Sits in her house on the route of the caribou and makes hats from the
ones that fall down or behind. Her house was full of this fur. To keep it
warm in autumn and winter she said.*

   But I should be home before then.

Sincerely,

Russell

Otto tapped the fur out from the bottom seam of the envelope. It fell
in little clumps, the way he had always imagined his own hair would,
one day; though, at eighty-three years old, he still had the same full,
white, head of it he'd had since he was seventeen. He pushed the scattered clumps of fur into a pile and ran his fingers over it, then picked
it up and rubbed it between his thumb and forefinger. Thicker than
a cat's or deer's, softer than a dog's or coyote's, in one direction it was
effortless and comforting, in the other it caught against the grain of
his fingerprints.

He was coughing a lot, now, these days. At first Oats would jump and
cower behind papier-mâché-Oats each time, but now she just carried
on licking or chewing or sleeping, not interrupted or bothered. And
mostly Otto didn't pay it attention anymore either, the little spasms
washing over his body as regular as waves. He really only noticed at

whatever point in the morning or night or day that he decided he had
to try to sleep, when, with the closing of his eyes, he became acutely
aware of each little thing in his body, of each cough reverberating like
a timpani roll, of his heart accelerating self-consciously like an ac-
companying snare. He'd catch sleep in the tiny snatches between. Five
seconds, ten seconds, two seconds, collected and piled together like
the clumps of fur from Russell, which he kept on the counter beside
the mixing bowls, ready for his next project: a full-size caribou onto
which he would paste the fur, on the head, around the eyes.

Otto got on the train and felt the pull of the ground under his feet, along the tracks, again, all the way to the edge of the country, then got off and onto a boat, which slipped across days and nights of drills and false alarms and real alarms, taking his turn at spreading the boot prints off the deck with a mop or a rag, singing and laughing, then dropping and lying flat against the planks at the call of the captain or someone else as something shot at them from above or below or beside and being grateful for the mopping, and, there, with his cheek picking up the grain of the deck, feeling like he might, just, if he listened hard enough, hear his parents talking or dancing just above or below all the shots and shouts. His hair stayed the same, this time, as he stepped off the boat, legs untrusting of solid ground, and swung his duffel bag, with dust from his mother's farm still in the creases, up into the matte green truck in a pile with the bags of all the others, who then bumped along side by side, knees touching, on the final leg of their journeys, this time.

The truck dropped Otto off in a small stone and sand village a few miles east from where he'd left his regiment, just over two weeks before. Does that mean we're winning or losing? he asked Gérald, who was showing him where he'd sleep, in an abandoned church vestry.

It means we're still moving, said Gérald. Back and forth, back and forth. We're not fighting with these boys, we're dancing.

Their numbers were thin. There was the gradual dripping away of those injured or lost, and there were the three who had not come back from their leave, whose families and wives swore they hadn't heard or seen anything of them. We're getting reinforcements sent in soon, said Gérald, chewing at a bit of skin near his little-finger nail. In a couple of days, just after you've all had a chance to readjust again. Gérald hadn't gone home; he'd chosen to stay, to hold and watch things until Otto and the others came back. I prefer to imagine what going home could have been like, instead of knowing what it really would have been, he said. I sat out here on my own, out on watch eight p.m. to eight a.m., and I imagined I was sitting with my wife all night, night after night after night, and *mon Dieu* she was beautiful, and it was so simple and so easy.

Etta walked over to Russell's. It was after work; she was still in her coveralls. It had been two days since Otto had left. Russell was bent down, pulling up thistle. Etta had no gloves so she found and pulled out dandelions instead. Pulling from the base, getting the roots. They threw everything they pulled into a big pile away from the good soil. You don't have to do that, said Russell.

I hate the emptiness of my house, said Etta.

Okay, said Russell.

A few days later, on the bus, Lucy Perkins said to Etta,

Do you hate the city?

You mean town? Where the school and the factory are?

Yeah.

No, I don't think I hate it.

I do, said Lucy Perkins.

The morning after that, Lucy Perkins was not on the bus. Etta took a seat next to a boy sleeping against the window.

After work she walked to Russell's. He was further down the land, still working on thistle. She walked out to where he was and got started on dandelions.

Mrs. Perkins came by yesterday, said Russell. He pulled at a thistle base with one hand. The leaves shuddered. He put both hands around it, right next to the soil, and pulled again, forcing out a cascade of roots twice as long as the plant. She's given up trying to sell; she said she was just tired. She said she felt ancient. Another plant, both hands, roots like uncombed hair. I said she looked the same, because to me she did. But she shook her head and said, No, Russell, no, I'm not the same, not at all. She said as their land's next to mine I might as well have it. She and Lucy are moving in with her sister in town, today or tomorrow.

Today, said Etta.

You spoke to them?

Lucy wasn't on the school bus. Etta broke the leaves off a dandelion stalk and put them in a separate pile for salad. Russell, she said, do you think—

I know. The letter carrier recognized the color of the envelope addressed to Mrs. Perkins, the feel of the tag inside. It's the only thing she delivers in Western Union telegram format, she said. It's so horribly obvious, she said. She was delivering to my aunt's just before, just one stop before, and had to go in and sit down and ask for coffee but not drink it, just sit at the table with my aunt, hoping time could stretch backward so she wouldn't have to do what she had to do. She finally left once the coffee was cold and half a day's work wasn't done. My aunt called round for me after that. To help her catch up. She told me then.

Yesterday?

The day before yesterday.

Etta pulled off some leaves and tore the stem; it bled thick white onto her hand. Russell, she said, he was from right here. Right where we're all from. It could have been any of them, any of us.

I know. And my aunt knows and Grace Vogel knows and the letter carrier knows. And Otto knows and Walter and Wiley and my uncle and Mr. Lancaster and Winnie knows too.

Etta wiped her hand on her leg and dropped the leaves into the salad pile. What did you say? About the farm?

I said I'd take care of it. That I'd keep the land active until they want it back. Mrs. Perkins said she never wanted to see it again, but I said, still, still, and she said, No, Russell, not at all. She said, You're all that's left, Russell. It's just you.

She was wrong. You're not all that's left. I'm here. I'm helping.

I know.

It's terrible, to just give up. It's horrible.

I know.

It makes me want to do things and do things and never stop doing. If we're doing we're living and if we're living we're winning, right?

Etta, let's go dancing tonight.

Okay. Yes.

Dear Etta,

Everything is fine. I made it over in one piece, the boat stayed up and I stayed on it. We are in this seems-to-be peaceful _____ until the new recruits come to bolster our ranks and spirits. In the meantime, there are double portions at dinner, and double socks and razorblades and blankets for all of us still here. The food is fairly terrible, but less so when you can actually eat your fill of it. So. Things are good. Except,

I miss your skin, Etta. I miss your hands and coveralls and bare legs and ____ and _____ and _____ and _____ _____ _____ and ____ for me. It is both easier and harder being here, now.

Yours, here,
Otto.

16

Sleeping under the moss that night with Bryony, Etta slipped into water dreams again. She was close to shore, needed to swim in, but her uniform was too big, rolled up at the wrists and ankles, coming unrolled every time she took a stroke. She could see land, see the rest of the boys there, gathering their things and marching away in pairs, across the beach and away, but she'd never get there because she had to stop and re-roll, wrists, ankles, again and again. Gérald was there too, on the beach, waiting for her, watching her; she wasn't sure how long he would wait.

She woke up at the sound of Bryony opening a cellophane bag of sunflower seeds. Oh good, good, said Etta, you're still here. Thank you for waiting.

Bryony smiled. She offered the opened bag to Etta. Barbecue flavor.

Etta took a small handful. Did everyone else go?

It's just us, said Bryony. Just like it was last night.

Last night we were all on a boat, said Etta.

A bridge, said Bryony.

A boat, said Etta.

Okay, said Bryony. Should we start walking?

Yes, said Etta, absolutely.

They stopped for a break around nine o'clock in the morning. They had walked silently together until then. Do you think he's coming back? said Etta.

Who? said Bryony.

James.

Oh. I don't know, Etta. I hope so.

You're not afraid of coyotes?

There are worse things.

Like what?

Bears . . . people . . . sharks . . .

There are some bears out here too, sometimes.

I know.

And people.

But no sharks.

Not as far as I know. Not yet anyway.

They finished drinking and stretching and leaving scent marks, Etta's far removed, separated from Bryony's. Ready to go again? asked Bryony. Etta was sitting on a rock, looking at a small, crumpled piece of paper.

You:

Etta Gloria Kinnick of Deerdale farm. 83 years old in August.

Bryony, said Etta, who was I this morning?

You were you, of course, Etta.

But was I?

I'm not sure.

I'm not sure either.

They walked through low forests and full forests, along rock-lined drops and broad open fields. They took off their shoes (Etta's sneakers, Bryony's tall leather boots) and made their way across shallow, pebbled streams and slick-wet slate gorges. They were away from towns and people again, and wouldn't need to stop for a few days at least. Bryony had taken off her burgundy blazer and tied it chunkily around her waist. It was very hot now through the drooping midsections of their days, and Etta had to eat more, more sugar, more quick-to-the-muscles food to keep herself awake and moving. She looked forward to streams and creeks, to water over her bare feet.

They were hiking through a north-bound stream, tingly with cold from the shins down, soggy with heat from the knees up, when Etta said, Hey, Bryony, what are your stories?

I don't have any, that's the point. She pointed her toes each time she brought a foot out of the stream, minimizing the ripples like a diver.

But you must.

I really don't.

Under all the layers of everybody else's I'm sure you do. You've just forgotten, maybe, or can't get to them anymore because they're so covered over.

Maybe, said Bryony.

Well, you can think about it, said Etta. And tell me if you re-member one.

Okay, said Bryony. They continued on for a few steps, Bryony lift-pointing with each one, Etta shuffling so as to keep as much of herself in the stream as possible.

They walked and lifted and shuffled and marched and walked and lifted and shuffled and marched, taking turns in front, moving north and east, keeping their distance from the American border. They camped just outside Saint-Elzéar-de-Témiscouata, in an abandoned barn surrounded by mustard flower.

In that night's dream Etta was swimming or dancing, she couldn't decide which, but it didn't matter because they were, really, the same thing, only in swimming the water was your partner, all around, ready, following, light and easy and heavy and comforting and there in your arms and you in its arms and if you opened your mouth to sing along to the music it would rush in and tell you its secrets and taste like wine.

In the morning she said, I want to go home.

Bryony was already up, was always up first. Home?

Yes, if they'll let us. I'm worried. I can't stop thinking about my father, mother, sisters, brothers . . . aren't you worried about your wife, Gérald? Isn't it stupid that we're here with each other and not there, with them?

No, said Bryony, it's not. It's not stupid, it's important.

Are you sure?

Yes.

So we keep marching?

Yes.

And tonight we'll find a bar and go dancing.

If we're lucky.

Okay, sighed Etta. She was sitting on the ground; she still hadn't gotten up.

Here, said Bryony. She took Etta's hands in both of hers and pulled her up to standing.

I miss them all so much, said Etta.

I know, said Bryony.

Otto was looking through the recipe cards, browsing for something he could make that he hadn't tried yet, something he had the ingredients for, when he found a card written out in Etta's young hand, in ink that had faded to a light indigo over sixty years. It was from when he had come home for good.

For Otto at night,

it said, in easy looping letters,

NEEDED:

20 flax flowers

1 mortar and 1 pestle

INSTRUCTIONS:

Take the blue flowers and crush and pulp them. Spread the paste on his eyelids, thick, weigh the skin down. Then have him sleep. And he will sleep easy and the dreams will stay away. In the morning the flowers will have gone dry and light and have turned to a powdery rust that can be brushed away as easily as hair or dust.

He put the card down apart from the others and headed out, weaving through his animals, to see if there were any late blossoms remaining on Russell's flax. He found four, collecting them carefully into the coffee mug he'd brought with him.

Back in the kitchen, he pulled the petals away from their stalks and dropped them into the mortar. As he crushed them, their color became brighter and richer. A good color for a beetle, he thought. He made a mental note to make beetles next. It was awkward spreading the paste on his own eyelids, and even more awkward feeling his way with eyes closed and heavy with paste out of the kitchen, along the hall, and into the bedroom. But once he was there, laid down on his back so as to not stain the pillowcase blue, he fell away, almost immediately.

Otto slept and slept, until night, then through the night and well into the next day. When he woke up, he brushed a hand, without thinking, across his face and rust-colored dust fell away around it.

He felt wonderful. He felt, for the first time in a long time, like his body didn't want anything from him. He made coffee and breakfast, then set about designing and crafting his beetles, and his hands didn't shake and his heart didn't race. While the first coat was drying, Otto went back out, back through his animals, to the fields to try and find more flowers. He had to go farther this time, and longer, but eventually he found two complete blossoms and one that had only dropped half its petals. He put them in a coffee cup with a little water so they'd be ready and fresh for that night.

And then he made the paste.

And then he slept.

The next day, he searched and searched up and down the overgrown rows of Russell's land, but couldn't find a single flower. The sun was hot and the top of his head pulsed with it.

That night his heart raced and his lungs jerked and jumped and he stared up at the sparkles in the stucco ceiling until he'd counted each one, breathing like a sprinter. Then he got up and walked to the kitchen and rinsed the big bowl and started a mix of flour and water in his pajamas and robe. His hands were shaking, but that was not such a big deal at this stage when he was just mixing. Later, when it came time to craft and sculpt, he would drink some coffee or take some ibuprofen or rye to try and calm them.

A few hours after sunrise, he started up the truck and drove to

the Co-op. They were just opening, just putting out the flower spe-
cials in buckets by the front door.

Good morning, said Otto. He walked slowly, carefully, from the
truck to the shop, on guard for coughing fits that could throw off his
balance and land him in the flower buckets.

Here for more flour?

Not today, Sheryl.

Paint?

Nope, not today, Wesley.

Sheryl was closest to the door, untying bunches of pink and yellow carnations. Here, she said, as she put down her flowers and held
the door for Otto.

Thanks, said Otto.

Be right with you, Wesley called after him, clipping the stems of
cellophaned roses.

Two minutes later, when Wesley finished with the roses, he
found Otto by the notice board. I just wanted to put this up, please,
said Otto. He passed Wesley a handmade notice. It said,

WANTED: FLAX FLOWERS

*Please contact OTTO VOGEL if you have/find any late
flax flowers in your fields or wild. Of some urgency.*

Of course, said Wesley. How long for?

Otto thought, calculated. Where was Etta? Quebec? Two weeks,
he said. Maybe more.

The bells on the shop's door rang and Otto and Wesley turned
to see Sheryl come in with the pruning scissors and a bucket full of
stem ends. She squinted toward the notice. Otto, she said, you having
trouble sleeping?

I'm all right, said Otto.

Because we got capsules.

Capsules aren't so good for your heart, said Otto. I'm all right.

Okay.

I'll put this up for two weeks then, said Wesley. Right in the middle, here.

And, here, take this, said Sheryl. She handed Otto a yellow carnation that was too short to fit in with the others.

At home, Otto put the carnation in a coffee cup, as all their vases were too tall for it. He stroked Oats's sleeping head and replaced some of the newspaper scraps in the side of the crate she wasn't using, then checked that the last coat he'd applied to his raccoon was dry. It was. Everything was dry here. He carefully picked up the model and carried it out to the yard to find a place for it. His eyes ached, hot. He'd find a shady spot in the living room or kitchen after this and would try to sleep again.

Beautiful raccoon, said a woman with mixed brown and gray hair all pulled back sharply. She stood between the narwhal and the trout. Underwater, thought Otto, though not really.

Thank you, said Otto. I thought I'd put it at that edge, there, looking at the trout.

That makes sense, said the woman.

But I don't want to sell, said Otto. It or anything.

That doesn't make sense, said the woman, but I know.

It shouldn't rain in the next two weeks, that would be very—Otto stopped to cough—unseasonal.

I know, said the woman. Though it could. But that's not why I'm here. She held one hand up to the narwhal's side, as if to pet it, but an inch away, not actually touching. I'm here because I thought you might want to talk about what could or should happen to your collection in the case of an unfortunate unforeseen event.

Otto nodded, waiting.

The woman stood, watching him, waiting.

Otto nodded again, waiting.

I mean, said the woman, I mean if you die, Otto. I'm here to ask if you might consider willing your collection to us, the gallery, should you die.

Oh, said Otto.

He thought. His left hand shook. He put it, with the other, behind his back. Then he said, I guess the first problem would be that they're mostly presents.

Presents?

Yes, presents. For Etta and for Russell. So I don't know if it would be appropriate to will them to someone else.

Well, said the woman, there must be some—

And, said Otto, the second problem is that, frankly, I just don't see who would be interested, of the gallery-going public. I mean, apart from you, of course.

Really? said the woman.

Really, said Otto.

Jesus! Otto! said the woman. Look. She turned around, toward the road, and pointed. A procession of cars and trucks were snaking slowly by, some with binoculars poking out their windows. Otto counted fifteen before his eyes started to blur. He lifted one hand from behind his back, and waved. An arm from out of the backseat window of a blue station wagon waved back.

Oh . . . said Otto, really?

Really, said the woman.

Huh, said Otto. And then, I'll think about it.

Thank you, said the woman. Before she left, she gave him another business card.

I've already got one, said Otto.

Well, now you've got two.

After she left, Otto sat down in the grass beside his raccoon and watched the cars crawling by. Apart from coughing, he stayed very still, like a statue, his hands behind his back.

The recruits arrived on a sleepy Saturday afternoon. Some of the resident soldiers were napping on borrowed beds or couches or lawns, some of them were throwing bits of debris they found for a dog who belonged to nobody. Otto was writing a letter, and Gérald was up on the roof of the church they were bunked in, watching, even though he wasn't on watch. So it was Gérald who first saw the trucks throwing up stones and birds from all the way down the road. So it was Gérald who was the first to know they were coming, then Otto, who heard him cry out,

Trucks!

then,

Etta, they're here! Finally. More soon.

And then everyone, all out on the one strip of street that was the beginning and ending of this once-town, all the soldiers at once moving together in a rolling, shouting, punching, exhilarated wave, down toward the trucks. The captains called for them to fall in line, but nobody really listened, and the captains didn't really care.

Otto wound up next to the second truck. All the current boys were gathered around the vehicles, shouting and jumping and clapping their hands against the warm metal, and all the new boys were inside, sat up strict-straight with eyes dead ahead. From the front seat of the front truck, a captain whistled. And then the doors opened and they all tumbled together, mixed, met.

Ralf MacNeil, said a boy with a halo of closely shaved orange hair, from Labrador. He shook Otto's hand vigorously. Really glad to be out here at last, really, really glad.

Lauren Ingersson, from Flin Flon, said the boy behind him, reaching around to take Otto's other hand. Hope you got better food here than on the boats.

Ralf and Lauren were swept on to the next group and Otto found himself faced with another pair of new boys, one with long, pale features and one with tight, dark curls. Hi, said the former, I'm Adrian, I'm—

Owen, said Otto.

No, Adrian—

Oh my god, Owen, said Otto.

No, sorry, it's—

Hello, Otto, said Owen.

Oh, said Adrian, you two know each other already?

Yes, said Otto.

Yes, said Owen.

And then the crowd surged and pulled and someone brushed into Otto's shoulder and he turned toward them but they were gone and when he turned back Adrian and Owen were gone too and in their place were more new, unmet faces, their bodies taut with the ecstatic tension of something going to happen. Over their heads, Otto thought he caught flashes of Owen's hair twenty or thirty boys away, but then again, Owen wasn't tall, and the crowd was always moving, so he couldn't be sure.

That night, Otto waited by the door to the town hall they used as a cafeteria while everyone filed in for dinner. Owen and Adrian were nearly the last ones in; they didn't know yet, thought Otto, that there was a very finite amount of everything here. He reached across Adrian, and pulled Owen out of the line, around the corner, into the unofficial coatroom.

Better food in here? said Owen.

What are you doing here? said Otto.

You just pulled me in . . .

No, not here, *here*, Owen. What are you doing *here*?

The same thing you are.

No, you're not.

I'm not?

You're too young, Owen. You're way too young.

They didn't ask about it. They don't care anymore.

But I do. And you should.

Well, that's nice, nice of you, Otto, but wrong.

Wrong?

Otto, there are other ways of being old, grown-up, other than just time. There are lots of things. I'm one of the oldest people I know. Sometimes it feels like I am the oldest of all. And that's not necessarily a good thing. But it's true.

Owen spoke in flat tones, his voice level, checked.

But thank you for your concern, he continued. It does mean something, it means a lot. It was shadowed in the coatroom, practically no light in here, just the bits that tumbled in along with the noise of dishes and voices from the cafeteria. Otto felt a hand on the small of his back, felt self-conscious about the sweat-wetness of his shirt.

I just don't want you to get hurt, said Otto.

A person can get hurt anywhere, said Owen. He leaned in just a little, just a little bit closer. I missed you, Otto, he said, I really missed you.

Okay, okay, said Otto. He inhaled and took a step backward, away. Exhaled. Sure. I missed you too, Owen. Sure I did. Now let's go see if there's any food left, okay?

Okay, said Owen, letting his hand drop, away.

. . . *So now Gérald and me are sharing our room again. We've got ___ new recruits who have been assigned to slip their roll-mats in the bits of space between ours. They seem nice enough. One, Patrice, speaks pretty well no English, so he and Gérald get along, and the other is a relaxed, good-natured West-coast boy called Adrian. He says some of the new kids were really wound up on the way over, getting excited to get over getting scared, and just getting excited just to get excited.*

And, of course, we were excited to have them arrive, too. I was. It's good to have distractions, and it's good to have their new hope.

Because I also have this awful idea, which I know isn't true, which I know is ridiculous. I have this idea that all these boys who have come to fill the places of the ones we've lost will fill their places exactly and be shot through or stabbed in the dark or blown up just like the last ones, exactly like them, one to one, and then new boys will be sent to replace them, and they'll be shot through or stabbed in the dark or blown up, exactly the same, and then more new ones, again and again. And we, the others, will just watch and know and not know what to say or do. Whether we should warn them or just let them enjoy the last bits of their tiny lives. And I don't know who it's worse for, them or us.

I know it's not real. But sometimes, when I'm so far away, that doesn't mean much.

Take care of yourself, and, if you see them, of Russell and of Harriet and Josie and Ellie and Benji and mother and dad and of yourself.

Here,
Otto.

Etta and Russell would go dancing every night now. They had asked around and made a list of all the events in all the villages and towns in the district. They rode on Russell's horses or in Etta's father's car. Despite his bad leg, Russell danced pretty well, just in half-time to everyone else. Etta didn't mind, it gave her more time to do turns. They started to recognize all the musicians, and tipped hats to each other walking in or out. Most of them were old men or farm girls. Everyone was exhausted from farm or factory work, circles under their eyes, calluses on their hands, but they still put on good shoes and pressed clothes and played and played and played and danced and danced and danced.

17

They had just crossed into New Brunswick, the air getting thicker, heavier with salt in the tiniest increments, only barely enough to notice, when Bryony said:

I have a brother.

Just that. They had been walking in relative silence, broken only by the brush of their legs against the tall wild grass, which left all-day-dew marks in affectionate stripes on their legs.

That's something, said Etta. That's a story.

No, said Bryony, it's just a person, not a story.

Well, it's something, said Etta. What else about him?

. . . well, he liked stars. Still does, I bet. Astronomy.

Is he an astronomer?

No, just likes them.

Okay. There was once a woman who had a brother who was in love with the stars. That's a story, isn't it?

Maybe. Not a terribly good one. And not really mine.

Well, what are you in love with?

The sea, I guess.

Even though you've never been there?

He's never been to the stars. Though he wanted to, when he was little. To be an astronaut.

What about you, what did you want to be?

I wanted to be him.

Not a journalist?

That came later.

And, where is he now?

Her Majesty's of St. John's Penitentiary. The one right on the coast.

There were approaching the district of Ciquart. Etta could just make out the banners and signs held out and above the small crowd waiting for them. They chanted, ET-TA! ET-TA! GO! GO! GO!

Oh, I, said Etta.

Don't, said Bryony. Don't worry about it. . . . Do you have any brothers? Or sisters?

Fourteen, said Etta. Eight brothers and six sisters.

The crowd was moving to meet them. Soon cameras were flashing and people were shouting and crying and giving Etta and Bryony bigger things, like a bag of dried apricots and bottles of homemade beer and an angel-food cake, as well as smaller things, like a stalk of dried lavender and half a melted tea-light and a silver baby spoon with the handle bent back on itself, and then, soon enough, Etta and Bryony were through to the other side of the hamlet, and alone again. They spent the rest of the day walking in their something like silence.

Two nights later, sometime around two in the morning from the feel of her body and the look of the sky, Bryony woke up. They were camped under a patch of white and yellow birch trees. She took stock: she didn't need to pee, she wasn't thirsty or uncomfortable or cold or hot, her blazer was still in place over her as a blanket, and there didn't seem to be any animal or insect on or near her. But she was awake. For some reason. Etta? she half-whispered, turning onto her side to face Etta's spot, two trees away.

Etta's eyes were open, staring open at her, past her. Oh, she was saying. Oh oh oh oh oh. Help me. Help me. Oh, oh. Oh! My ear. My ear! My ear my ear my ear. Oh god oh god. Oh oh oh.

Etta, what's wrong?

Oh god! Oh god oh god!

Etta! I'm here. It's Bryony, here, what—

I'm on fire! My head! Please!

Etta, please, I don't know—

On fire! Now Etta was on her back. Her arms and legs shook and flailed like she was drowning. Bryony couldn't get close. My ear! My ear! My ear! My god! My god! My god!

Okay, said Bryony, stay here. Just, stay here.

She opened one of their bags, the closest one, and threw out buttons, paper, pens, a ring, a plastic horse, a child's shoe, all onto the ground, until she came to a water bottle. She fumbled the cap off, then turned back to Etta, My ear my ear my ear my, and poured the water slowly, deliberately, onto Etta's right ear, letting it pool under her head. There, she said, there, there, there, pouring and pouring until Etta's breathing became regular and she stopped moving and yelling and just stared up, straight up.

He's dead, you know, said Etta.

Shhh, said Bryony.

He's dead.

Listen, I'll tell you a story.

I can barely hear you.

I'll speak clearly.

Okay, okay.

And then Bryony took a breath, and then she told a story:

Okay. Once upon a time there was a family. In suburban Ontario, where so many families were, or, are, I guess, but this family
was special, maybe just because it's the one we're going to talk about,
but, well, that's something. There was a mother and a father and a son
and then, just a couple years later, a daughter too. And the son would
spend evenings, before bedtime, out in the yard with his mother and
the telescope, and the mother would point the telescope at just the
right place, somehow she knew, just the right space, and tell her son
to look and he would look, closing one eye and pressing the other one
up to the lens, seeing things so far away he could only understand if
he thought in numbers and not in thoughts. So the mother pointed
and the son looked and the daughter watched them through the window, night after night.

And I watched them and wanted to be with them and wanted
to know what he was seeing, night after night, until one day when
everyone was doing something else, distracted enough that I was able
to wander unnoticed to the backyard and pull up a green plastic lawn
chair and climb up onto it and stare into the eyepiece of the telescope.
All I could see was a vast blur of blue. Oh, I thought. The Sea. Of
course.

Two years later the mother died, long and slow and dripping, her
body slowly eating itself in the way the bodies sometimes, often, do.
And we just watched, because that was all we could do. We were not
doctors and the doctors themselves couldn't do anything. They sat
beside us in hospital rooms and we all watched together.

A couple of weeks after she died I asked my brother to show me
how to use the telescope, to point it for me, but he wouldn't. He was

nice about it. Just said, No, Bryony, I can't, even though I still saw him looking through it, late at night.

The father was good and kind and raised his kids well despite being alone and everyone grew up together relatively happily, the son thinking the constellation-straight thoughts of numbers, the daughter thinking the wet-heavy thoughts of the sea.

When he was eighteen the brother moved away to go to university. Engineering in the East. I missed him like crazy. I was still in school, still young and at home. His absence throbbed for the first few weeks like starving, then less, then less, then life pushed on and I continued as an only child to an only parent.

He didn't come home at Christmas, so I wrote him a card. Do people really become astronauts, still? I asked him, inside. Isn't that era kind of over?

His reply came three weeks later, at the end of the holidays. Yes, it said. People still do.

Back at school that January, I was talking to an older girl between Career-and-Life Management and Sports. She was barely a friend, Bette Robbins with the fuzzy blond hair. I told her that Christmas had been all right, but not great because my brother hadn't come home.

Of course not, she said. They wouldn't just let him out.

Of course they would. Reuben's sister came home from the University of Alberta.

They wouldn't let him, Bryony, because your brother's not in university, he's in jail.

No, he's at university.

Jail.

University.

Jail.

*   *   *

The girl waited a week and then asked her father. And her father said, I'm sorry, Bryony, I'm sorry. . . . And then he said, They have classes there, for them. He can take classes in there. Engineering. And he said, I'm sorry, I'm sorry, I'm sorry, I'm, I should, I should have—

And the girl said, No, Dad, it's okay. No, no.

And that's all they ever said about it. Not why. Not for how long.

So I waited and waited and waited and eventually my father died too and all was quiet, nothing but quiet from the East, and eventually I was an adult and got an adult job and met you, walking east, to the water, and you said, I have a sister, and, You can come too. I can't, thought the woman, even though she had a far-away sibling too, so far away, I just can't, she thought, until one night she looked up at the sky and the stars she still didn't know the names of, one night, not long ago, not long at all, and realized, yes. Yes I can. Of course I can. Of course I have to. I will. It wasn't a big discovery. It was terribly, wonderfully, small. And, and here I am, Etta. And here we are.

Etta was asleep. Bryony pulled her coat back up over her, then lay down beside her. She stared up through the birch leaves, counting the stars and stars and stars until, finally, she fell asleep too.

When she woke the next morning, late, after the sun was already full, Etta was up, sat on the long body of a fallen tree. She had her hands over her face and was crying into them.

Hello, said Bryony. Good morning.

Etta didn't look up, just kept weeping.

Is it your ear? asked Bryony. Is it still bad?

It's my fault, said Etta. She spoke through her hands, through her sobs, in wet, shallow breaths. He was following me.

Who was?

Owen, said Etta. The skin around her ear was red and white in splotches; she kept scratching at it.

Are you sure, Etta? said Bryony. Are you sure it was *you*?

I am sure, said Etta. She was heaving a little, shaking, from the exertion of the crying, her skin all transparent brown-blue in the daylight. She looked, for the first time, as old as she was.

Absolutely? said Bryony.

Absolutely, said Etta.

Okay, said Bryony. But, we still have to eat. She opened one of her bags and took out a packet of crackers and the apricots. Here, she said, as she handed them one at a time, one cracker, one apricot, one cracker, one apricot, to Etta. Here, here, here, here, here. Then she took the second water bottle, the one she hadn't emptied last night, unscrewed the cap, and passed it to Etta. Here. Etta drank and drank.

Now, said Bryony, we have to walk.

Without the others? said Etta.

Without the others.

They walked west, backtracking. Bryony led, and Etta followed a few steps behind. They made it to Grand Falls Hospital And Care Home a few hours before sunset.

Bryony sat Etta down in one of the lobby chairs and approached the welcome desk.

Hello, said the reception nurse. He was enormous, maybe seven feet tall. Dark skin and hair. Can I help you?

She's lost herself, said Bryony.

The nurse nodded. Are you next-of-kin? he said.

No, said Bryony. I'm sorry.

The nurse slid a form across the desk toward her, leaving his hand on it longer than he needed to. A comfort.

I really am sorry, said Bryony. I really, really am.

I know, said the nurse.

Those are her things, said Bryony, to be kept with her. She motioned toward the little pile at Etta's feet. A worn bag, a coat, and

A gun? said the nurse.

No bullets, and rusted through inside and out. Just a toy.

Okay, said the nurse, that's fine. I'll be sure it all stays with her.

Once all the forms were filled in, they walked with Etta to a small room in the middle of a hall of similar rooms. Etta sat down on the bed. Bryony sat beside her. The nurse stood back, just inside the door. I'm going on to St. John's now, Etta, said Bryony.

To the jail, said Etta.

Yes, said Bryony.

Okay, said Etta.

I'll come back here afterward, on my way home, said Bryony. She looked at Etta, then at the nurse. They both nodded.

Good luck with your brother, said Etta. I'm sure he is sorry. I'm sure he is.

Thank you, said Bryony.

Goodbye, said Etta.

Goodbye, said Bryony.

After Bryony left, the nurse walked Etta back halfway down the hall to a door that was a slightly darker green than all the others. The showers and toilets, he said. Let's get you proper clean. Are you okay to undress yourself? Deal with the water?

I'll be fine, said Etta.

The taps are all safety, he continued, you can't get burned. And the towels are folded in a pile in the cupboard by the sinks.

I'll be fine, said Etta.

Good, good. I know it. Just making sure. I'll wait out here till you're done. I'll walk you back to your room after.

I think I can—

Of course, I know. I just like the company.

As she pushed open the door into the washroom, Etta remembered, turned back to the nurse. Do you know if Gérald is here too? If he's okay?

He's fine. He's gone home.

You're sure? The boy with the accent? The torn-up trousers?

I'm sure.

Okay. Be kind to him. He seems hard and mean but really he's just scared, he's really scared.

Okay. I will, we will. And, for now, I'll wait here. Right here.

Okay, right here.

That night Etta slept and slept. Her legs and her feet and her hips all so tired, all at once. She slept through midnight, when the nurse came to check on her, through morning, when another nurse, Sheila, with five grown daughters of her own, came by with tea and eggs and juice and toast, leaving them on the table by the bed, through afternoon, when Sheila looked in again with more tea, through to night again. It was dark when Otto woke. He stretched his legs and toes under the sheets. There was just a bit of light in a thin strip from under the door and a bit of light in pale tones from through the window's curtains. He looked around the room until her eyes adapted, then got up and stretched his legs and toes again, feeling strong, alive. He made his way to the door and out into the hall to find the bathroom. Three doors down, dark green door. Although it was fully lit, there was no one else in the hallway. All quiet.

In the bright light of the single bathroom stall, Otto took stock. He was wearing a half-fabric-half-paper gown, in the same light green as the door to his room, the same light green as the regiment's trucks. So they know who I am, thought Otto. There was a bandage on his ear. He touched it lightly, still painful. He ran a hand through his hair and came away with a few loose strands, bright white.

When he went to use the toilet, Otto found he was wearing a diaper. He took it off and put it in the bin by the cistern, emptied his bowels and bladder, flushed, washed his hands, and headed back to his room.

Once there, he sat on the bed, awake, up. He wasn't tired at all. He listened to the rhythmic rustle of his paper gown moving with his breath, to the click of a clock, to the rise and fall of the wind outside, like singing. Except it was too long and regular and thick to be wind. Too solid. Otto went to the window, opened it as far as it would open, three inches, and listened again. Familiar, nostalgic. He carefully felt his way around his ear's bandage until he found the end, then unwrapped it around and around until he felt the air and sound on it, twice as loud, starting low, then rising up, then falling down again. Coyotes, said Otto, to the room, the clock, the wind. Like home. He pulled the room's one armchair across and around so it was facing the window, sat down in it, and listened.

At midnight the first nurse knocked gently on the door, then opened it a crack. Midnight check-in, he whispered. Then, noting the empty bed, Etta, you're up?

Yes, but I'm fine, said Otto.

You moved your chair.

Yes, but it wasn't heavy.

Okay. Call me next time. To help.

Okay, said Otto, as the nurse closed the door and left him alone again.

Otto was still in his yard, still beside the raccoon and the trout, when his neighbors, the ones with the girl with the guinea pigs, pulled out of the slow parading line of vehicles along the lane and down onto Otto's front drive. Otto recognized the car, dark blue, large and practical. It pulled all the way up to where he was sitting, carefully negotiating the sculptures. The back door opened first and the little girl jumped out. HelloMisterVogel! she said, then ran past to the raccoon, stroked it once down to the end of its tail, then cut back across to the wolf, petted it cautiously between the ears, then away toward the grouse, and so on. She was with the gophers before her parents were out of the front doors of their car. Afternoon, Otto, said the girl's father.

Afternoon, said Otto.

Afternoon, Otto, said the mother.

Afternoon, said Otto.

Guinea pig treating you well?

Yes, quite well. She mostly sleeps and licks.

Yeah, said the father.

Tell me about it, said the mother.

Doesn't look like Russell's back yet, hey? said the father.

No, said Otto. He's not. He's way up north.

I see, said the father.

In any case, said the mother, I've brought you something. She reached back into the car, into the backseat. They're fairly wilted now, but, well, I thought you might still want them anyway. She brought out a coffee tin with three sad-looking flax flowers, half-petaled, in it. I saw your sign, she said. Behind them her daughter ran from the golden eagle to the foxes to the red squirrel.

Oh, said Otto. Yes. Yes, thank you.

Not much, but all I could find on our land.

She looked all afternoon, added the father.

I'm sorry there's not more, said the mother.

No, no, these are great, said Otto. Thank you. Really. He eyed the flowers, counting the petals in his head. They shuddered limply in the wind. Hold on, thought Otto, just a tiny bit longer, please. Well, he said out loud, I'd love to have you in for coffee, but—

No, no, said the father. Thanks, but I'm afraid we've got to run off. We've got swimming lessons in town. He turned away from Otto, toward his daughter, who was now dodging between grasshoppers. KASIA! he shouted. Swimming! She ignored him. Three steps, touch-a-hopper, three steps, touch-a-hopper. Her father shrugged and tramped off toward her.

Once he was gone, the mother took a step closer to Otto, coffee tin in her hand, and said, You all right, Otto?

Some trouble with sleep, said Otto. And with being very old.

I could make the paste for you, if you want, drop it off after dinner.

No, said Otto. I like doing it. It's fine, I'm fine.

Otto, you haven't moved since we got here, this whole time.

No?

No. Tell me, can you stand up?

Now?

Yes, now.

Otto hesitated. No, he said. I can't. Not right now.

Okay, said the mother, I'm going to help you. We'll make it look natural, just walking and talking.

No, it's fine, said Otto. You really don't . . .

Yes I do, said the mother.

She wasn't a large woman, but she was strong. Solid legs, arms, core. From swimming, she said. She put an arm across Otto's back, her fingers reaching around just below the armpit, rocked his weight back onto her, and lifted. He came up quickly, easily, like an empty jar she expected to be full.

Can you walk? she asked.

I don't know, said Otto.

Okay, let's just try then. She took one step forward with her right leg and Otto followed. Right, okay, good. Then left, okay, good. Then right. Then left.

I'm just tired, said Otto.

Left, said the mother, and right.

Kasia, having now tagged every animal, came bounding back toward them just as they reached the front door.

Where are you going? she asked.

To see Otto's guinea pig, said the mother. He was going to show it to me.

Great! said Kasia. I LOVE guinea pigs!

Her father followed a few steps behind. He caught his wife's eyes over their daughter's head. Should I wait in the car? he said.

No, no, it's fine, really, said Otto. Everyone can come and meet her.

Do you have any kids too? Any toys? asked Kasia.

No, said Otto. Sorry. Just the one guinea pig.

Well, that's sad but okay I guess, said Kasia. For now.

They gathered around Oats's orange crate. She was sleeping. They do that a lot, said Kasia. Mine too. Don't worry. She put her hand into the crate and patted papier-mâché Oats. I like this one, she said.

Before they left, the mother put the coffee tin of flowers on the counter, just behind where Otto was leaning. Can you lift your legs on your own? she whispered.

Yes, whispered Otto.

Show me.

He lifted his left leg. Three inches off the floor, maybe four.

Okay, whispered the mother. Okay?

Yes, whispered Otto, okay.

After they left, Otto got a pen and paper, and, still standing up in case sitting meant sitting forever, wrote:

Dear Etta,

We have good days and bad days. You told me, once, to just remember to breathe. As long as you can do that, you're doing something Good, you said. Getting rid of the old, and letting in the new. And, therefore, moving forward. Making progress. That's all you have to do to move forward, sometimes, you said, just breathe. So don't worry, Etta, if nothing else, I am still breathing.

You must be almost there, must be close. I hope you are. I hope you're seeing everything.

I am just writing to tell you: I am here, don't worry. I am here, breathing, waiting.

Otto.

Then he made the flax paste, spread it on his eyes, and slept and slept.

Russell stood on a round, flat rock. It was the tallest thing for miles and covered in orange and green and gray lichen. The woman beside him was tiny with wrinkles like fireworks around her eyes. She wore a skin and fur coat that blended into her own white hair. She had her hand on his shoulder. THE HERD SHOULD COME FROM OVER THERE TODAY, she shouted. The wind was so loud Russell could barely hear her. SOMETIME IN THE NEXT SIX HOURS, I BET. They both sat down on the rock, careful not to scrape the lichen. YOU HAVE NO WIFE? she shouted.

NO, shouted Russell.

YOU'RE HAPPIER ALONE, LIKE ME, MAYBE, she shouted.

YES, shouted Russell. YES, MAYBE.

They stayed in the village with the new recruits for almost a week, and then, for no reason that anyone would tell them, Otto and Gérald and everyone else were woken at four in the morning on the Sunday, still foggy out, still cool, to hastily dress and pee and pack their things, and start marching west.

Owen caught up to Otto in the line. Do you know where we're going?

You're not allowed to break the line like that, you'll get smacked or made to take the back, said Gérald, from beside Otto.

It's okay. I know. Do you know? Where we're going? Why?

No idea, Owen.

Aucune idée, said Gérald.

Does this happen a lot? All normal, then all of a sudden, no warning, up and go?

Sometimes, said Otto.

Look, said Gérald, this is not bad. This is better than leaving because they're peeling away your watchmen and city guards. Or breaking into sleep rooms at night and slitting throats. This is a nice morning stretch.

Oh, said Owen. Does that . . .

But that's still not so bad, still better than when we're the ones sneaking in. Better than standing at a window, watching the Adam's apples of two strangers go up and down in sleep, knowing they'll have the chance for six, maybe seven more breaths before your knife slides right through them, so they don't have the time or means to cry out, just only barely time to open their eyes to see you, to feel their own heartbeats swell and die in their necks—

Jesus, Gérald, said Otto. Turning to Owen, We don't, it's not so—

It's okay, said Owen.

And, said Otto. Even if we do . . . Then he stopped, sighed.

Look, said Gérald, it's just like chess. Sometimes it's our turn to be moved, either aggressively or defensively. Sometimes we're not moved for ages. Sometimes we're moved back to a place we've just been. It all seems random from here, but from above, for those who can see the whole board, it probably makes sense. There very well could be a strategy, a plan. The thing to know, *mon petit* Anglo, is whether you're a queen or a pawn.

Owen looked to Otto, said, A queen or a . . .

I don't know chess, said Otto.

They marched on in silence. Owen stayed with them.

After another thirty-six steps, he was spotted as out of place, and made to take up the back of the line.

It won't be for long, said Otto. I'm sure we must be just about there.

After Owen left, Gérald said, Just about where? Do you have any idea where we are?

No, said Otto. But we must be just about somewhere.

He's a funny one, you know, said Gérald. I wouldn't spend too much time too close to him.

I know, said Otto. Don't worry. I know.

They walked until dark, and then through it for some hours until given the call to stop and camp up. A low, dull fire was made in a covered spot, unseeable from every angle except straight on, and food was warmed and distributed. Everyone was exhausted, but no one was ready to sleep; they sat around the fire in spiraling layers, as close to it as each could get, talking lowly in twos and threes about nothing, because they'd been together through night and dark and everything in-between for so long that the only thing left to talk about was nothing. And then, sometime between dinner and sleep, from somewhere between two boys arguing over nothing and three boys comparing stories of nothing, Owen started to sing,

Though April showers may come your way
They bring the flowers that bloom in May

So if it's raining, have no regrets,
Because it isn't raining rain you know
It's raining violets.

And where you see clouds upon the hills,
You soon will see crowds of daffodils,

So keep on looking for a blue bird
And listening for his song,
Whenever April showers come along.

So just keep looking for that blue bird
And listening for his song,
Whenever April showers come along.

Light, rich tenor. Just like in Etta's schoolhouse. He was looking right at Otto. Otto fell away from his conversation.

And eventually everyone stopped talking and listened, some of them joining in, some in harmony and some barely finding the melody, and some just sitting silent, watching the music like a film.

The next morning as they packed up the song went round in Otto's head. And around while they started marching, and around as they continued on through the hot dry fields of tall grasses and tiny orchids, as they stopped and camped out for a second night, no fires or noise allowed this time, straight to bed after a silent meal, so that the sound of the song in his head mixed with the sound of the sea, just on the other side of the bluff they were tucked in behind. They were back at the water; the unseen feel of it rocked Otto to sleep like a lullaby.

The morning came before morning. It came with light that wasn't the sun and speed and noise and a hand through Otto's tent, down on the canvas, falling into him, pinning the wall down in a hand-shape so that he had to roll out of the way and spring up against it, pushing the deadweight away from him, and out into the bright non-sun light and non-morning noise, struggling his boots on and following the wave of everyone up over the bluff and down toward the sea, where, before the water, there was a sea of men, everywhere everywhere swirling, pouring in so the line between sea and land was blurred, was gone, was only bodies, and because everyone was shouting, Otto was shouting and up to his ankles, his knees, his hips in the water, get in! get in! get in! and get them out! someone is yelling everyone is yelling, in! and out! and boats and boys and men and boys, breathing in the water, spitting out the water, and everything loud and so much color, but darkened and getting darker and you better get down get right down, down, deeper, deeper, deeper and the water warmer than he'd expect, rhythmic, and, in his head, the song still going around and around, and the water's still black because it's still just sunrise just before and half the shouts and half the bodies and half the uniforms are familiar, are what he's been taught to know and the other half are the other ones he's been taught to recognize but for different reasons and both are shooting and screaming all are shooting and screaming and something or someone is exploding in the water, how can things explode in the water? And a stab of noise of light of steel in the side of his head in the right-hand side his ear in his ear and then something against his stomach like a fist but bigger, heavier, a body thrust into his, upside down in the water, he has one hand on his head, his ear, is squinting to see through the light that is everywhere just everywhere, and uses the other hand to reach down, to flip the body around and the cheeks puff out and cough out water and it's Owen, Owen from home, and he's just tiny, and he coughs again and water rushes into his open mouth and maybe he's bleeding from the chest, just below the chest, the very center of him, and Otto drops his hand from his head and uses both arms to lift and pull lift and pull Owen out of the water away try to get away somewhere quiet and dark shouts help please! Please! And his shouting is like harmony to all the other shouting, everyone is shouting, even those who weren't singing, who were just watching, before, have now joined and everyone is shouting and it rises up together and fills Otto's good ear and the air and fills everything.

Owen is dead before Otto can put him down. There is no quiet place to put him. No clean place no quiet place. He puts him on the beach, beside the others. His eyes are open. Otto knows he's supposed to close them, but he can't. He leaves the eyes open. It's my fault, he says.

And, even though Owen is dead, he says, *It isn't.*

And Otto says, It is.

And Owen says, *Maybe.*

And then Otto's ear flashes white through his head and down his whole body and he wants to kiss Owen but he doesn't and instead he runs, runs back up the bluff, back over to where he had camped, past there, away and away and away.

Otto ran for forty minutes; seven thousand and two hundred steps. He ran until he found a British Armed Forces truck, parked off the side of an empty road. He jump-started it, just like so many tractors, threshers, trucks, before, and drove inland until the next big town, where he got out, found the darkest room he could, and, even though the sun was barely up, ordered rye whiskey, and even though the sun was barely up, they gave it to him. Otto stayed there all day. Sometime around sunset Gisèlle came in. She wrapped her arms around his neck and he ran his hand up her legs, no nylons, just a painted-on line, up the painted-on line, and she smiled and said, Yes? and led him away, down the street, around the corner, and up to her room. Otto ripped at her clothes like they were the burning in his ear. Tore into her like she was the blood-dark water.

Later, as he slept, Gisèlle bandaged Otto's ear, wrapping clean white cotton around and around and around.

He spent the next weeks between those two rooms, the bar and Gisèlle's. He realized, briefly, sometime around Saturday, that he couldn't go back. He'd heard stories, crouched around the radio with Russell, of soldiers like him shot unceremoniously in flowered fields. So, it was the bar and Gisèlle's, back and forth, simple, easy.

It was in the bar, sometime around the middle of a week, sometime early evening, when the most beautiful woman Otto had ever seen walked in. Her nylons were real. She smiled at the bartender, familiar, recognized, and sat at a table near the back of the room, alone. Otto, at the bar, finished his drink, pushed the glass away from him, and went to her.

My god, he said. Winnie.

Hi, Otto, said Winnie. She stood to embrace him, he didn't even lift his arms to her, heavy, hanging, like a child, his head on her shoulder. You smell terrible, she said.

I know, he said. You smell wonderful.

I know, she said.

They sat across from each other, she with red wine, he with nothing. They think you're dead, she said. In the ocean somewhere.

I might as well be.

That's crap. And you know it. Don't be an idiot, Otto.

They think you might be dead too.

It's not the same.

Have they sent a letter? To Mom?

Not yet. There's backlog.

How did you know I wasn't? Dead?

It's my job to know things. I asked around.

Do you know Gisèlle?

Of course. It's her job too.

Oh. And, and you're okay?

I'm fantastic, Otto. I am so much better than I thought I could be. You're the not-okay one.

They worry, at home, about you. A lot.

They shouldn't. You can tell them that. But nothing else. Anyway, it's you that needs worrying about. Gisèlle will need to move on soon. She's got a backlog of cases, should never have spent this long on you. . . . Then where will you sleep?

She didn't say she was going.

She doesn't say a lot of things. Look, I think I can make it okay for you, okay for you to go back without problems.

I don't think I can.

You can.

I don't know.

You can. It won't have to be for long.

Okay.

Okay?

Okay. Thank you, Winnie.

She reached under the table to Otto's hand and squeezed it. Geez, Otto, she said. Of course.

That night, Otto took a pen from Gisèlle's bedside table, and some bar napkins from his pocket, and wrote:

My Dear Etta,

He wrote the marching, he wrote the singing, he wrote the camping, the morning, the water, he wrote the boats, the crowds, the water, the ear, the water, Owen, the water, the water, the water.

Tan-lines of factory grit between her ankles and socks, wrists and hands. Through the window she could see Russell, on his horse, making his way down the track. Early.

He waited, on his horse, in the yard, while Etta finished getting ready. Putting away dinner dishes, pinning her hair back, tying up boots. Are you sure you don't want to come in? she called out the open front door. Wait with some coffee?

No thanks, said Russell.

He never came in. He always came early.

Etta had two dresses for dancing, one green and one blue. Tonight she wore the darker one, the green. The pleated skirt flared and fell as she boosted herself up onto Russell's horse. A small, sudden pain in her lower stomach as she landed. You okay? said Russell.

Etta breathed into it. Fine, she said. Let's go.

After the dance, Etta and Russell walked back to where they had tied the horse. It was just past eleven. Russell carried his hat in his hands. Everyone else had gone other ways, either back into town, or to the lot where the trucks and other horses were all parked. Russell was afraid that someone might mistake his horse for theirs, so they always tied up somewhere else, somewhere away.

Usually it was Russell who set the pace on these walks to and from the dances, for whom Etta would wait, but tonight she could barely keep up with him. She took two steps, stopped, breathed, took two steps, stopped, breathed. Etta, said Russell, really, are you okay?

I don't know, said Etta.

They were walking along the backs of houses, all dark. Fields on the other side. Etta stopped, crouched down, put both hands flat against the ground for support. Breath. Breath.

Okay, said Russell. Okay, okay. Okay. I'll go get the horse. You stay right here. As fast as I can. Okay.

Etta breathed and breathed and nodded okay.

Her eyes were closed. She listened until Russell's footsteps were ten seconds out of hearing, then used her hands to push up off the ground, and walk, two steps breath, two steps breath, to a hedge growing up along the back fence of one of the dark houses. She pulled aside the stiff, dry branches and slid in behind it, her skirt catching in worried bunches. Once she was in, all the way hidden, she crouched down again, hands on the cool, almost damp, ground. Every bit of her from her chest to her thighs was pulsing, and squeezing, pulling her in. She curled down into a ball, laid her head on the ground. There was just enough space between the plant's dense base and the fence. The soil against her temple felt perfect cold and soft and unmoving. She counted the weeks, one, two, three, four, five, six, seven, almost eight. Almost eight weeks. Fifty-five days. She counted them up and down and up and down. With each one she mentally folded and put away one of the names she had allowed herself, quietly, one week at a time, to consider, like bright, colorful things gone dark. Fold and away. Fold and away. Her body pulsed and the spot beneath her was wet.

She heard Russell get back a few minutes later, heard the scramble of the horse as he jumped off. Etta? Etta? Heard the creak of his knee as he bent down, looking for her boot steps. Heard the horse sniff and wander. Heard the branches crack and pull again. His sharp intake of breath.

Calm down, Russell, it's all right. I'm not dead. As Etta spoke little bits of soil stuck to the dampness of her lips. I've got a stomach-ache, and need to lie down is all.

On the other side of the hedge was the sound of the horse happily eating the crops in the field.

Right. Okay. Do you want to stay here or go home?

Let's stay here for a little while.

Okay.

Russell backed out of the hedge and stood on the other side, with the horse, for thirty-six minutes. He patted the horse down with his hands, running over all her back and sides until she was completely smooth and clean. It's okay, it's okay, he whispered to her as he went. After thirty-six minutes, Etta uncurled herself and said, through the branches, We can go home now.

You're sure? said Russell. He didn't look down to her skirt, her legs.

I'm sure. I'm just fine, now. Back to normal.

At home, after Russell had dropped her off and ridden away, Etta undressed and threw everything into the sink. Her underwear, her dress, her stockings, everything. All turned red and red and red. Impossible to scrub out. After they had dried, still red, she bunched them together into a steel bucket out in the field behind her house, where, along with a letter to Otto, written but not sent, she burned them all, watching as the sides of the bucket, and then everything else, turned ashy black.

The next day there was a letter from Otto.

My Dear Etta,

it said, full of rectangular holes, neat as windows.

Then, because of all the holes, it said nothing at all.

They didn't dance for two weeks.

On the fifteenth night, Russell rode to Etta's. He swung his bad leg around and down and lowered himself off his horse, tied it to a tree by the schoolhouse, and called through Etta's open front door, Etta, it's me. I want to come in this time. Etta came to the door, still in coveralls, with Otto's letter in her pocket.

The thing is, he said, Otto's not here, and I am. And I will be here tomorrow and the day after and the day after and the day after that. Right here.

Etta stepped outside and closed the door after her. She held out a hand. Here, she said. Her left hand. Russell took it in his right. You can't come in, said Etta, but we can stay here, on the steps.

So they stood on the steps and he held her hand and when they got tired they sat on the steps, and he held her hand. And he held it hard so that Etta could feel the blood throbbing through each finger, down across her palm and up her wrist, but she said nothing. It should hurt, she told herself. It should.

When Russell left, Etta had to use her other hand to pull her fingers out of their held position.

All the next day at the factory she would catch them curling back, and would have to pull them straight again and again.

She wrote back,

Otto,

It is harder, now. I wait and I work and I wait and I work and I work and I work and I wait and I wait and I wait and I wait and I wait.

The next night Russell was there again, early. Are you sure, he called, from ten meters away, on his horse, in the yard, that you want to dance? That you're okay to?

Yes, Etta called back, I am absolutely sure.

They danced in a new way. Before, even though Etta was always tired, she kept her head up, looking over Russell's shoulder, but this time, tonight, she let it fall, let it rest down in the warm place where his neck and shoulder met, where she could feel his heartbeat through her cheek.

They left the dance early. In the mustard field between the parking lot and their horse, they stopped walking and Etta kissed Russell's mouth and Russell kissed Etta's neck and Etta used one hand to find the zipper on her last, blue, dancing dress while the other hand worked down through a handkerchief in her pocket to the smooth fish skull inside it, saying oh, oh, oh, as it met her warm skin.

Etta got off the bus and walked up the drive toward her house. She was smiling. Russell would be there in half an hour.

The official letter, a familiar muted uniform green, was on her doorstep, held down from the wind by a small pile of pebbles. She almost stepped on it.

She didn't pick it up. She sat next to it on the step, almost touching but not. She stopped smiling. She closed her eyes.

She was still like that when Russell arrived, twenty-six minutes later. He got off his horse, tied it to a tree, the one all the students' dogs used to congregate around, and walked toward her, first eagerly, then, noticing the letter, more and more slowly. You haven't opened it, he said.

I'm not his wife, said Etta. Or his family. They shouldn't have sent it to me. It must be a mistake.

Russell sat down next to her, on the far side of the letter. He left his hand open and close so she could take it if she wanted, but she didn't take it. I still want to go dancing tonight, she said. If you do.

Yes, said Russell.

Will you pick it up and take it inside and put it on my table so it doesn't blow away?

Russell reached over Etta and pushed the pile of pebbles down the steps. He picked up the truck-green letter and rocked crookedly up the remaining step and into the house. Before he put the envelope on Etta's table he held it up to his chest, crushing a palm-shaped indent over the center where the name and address was written. He felt his heart beat through it. Thick and fast and horrible.

When he got back he said, Do you want to change your clothes?

No, said Etta.

Are you hungry?

No, said Etta. She took his hand. Let's go, she said.

Everything at the Kenaston school gymnasium dance hall was familiar. Every person and every song and every step. Etta and Russell danced to every single number, and only danced with each other. The clarinet and trumpet and piano and drums and fiddle and their footsteps on the dance floor; Etta opened her ears and closed her eyes so she heard nothing else.

*   *   *

At the house, after, Russell waited on his horse in the yard. I'll stay here, he said. You can come and get me or not.

Etta closed the front door after her. Through the window she could see Russell's horse eating dandelions. She sat at the table and slid her finger under the paper-glue seal, breathed the smell of it. The paper inside was folded in perfect thirds.

18

Through the window of a care home five hundred and ninety-nine kilometers from the harbor of Halifax, three thousand, three hundred and seventy-nine kilometers from Davidsdottir, Saskatchewan, a coyote howled and Otto listened. He listened and waited as the howling got louder and closer. Listened and watched until he could make out the texture of rough fur, and then the silhouette of a triangle face, and then the smell of wet warm breath. And then the coyote was right there, under his window.

Etta, said the coyote. *There you are.*

Who?

Check your pocket, said James. *The left pocket of your coat.*

Otto turned away from the window and looked over the room. There was a stack of folded clothes on a dresser against the far wall, near the door. He walked to it and ran his hand over the clothes one at a time, top to bottom, underwear, bra, tights, dress, sweater, coat. He pulled the coat out of the pile, careful to keep everything else in place, and felt through the left pocket. A coin, a ring, a piece of paper.

The paper, Etta, said James.

He took out the paper, unfolded it. There were dark-set stripes of dirt and wear along the creases. He brought it back to the window, where there was some light from the night to read it by.

Etta Gloria Kinnick of Deerdale farm. 83 years old in August, said James, at just the same time as Etta read it.

Family:

Marta Gloria Kinnick. Mother. Housewife. (Deceased)

Raymond Peter Kinnick. Father. Editor. (Deceased)

Alma Gabrielle Kinnick. Sister. Nun. (Deceased)

James Peter Kinnick. Nephew. Child. (Never lived)

Otto Vogel. Husband. Soldier/Farmer. (Living)

Russell Palmer. Friend. Farmer/Explorer. (Living)

Etta Gloria Kinnick, said Etta.

Etta, said James, *let's go.*

Etta pulled off her nightgown and put on her underwear, her bra, her tights, her dress, her sweater, her coat, and her running shoes. She found her bag and rifle and put them by the window. She made the bed and placed the folded paper-fabric nightgown at its foot. She reached into her right coat pocket, found a fish skull, and used the sharp end to cut a square in the window screen. She climbed out, then pulled her bag and rifle out after her.

We're not too far now, are we?

Two weeks, maybe. Not far at all.

Otto slept from six p.m. until eleven the next morning. After waking, still on his back in bed, he brought one hand to his heart. Slow, normal. I could just stay here, he thought. Just like this until she gets home. And then? And then I will get up and we will see to winterizing the garden together, or, I will move over and she can lie down too. He lay there for half an hour, then started coughing, which made his heart race, which made him need to pee and too hot for the covers, even just the sheet. He got up, put on his robe, and went to the washroom. Water on his face to wash off the flax powder. He used a wet hand to comb his hair, slicking it down, finding his part. He squinted at the mirror, blurring the details.

Then he went into the kitchen for coffee and found Kasia at his table, with Oats in her lap.

Hi, she said. She's really friendly.

She doesn't like to be awake in the day, said Otto.

I know, said Kasia, but I'm being really gentle. She's still sleeping, just on my lap.

Otto looked down at Oats, Oats looked up at Otto, her claws making little pulls in the cloth of Kasia's yellow corduroys.

Okay, said Otto. How did you get in?

I thought the door would be unlocked, so I tried and it was. Mom told me to bring you these and said you might be sleeping so I was just going to play with Oats until you woke up.

There was another coffee tin on the table, holding two more half-dead flowers.

Thank you, said Otto. That's really nice of her. I hope she didn't spend too long—

Don't worry, she loves the excuse to be out.

To be out?

That's what she says. She says, I love the excuse to be out. I do too.

Do you go with her, looking?

Oh, no, I mean here. And in your yard.

Of course. How long have you been here?

I don't know. I have a watch but it doesn't have batteries.

Long enough to be hungry?

Probably. What kind of food do you eat?

Mostly pickles, lately.

That sounds great.

Kasia held her pickle up to Oats, who pulled her eyes and nose in and away from the smell. Not hungry, said Kasia. She was careful not to drip too much vinegar onto the guinea pig's head as she ate. Hey, she said, between bites, you know what sculpture you should make next?

No, said Otto, what sculpture?

A child-sculpture, said Kasia. Like, a girl or boy. A kid.

Otto's heart flared again and set him coughing so his eyes watered and he had to sit down. Yeah? he said, after it had passed.

Yeah, said Kasia.

The morning after he'd met with Winnie, Gisèlle shook Otto awake. Her hair was up and back and she was wearing a Voluntary Aid Detachment nurse's uniform. If we're going to do this, she said, we have to do this now. No more sleeping. Her accent was gone.

Okay, said Otto, sitting up, standing up, pulling on his trousers and buttoning his shirt, okay, thank you.

Put your hand to your ear, like it's still ringing,

It is—

and your other arm around mine, like this, like I'm leading you. Good, yes, okay, let's go.

They walked out into the full morning light, light that Otto hadn't seen for weeks, down streets and up avenues until the people on the sidewalks and roads were no longer just old women and children, but men and boys, American, English, Australian, French, and Canadian, on crutches, with eye patches, missing arms or legs or noses, and, among them, a flurry of young women nurses, all dressed exactly like Gisèlle. Gisèlle led Otto deftly between them, looking straight ahead. They walked up to an old stone building. It looks like a church, said Otto.

It's not a church, said Gisèlle.

They walked up the steps and in the front door, Gisèlle nodding briskly at the matron manning the check-in desk before they continued across the lobby and through some swinging doors into a long hall. Room one-oh-six, said Gisèlle, on the left. They made a sharp turn into a room lined with beds, five on each side, divided by curtains. Boys, some awake, some asleep, were in all of them except the third one on the right. There you go, Private Vogel, said Gisèlle, leading Otto to it. Back to bed. Would you like help with your boots?

Oh, said Otto. No, I'll be fine. He unhooked his arm from hers and sat down on the bed, letting his other hand drop from his ear. It was tingling from being up for so long. I can manage.

Gisèlle unbuttoned his shirt as he undid his boots. Trousers too, she said, you know the drill.

The other soldiers, the ones who were awake, paid them no attention at all.

There you go, in you go, said Gisèlle, pulling back the cot's tight white sheets. She folded his trousers and shirt and placed them, with his boots, under the bed. Then Gisèlle leaned in low over the bed, her breath on Otto's cheek.

Goodbye, Otto, she said. You really were one of my favorites. Your chart is in the envelope at the end of the bed. There's a letter from Winnie in your boot. You really were.

She leaned in further and kissed him, silent and fast, on the side of the mouth. Really.

And then she straightened up, pulled the sheet up to his neck, and walked off, looking straight ahead.

Once she had gone, Otto waited, counted to a hundred and down again, then sat up and reached across his legs to the envelope that held his chart. It looked like all the others at the ends of all the other beds. Inside was his name, rank, unit, hometown, and condition: Severe Ruptured Eardrum and Psychological Shock/Trauma. It was date-stamped three weeks and two days ago. Otto slid it carefully back into its envelope and reached around to his boots. A small, folded bit of paper in the left one. It was an old train ticket, Saskatoon–Halifax. On the back it said, in black pen,

*It's sorted. You'll go home soon. Take care of yourself until then. Take
care of everyone else after. My love to Etta. It was good to see you, Otto.
Let's do it again, after all this.*

Otto refolded the ticket along the original lines and put it back in his
boot, then stretched out under the thin sheets, closed his eyes, and
went to sleep.

When he woke there was a doctor standing over him with a nurse
beside. Oh, right, said the doctor, he'll be the transfer. Send notice
Western Union, that's fastest. Out just as soon as all okay in the ear
and the head. Keep an eye on and let me know. He turned from the
nurse down to Otto. Hey, Vogel.

Yes? said Otto, unsure if he should sit up or not, what was polite.

Can you provide us an address for back home?

The Teacher's Cottage, Gopherlands School, Gopherlands, Saskatchewan, Canada, said Otto, without sitting up, without having to
think at all.

19

And Etta and James walked. East and south. The smell of salt, the feel of water in the wind.

And Otto cleaned out his bowls and spoons and made table space. He mixed flour and water. He tore the last of his newspapers into long, thin, strips.

And Russell drank dark coffee in an almost empty café where a man even older than him drew invisible lines on the plastic tablecloth with his finger: this road and then this road and then this road and then you'll get to the airport. Two flights a week.

Stand up, said the nurse.

Okay, said Otto. He pulled his legs free of the sheets, out of the bed, and stood up.

Good. Can you walk to the far wall and back?

I think so, said Otto. He walked to the far wall and back.

Good. Can you tell me your whole full name?

Otto Vogel.

No middle name?

Well, sometimes 7.

Seven?

Never mind. No middle name.

Good. Can you touch your toes?

I think so, said Otto. He reached out, bent at the waist, looked down toward his feet, and felt them rush up at him. His head snapped back, he fell onto the bed.

Okay, said the nurse. That's fine. Can you go to the window and tell me what you see?

I don't know, said Otto.

Try, said the nurse.

Otto walked to the nearest window, by the bed of a boy with both eyes bandaged. I see the sky, said Otto. Tops of trees, spires of churches.

And down below?

No, said Otto. I can't.

No? said the nurse.

No, said Otto.

Okay, said the nurse. That's fine. You can come back here. You can sit down if you want.

Thank you, said Otto.

The nurse sat on one side of him, his left, and whispered, Can you hear this?

Yes, whispered Otto.

Then she got up and sat on his other side, his right, and Otto felt the soft wind of her breath and heard nothing.

Okay, said the nurse, standing up again. That's just fine.

The next day both the doctor and nurse stood over his bed again. Hey, Vogel, said the doctor, have you got anything you need packed up? Any personal items apart from these clothes?

No, said Otto.

Okay, said the doctor, good.

The nurse walked Otto to the train station. Her arm over his just like Gisèlle's. If it gets too loud, she said, remember: She held her hand, the one that wasn't leading him, up to her ear and pressed, closing her eyes and frowning.

Yes, said Otto, thank you.

Before dropping him off she said, Has your hair always been that white?

Yes, said Otto.

Otto bought a sandwich and a coffee from the station café and took them to eat and drink outside, on the platform, where the wind from the trains made it cooler and easier to breathe. His train was due to arrive in thirty minutes, going west.

There was only one sheet of paper, and on it only three lines. It did not have any holes in it, not one. Etta ran her finger along the folds, flattening until they were barely visible. It said,

> *Pvt. Otto Vogel has been dispatched with injuries.*
> *He will be aboard the Canada-bound HMS Nova Scotia due September 14.*
> *He has requested you be informed of this.*

Etta walked to her kitchen window and pressed the letter up against the glass. Russell pulled the reins, steered his horse away from the dandelions and to the window. He read the three lines then looked up to Etta. Through the glass, his skin looked uneven, old.

Oh, he mouthed.

Yes, she mouthed back.

Oh thank god, he mouthed.

Yes, she mouthed back.

20

She could hear the brass band from a few miles out. Could make out the banners and bunting. *They're even more excited to see you than ever*, said James.

I'm going to go around, said Etta. I'll meet them on my way back.

She followed the outer edge of the peninsula, water on one side, the backs of houses on the other. From over the houses, she could hear the band playing "Make We Joy." It was out of time with the waves. Etta hummed along.

Halifax is pretty nice, said James.

Otto tested the little girl's hair to see if it was dry. It looks dry, said Kasia.

Yes, it is, said Otto. It's done.

They carried her carefully out the front door to the yard, Otto holding the shoulders, Kasia helping with the feet. Right here, I think, said Kasia. So it's the closest one to the house.

Okay, said Otto.

They positioned the statue right there, then sat down together on the front steps.

This is a great collection, said Kasia.

Thanks, said Otto.

Can I have it if you die?

Okay, said Otto.

The HMS *Nova Scotia* was a beautiful ship. Isn't it beautiful? said Otto to the soldier beside him in line, on crutches.

Looks like the rest, said the soldier.

Otto had trouble keeping his balance on deck, but spent most of his time out there nevertheless, clutching the rail. The wet cool air matted down his hair and condensed into heavy drops down his neck.

Etta ironed her blue dress and pinned her hair away from her face, leaving it to curl down to just above her shoulders. Because she didn't have any better shoes, she polished her boots until they looked almost new.

When they reached the tip of the peninsula, Etta climbed over the safety fence and James slid under it, out onto the bed of flat gray stones dipping down into the water. *I'm going to stay here*, said James from the top of the rocks. *Be careful.*

Of course, said Etta. She left her bag and rifle on the stone beside him.

After Kasia went home, Otto did the dishes until all that was left on the counter was the coffee tin. He pulled the petals off the flowers, six petals altogether, and put them in his mortar.

Otto took two trains, one from Halifax and then one from Regina. He sat by the window with a letter open on the tray in front of him.

Just remember to breathe,

it said.

Russell loaned Etta his horse to get to the station in town. You look beautiful, he said.

You should come too, said Etta.

No, said Russell.

At the place where the big stones turned small and met the water, Etta took all the things out of her pocket, a paper crane, a bobby-pin, a nickel, a green ribbon, a locket, a small plastic soldier, a perfectly round pebble, a button, a photograph, an arrowhead, a ring, a stalk of dried lavender, half a melted tea-light, and a silver baby spoon with the handle bent back on itself, and put them in a line. She watched as a wave pushed in over them, and then pulled them away. Then she took off her shoes and stockings and dress and stepped into the water.

Otto spread the paste on his eyelids and felt his way down the hall, into the bedroom, and into their bed. He flexed his stocking feet against the blankets and then let them relax.

He breathed easy and deep six times in a slow ritardando.

And then he stopped.

And then he was underwater.

Gray water, but not cold and not loud. Otto could see Etta's feet and ankles and knees, closer to the shore. He swam toward them. Once he was close enough that she noticed him, she dove down to meet him. They sat together underwater on the rocky sandy floor.

I missed you, said Otto.

I know, said Etta. I'm sorry. She pushed her fingers into the wet sand. I'm going to miss you.

I know, said Otto. I'm sorry.

But I'll be okay.

You're sure?

Yes. It's a loop, Otto. It's just a long loop.

The water blurred their faces so they could be any age.

They sat like that until Etta had to breathe. She turned and kissed Otto, his mouth already full of salt water. She squeezed his hand twice,

one,

two,

then let go and squinted her eyes and surfaced.

She was facing out, away from the land. Everything was gray and green and moving as far as she could see.

Otto's train was due in seven minutes. Etta stood on the platform and waited for the wind it would bring.

THANK YOU

Thank You

Ione and Rick and Erin and Chris Hooper, my mountains
Charlie Williams, my balance

and

The endlessly helpful Cathryn Mary Summerhayes, Annemarie
Blumenhagen, and Claudia Ballard at WME

The inspiring and obliging editors, Juliet Annan, Nicole Winstanley, and
Marysue Rucci

and

Bren Simmers and Claire Podulka for the thoughts and words
Isabelle Casier for the French

and

Uncle Peter for the books
Aunt Gloria for the recipes

and

The Vermont Studio Center for time and place and people
The Canada Council for the Arts for opportunity

and
of course

Caroline and Ted Old, and, with them,
The happy burden of history, connectivity, and
Saskatchewan.

ABOUT THE AUTHOR

Described as "Amélie Poulain with an old suitcase full of futuristic gadgets, a viola, and an accordion," Emma Hooper is a musician and writer. As a musician, her solo project *Waitress for the Bees* tours internationally and has earned her a Finnish Cultural Knighthood. Meanwhile, as an author she has published a number of short stories, nonfiction pieces, poetry, and libretti, as well as a number of academic papers and presentations on a range of things from retro-futurism to gender studies in pop music. Emma is currently a research-lecturer at Bath Spa University, in the Commercial Music department. She lives in the United Kingdom but goes home to cross-country ski in Canada as much as she can.

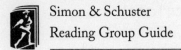

ETTA AND OTTO AND
RUSSELL AND JAMES

EMMA HOOPER

INTRODUCTION

Otto Vogel wakes before dawn on his farm in rural Saskatchewan, Canada, to find a letter from his wife, Etta. She has left home but will return if she can; she has never seen water and has gone to find the ocean. When their beloved neighbor, Russell Palmer, learns from Otto that she has left, he embarks on a mission to find her. Her husband chooses to stay home.

The two men had formed a deep bond as boys after an accident on a tractor left Russell partially crippled. Thereafter they alternated days at the schoolhouse, which was run by a young teacher, Etta Gloria Kinnick. Then World War II came, when Otto and every other young man in town (except Russell, because of his disability) was called to serve. As time passed, Etta learned of Otto's war experiences in tender correspondences that blossomed into romance when the young man returned on leave. Russell supported Etta emotionally when she suffered a devastating loss, but Etta chose Otto, not Russell, as her husband. Thereafter the three shared a warm friendship into their latter years.

Now eighty-three-year-old Etta makes her way on foot toward Halifax in the east, taking on as a companion a somewhat tame coyote, whom she names James; her friend Russell, hoping to dissuade her from her mission, tracks her down, but she refuses to turn back and goes on undeterred. Otto, who knows in his heart that Etta must do as her own heart dictates, diverts his unease and sadness by taking up the craft of papier-mâché, at which he excels; and the two men await the outcome of Etta's quest.

TOPICS AND QUESTIONS FOR DISCUSSION

1. One day during their childhood years, Alma impressed her little sister Etta with a display of whitened fish bones, which Etta found strikingly beautiful: "What language do fish speak?" she asked. "Probably French," said Alma. "Like Grandma." Does the scene contain a clue to Etta's late-life journey?

2. During the journey, James the coyote begins to speak to Etta in human language; a little boy who has seen Etta says she was "maybe a witch or maybe a lady-Santa-Claus." We are in a world of magic realism. What other subtle magic do you see in the novel? What role do you think this stylistic choice plays in the narrative?

3. Otto and Russell first learn about the war abroad through radio interviews, in which they hear a story about imprisoned children and babies who float through the prison window because they are so light from malnourishment. Discuss the meaning of this story. Where else in the novel do you come across storytelling or oral history?

4. Etta and Otto have long corresponded by letter, beginning with Otto's letter from the European front and continuing much later while Etta is hiking to the ocean. In what ways do letters at the beginning and the end of their relationship mirror one another? Why do you think Emma Hooper chose the epistolary form to convey many of the details in her novel?

5. When Russell finds Etta and tries to convince her to come home, she responds: "You're not actually here to fetch me. . . . You're here . . . because it's your turn, finally. It's sad that you felt you needed my permission for that, but, oh well. Go, Russell, go do whatever,

wherever. Go do it alone, and now, because you want to and you're allowed to and you can." What has Etta learned on her trek that prompts her to encourage Russell to travel? What meaning do you think Russell is seeking when he rides north in search of caribou?

6. In the course of Etta's travels, she becomes a celebrity—as does Otto, at home, though both would rather have pursued their endeavors privately. What qualities do Etta's pilgrimage to the sea and Otto's papier-mâché projects share? What qualities distinguish them? What might these august achievements say about the nature of celebrity?

7. Russell does not return to his farm before the end of the novel, but in the latter part of the novel he sends a letter to Otto estimating that he "should be home" before autumn; then, still later, he is shown soliciting directions to the airport. How might his travels in the Northwest Territories have changed him?

8. In one of his letters, Otto admits to Etta that he has "this idea that all these boys who have come to fill the places of the ones we've lost will fill their places exactly and be shot through or stabbed in the dark or blown up just like the last ones, exactly like them, one to one." His vision betrays disillusionment in the face of unremitting death on the battlefield. Do you think this is the author's statement about the nature of war? How have wars affected you or those close to you?

9. As Etta's journey gains national media attention, a journalist named Bryony decides unexpectedly to travel alongside her. Do you think Bryony's account of her brother's troubled life helps to explain that decision? Compare the loss of Bryony's brother to Etta's loss of her sister Alma.

10. At home, when husband and wife slept in the same bed, Etta tried to "sleep without any part of her touching any part of [Otto]," so that she would no longer be pulled into his dream. What was the dream? And as she lies in a hospital bed late in her journey, for a while her husband's identity replaces her own. How do you interpret this phenomenon?

11. In the final pages, Etta enters the ocean at last. At home in his bed, Otto breathes "easy and deep six times in a slow ritardando," and then he is "underwater." How do you interpret the lovers' meeting underwater, and their tender words as they sit there together? Why dos the author return to the past in the final lines of the novel?

ENHANCE YOUR BOOK CLUB

1. Etta's list of items she brings with her gives the reader a sense of what she values in her life. Create your own list of necessities as if you were embarking on a personal journey, and compare your own list against the lists of others.

2. Write out a travel itinerary for a particular site you hope to see in your lifetime. How far would you be willing to travel on foot to reach your destination? How would leaving home abruptly, as Etta did, affect your friends and family?

3. Emma Hooper performs as a solo artist under the name Waitress for the Bees. Explore her music on the Internet at http://waitress forthebees.bandcamp.com/ and compare the style and imagery to that of *Etta and Otto and Russell and James*.

A CONVERSATION WITH EMMA HOOPER

You wrote the novel using three different points of view and alternating narrative timelines. What challenges or rewards did this intricate structure give you as you worked?

They say "A change is as good as a rest," and I found this to be immensely true while writing this book; being able to swap between times and voices ensured that whenever I hit a wall with a certain person or plot, instead of having to quit for the day and go for a run or a bowl of cereal, I could switch perspectives or time frames for a renewed sense of energy and excitement. The hope was that it would work the same way for readers.

The challenge was not getting lost or tangled up in my own story lines. There were certainly times when (like Etta) I had to stop and think, "Wait . . . who's thinking this? Where are we? *Who* are we?"

The reader suspects that when Etta pulls out a piece of paper annotated with her name and the names of her family members, she is slowly losing her memory. Yet Etta is haunted by dreams of her husband's suffering in a war that occurred half a century ago. How did you balance the roles of memory and forgetfulness in a novel with an aging protagonist?

One of the things that is most striking to me about memory loss is how sufferers often lose the present, the short-term, while staying firm and clear in the long-term, the distant past. I wanted to explore this idea one step further, with Etta losing her own memories, and with them her sense of self, and soaking up Otto's instead, particularly those distant, long-term memories of war and water. This is ultimately what spurs her to undertake the journey for herself, to rewrite the history she's remembering on her own terms.

You grew up in Alberta, relatively close to the fictional home of Etta, Otto, and Russell. How did the geography of Canada inspire your writing? Did you draw from personal experience when mapping out travel in the novel?

My mother's family is from rural Saskatchewan (to be honest, most of Saskatchewan is rural), and I spent many, many childhood vacations there, out walking in the wheat and sun (and mosquitoes). It's a landscape unlike any other I have encountered, with a dry emptiness that is so vast and striking. Even though it's not where I spent most of my time growing up, when I'm nostalgic for home it's for these sorts of open spaces, that kind of dry air.

I have never walked across Canada from that point, but I have taken the train all the way from Alberta through Saskatchewan, Manitoba, Ontario, Quebec, and New Brunswick to the water, observing the drastic changes in landscape as well as the just-plain-massive hugeness of this place, which all counts as "home."

You tightly intertwine the lives of Etta, Otto, and Russell from childhood, but James shares a relationship only with Etta. At what point did you realize that a talking coyote would be Etta's guide during her journey?

I tend not to plan ahead very much in my writing, so I found out about James at just about the same time as Etta did; I like letting my imagination take over as a sort of cruise control in that way, asking myself as I write, "So, what happens now?" . . . "Oh, she meets a coyote.". . . "And then?" . . . "He licks her feet." . . . "And then?" . . . "He talks." . . . "And then?" etc. Writing a novel for me is just really asking "And then?" over and over again and trying not to question or doubt my own crazy answers.

Folklore and magic realism feature prominently in the novel. How do you think these traditions have influenced you as a writer? What authors have inspired you most?

My imagination runs away with me a fair amount in "normal" life . . . The other day I saw some metal piping hanging from a window and I thought: those look like robot arms . . . like robot arms hung like carcasses at a butcher's . . . like we eat robots like we do animals . . . hmm . . . and then I'm off, imagining what that world would be like, getting to invent and, at least temporarily, inhabit it. A whole other world! It's very exciting. I love the idea that you can imagine anything, *anything* you want and then work backward to make it work within a comprehensible universe.

I also had a moment recently when I saw some garbage bags by the side of the road that looked like sea lions. I knew they weren't, actually, but it got me imagining a world where we'd put sea lions out at the side of the road every week. Why? Why not? This is one of my very favorite parts of being a writer.

I've been inspired by many authors in many different ways. Reading Dave Eggers in university opened my eyes to the idea that narrative form could be playful and nonlinear, and that comedy and tragedy could work off each other within the same work. Márquez made the magical mundane in a really beautiful way, while Borges was the first to show me how prose could reflect on itself in structural spirals. Right now I'm very fond of Karen Russell and the half-real half-imagined universes her writing occupies.

How would you best describe your process? Do you keep a single space dedicated to writing, or do you move around? During what time of day do you find yourself most productive?

I try to have a dedicated space. I have a great little loft with a lovely old desk and a rug with owls on it and a handmade-by-a-child pencil jar; however, I almost never use it. I do a lot of my best writing in little bits and pieces between other things. On trains to London or in scrappy notebooks in the middle of walks, or in dim, sticky bars during band sound checks. When I do work at home, it's most often on the floor. I really like curling up on rugs with my laptop for some reason. Maybe because I had cats as a kid?

I do, also, like café writing. There was a period of time when every week, my friend Simon and I would agree to meet at a new, different café in Bath, and sit at different tables and not speak to each other. The idea was that the peer pressure of having the other person there writing/working would spur us on. And it worked (for me at least). We would agree on a stop-time, and, once that rolled around, we'd quit working, go sit at the same table, and allow ourselves to socialize a bit. At this point we'd also give that particular café ratings according to things like level of noise, tastiness of hot chocolate (which is what I usually ordered), availability of gluten-free snacks (which is what Simon usually ordered), etc. We put it all into a giant spreadsheet we still have somewhere. . . . It's worth noting that this is something I kept up when I moved to London for a year and was working on the book's edits. In this case it was my friend Jason I'd meet, fortnightly, and we'd share one silent table instead of two (London cafés are more crowded), but the overall formula was the same. And we've got a spreadsheet of café ratings for London too.

As for time of day, any but the middle, really. Morning and night are great. During the middle of the day I'm too distracted and just want to run around or nap. (Usually I'm meant to be giving a lecture or playing a rehearsal or something like that, though—sadly.)

Otto's descriptions of war focus more on emotion than the details of combat, and censored fragments of letters and dreamscapes in the novel make his experiences impressionistic. These qualities lend your war scenes a sense of universality. What message about war in general, beyond the conflicts of World War II, do you want your readers to take with them?

My hope was, and is, that the impressionistic nature of the scenes would blur any definite details, so there are no concrete things to hold onto like "good guys" or "bad guys" or clear-cut right and wrong. People talk of "the fog of war"; I was hoping to depict something along those lines—"the blur of war," where there are no certainties, no easy-to-pin-down exact signifiers, more visceral than academic, like wordless, instrumental music, or like Otto's letters with all dates and people and places, all distinct references, removed.

You are an accomplished musician and educator who wears a lot of hats. How has your formal training in music influenced your writing? How has your prose influenced your songwriting?

Well, I *do* hold unreasonably high standards for lyrics . . . I have song-writer friends who are afraid to show me theirs for fear of harsh criticism . . . (though actually they're all amazing, my songwriter friends: check out Cajita, for example—beautiful, with great lyrics).

Rhythm is a big part of my writing. I'll often go back and change phrases because they have too many or not enough syllables, or the emphasis falls in the wrong place, regardless of the actual meaning of the words. The rhythm of prose can pull you in and along, just like it can in music. This is something that people acknowledge in poetry, I think, but that gets less attention in prose. However, I think it's equally important in the latter, maybe even more so, for me, since long chunks of writing need that rhythm to keep pulling you along and through, both as writer and reader. This explains, among other things, my love of repetition.

Otto's newfound hobby of papier-mâché is a unique development for his story line. From where did the idea originate to incorporate this craft into his anticipation for Etta and Russell's return?

There are two answers to this question, the superficial and the slightly more deep. Superficially, papier-mâché is *fun* and I love it. Who doesn't like making and smashing piñatas? I won my grade 8 science fair by making a papier-mâché dolphin to scale with all its organs in place . . . I think doing and making hands-on crafts is good for the head and the heart. On another level, a running theme in this book is the "swap" that Etta and Otto are undergoing, both in terms of the stereotypical gender roles of their generation, and also the roles they've played throughout their own specific lives. Etta does this by "doing" and "going," and Otto by "creating" and "nurturing." Hence, for Otto the papier mâché (and the baking, and the guinea pig too).

Each character responds differently to Etta's choice to walk halfway across the country, and she is received variously with humility, anger, hope, and sensationalist conjecture. What do you want readers to take away most from her bold decision?

In the words of my Etta, I would love for them to "go do whatever, wherever. Go do it alone, and now, because you want to and you're allowed to and you can." For readers this could mean writing a book or starting an astronomy degree or cutting their own hair or learning Mandarin or any other thing they've always wanted to do.